Catch It Spinning

Claudia J. Severin

CATCH IT SPINNING

Copyright © February 2021

Claudia J. Severin

Published by Pella Road Publishing

Lincoln, Nebraska

ISBN: 978-1-7342-1483-3

Catch It Spinning is a work of fiction. Any references to historical events, real people, or real locales are used fictitiously. Other names, characters, places, and incidents are the product of the author's imagination, and any resemblance to actual events or locales or persons, living or dead, is entirely coincidental.

Claudia J. Severin

https://claudiaseverin.net

DEDICATION

For Pamela, Linda, and Debra, who taught me to twirl a baton in high school. I wish you lives filled with lucky catches.

CONTENTS

ACKNOWLEDGMENTS

I wish to thank the past residents of Eastridge in Lincoln, Nebraska for their inspiration. The atmosphere and setting are accurate for the time period. It was a friendly, safe place to grow up, to stroll through the neighborhood, to ride your bicycle, to drive your parents' huge car around in a time before seatbelts or speed bumps.

I thank my friend, Paula Kucera, for recounting her personal experiences that served as a basis for part of Yvonne's story.

I thank JustWrite Communication for their editing, and the encouragement of my family. Cover credit belongs to Melanie Severin.

CATCH IT SPINNING

Twirling the baton was relaxing sometimes. It was hypnotic letting the sleek cool bar of silver slip around her fingers or glide across her waist to cast shadows on the lawn. When she spun it horizontally doing helicopters, it toyed with the changing light of the setting sun. She'd practiced many hours since last summer and had conquered wrapping her baton around her elbows and knees, flipping it around an outstretched wrist, and flicking it from her right to left hand. It caressed her body like water tumbling off a wall.

Her challenge now was tossing the baton. Oh, she knew she could twirl around the world, releasing the baton at the apex of the second revolution and it would continue rotating twenty feet above her in the air. Any higher and she would hit the telephone lines that skimmed five feet above the weeping willow in her backyard. What she had trouble mastering was getting that circling baton to return to her so she could catch it without moving her feet. In a performance on the field, it shouldn't look like you were chasing a fly ball. No, she had to have control over its ascent and descent, regardless of the sun, wind, or temperature. If she released it eighteen inches in front of her body, she needed it to come back to the exact same place, like a boomerang. In her sixteen years, she'd learned to control as many things in life as she could. Without self-control, she might end up a victim. She might be hit with her own baton. And that made one nasty bruise.

CHAPTER ONE

April 13, 1968
Lincoln, Nebraska

"Do you love me, Yvonne?" Dick Dunn asked her. They were parked on a dead-end residential street overlooking a city park near their Eastridge neighborhood. He scooted to the middle of the front seat, away from the confines of the steering wheel.

Yvonne Marie Edison murmured as he pushed her thick mane of hair in front of her shoulder and ran his lips past the nape of her neck. "You know I love you. I am wearing your class ring." The third finger on her left hand sported Dick's Capital High School ring, pink yarn wrapped around the band, so it fit her finger rather than his.

He wrapped one hand behind her head pulling her mouth to his. His lips demanded and his tongue invaded as he shifted her onto his lap trapping her head between his hand and the ceiling of his 1959 Chevy Impala. She felt a prickle of heat as he ran the other hand under her ribbed cotton sweater. There was a subtle hint of the Brut cologne she'd bought him for Christmas when he pulled away to catch his breath.

"If you love me, Baby, you should prove it."

That stopped Yvonne cold. She leaned away, blinking at the image of Ann Landers and Abigail Van Buren each waving a big red flag beyond the Impala's massive fins. She knew that she'd read that line before in each of those ladies' advice columns. She never missed them in the *Lincoln Star* or the *Lincoln Evening Journal*.

"My boyfriend says I have to prove my love to him by going all the way," was how the lovelorn letter usually read.

"Dump him!" was the advice columnists' oft-repeated reply. "He is using you."

"What are you talking about, Dick?" She had to give him a chance to explain. Maybe she had jumped to the wrong conclusion. She slid off his lap and pulled her sweater back down.

He drew her back by slipping his hand around the waistband of her bell-bottom denim trousers. "Come on, Yvonne. You don't want to be a virgin forever, do you?"

"That's what he said?" Debbie Adams asked, the next afternoon in the band room. Yvonne never kept secrets from Debbie, although she wasn't sure the confidence was always reciprocated. "What did you say?"

"I told him I planned to be a virgin at least through my seventeenth birthday. He took me home right afterward. I don't know what has gotten into him lately. I used to think he was romantic when he kissed me. Now it seems like he is after something more every time we are alone. Was Barry like that?"

Debbie sighed. "Barry didn't think of me that way. I was kinda glad when he stopped calling me. A friend who goes to his church told me she saw him with another girl after choir practice last week. I guess he has moved on."

Debbie didn't give herself enough credit. She was a beautiful blonde, slightly plump, but in a Marilyn Monroe sort of way. Not that Debbie acted at all like Marilyn. She was friendly, but not flirtatious. Yvonne's family had moved into the house next to Debbie's on Mulder Drive nine years before. Within days, they'd become best friends.

Yvonne and Debbie got their batons out of the band director's coat closet. Mr. Humphreys, their band director, could be one of their staunchest supporters, but most of the time, he acted like he'd forgotten to take his daily sedative. His anxiety was so bad it often made Yvonne nervous and she noticed it was worse whenever Barbra was around.

Barbra Simpson was a senior twirler. They found her cuddling with her boyfriend, John Anthony Turner, on a bench in the hallway where five girls were practicing for the impending auditions to be twirlers next year. Her parents had named her Barbara, but she had changed the spelling to imitate Barbra Streisand.

Barbra looked up when Yvonne and Debbie approached. "You two have a lot of work to do with this bunch. Mr. Humphreys told me and Joann we don't have to stay as long as you juniors are here."

"He said you were excused? I think the seniors helped with practices last year." Debbie set her jaw.

"Mr. Humphreys likes me. I may as well take advantage of it. If I bat my eyelashes at him, he turns six shades of red and starts stuttering. The old goat!" With that, she took John Anthony's outstretched hand and headed for the parking lot.

"What did I miss?' Joann Walters walked up to the twirler group as Barbra left. "Are you going over the eight basic twirls?"

"Barbra just informed us you two seniors are excused from teaching," Yvonne said.

"News to me. Let's get to work." Joann was not the beauty Barbra was, but she was as agreeable and dependable as they come.

Most of the girls who tried out for twirler already played instruments in the marching band, so they knew the standard songs that were played at every football game, pep rally, and basketball game. And they knew how to march, to flank right and left, and do an about-face quickly. Yvonne played flute and Debbie played clarinet in the band when they weren't twirling.

Five girls were still vying for two spots as twirlers. Two

hopefuls stood out as having real twirler potential: Linda Bridges and Nancy Evans.

Linda was athletic, boyish with a dishwater blonde super-short haircut similar to British supermodel Twiggy, but without the spider-leg eyelashes. She could do cartwheels and a toe touch while jumping in the air. She might have gone out for cheerleader, but Linda was not the cheerleading type.

"I wish they had real inter-school sports for girls as they do for boys. I like volleyball, gymnastics, and running track, but I don't know why we can't compete against other schools. It doesn't seem like it is worth the effort when no one sees your afterschool events. The boys have to compete for a spot on a varsity team. They let anyone participate in the intramurals. They act like we should do this sports stuff for the exercise to keep fit and trim. It seems like a double standard to me," Linda had told them when they asked her why she was auditioning for twirler. "I thought about trying out for cheerleading, but it's so girly-girly. At least playing the trombone, I get to wear a uniform just like the boys and stay warm marching on the field in November."

"But you know the twirler uniforms have short skirts?" Debbie said.

"Yes, but at least I see the twirlers wearing white boots up to their calves and they usually wrap blankets around their legs in the stands. Cheerleaders probably can't feel their legs by halftime!" Linda grinned. Linda didn't smile shyly like most girls. Linda threw her head back and showed all her teeth. It reminded Yvonne of how her own older brother, Clark, grinned boldly, radiating confidence.

Nancy, on the other hand, was mysterious, if you bothered to notice her at all. She was as enchanting as the oboe she played; one of the most difficult of all the instruments because it had two reeds. The oboes made a beautiful sound, but the only time Yvonne ever heard them was when Mr. Humphreys asked them to play alone.

"Tell me, Nancy. What made you want to be a twirler?" Yvonne had asked her in the interview.

"The twirlers seem to be having fun. When you are marching on the field in the band, you have to worry about the formation, what music you have to play, and whether your hat is going to fly off in the wind." Nancy pushed her eyeglasses back up her nose. "The twirlers seem to be creating their own tableau, separate but complementary to the band's presentation."

"Gosh, I never thought about it like that," Yvonne had said, making a mental note to look up the word 'tableau' in the dictionary when she got home. There was more to this girl than met the eye. Not that there was anything wrong with what met the eye. Nancy had straight auburn hair halfway down her back which she usually kept out of her face with a white ribbon. And enormous emerald green eyes like an exotic leopard. But those cat eye spectacles needed to be updated. They reminded Yvonne of her Aunt Tilly's glasses; not a good look for sixteen.

"I think Linda and Nancy are the frontrunners," Debbie said, as she and Yvonne piled into Debbie's turquoise 1962 Volkswagen Bug after the practice session. "Janet and Susie are doing pretty well too, but they have missed some practices. I doubt they'll catch up before tryouts. Mary doesn't seem to have the right coordination, from what I have seen—" A loud grinding sound interrupted her as she shifted gears.

"You should have your transmission looked at, Debbie," Yvonne said. "Has your dad heard that yet?"

"Only every morning when I leave. He said he's going to take it to the shop but once he starts checking his building sites, he doesn't have time."

"You're probably right about the twirlers but I am secretly rooting for little Susie. She comes from a nice family," Yvonne said, then shifted subjects as Debbie shifted gears. "Are we all set for the slumber party at your house on Friday night? Do you want me to bring my albums? Four Seasons? Rolling Stones? Supremes? Petula Clark? Oh, I know you want some of the Lesley Gore albums."

"Bring them all. It will drive Daniel crazy."

Debbie's twin brother, Daniel, didn't share her taste in music. He played classical music on the piano proficiently, although he would sometimes strum folk music on his guitar. He stuck to the French horn in both the band and orchestra.

CHAPTER TWO

Friday night's slumber party would be the twirlers' last one before school ended; their last chance to have a party that included the graduating majorettes. Debbie had also invited some of the other junior and senior girls in the band.

Debbie's parents had given the girls the run of the walkout basement, and they danced, sang, ate pizza, and drank Coca-Cola. They did "The Pony" around the room singing, "It's My Party" along with Lesley Gore. Debbie even jumped up on the hassock to do "The Jerk."

Debbie's mother informed them it was time to turn down the music around eleven o'clock. That's when the gossip started.

"Did you hear about Patrick Jeppers?" Rosemary Adkins flipped her light brown pageboy and wiggled her overly tweezed brows. Rosemary was a senior flautist who sat by Yvonne in the band.

"He got suspended, I heard," Barbra said.

"For smoking. In the boys' bathroom. Not even outdoors." Rosemary's lips curled.

"I thought you and Pat had a thing going, Rosie," Debbie said.

"Ancient history," Barbra said. "He threw her over for Marcy Bellmore. And they lasted about two weeks." She ignored the color draining from Rosemary's face.

"Who are you going to prom with, Debbie?" Joann asked, trying to focus on something more pleasant.

"I don't know him very well. He is a friend of Daniel's from Youth Symphony. His name is Keith Pritchard, and he goes to Southeast High. Their prom is on the same night, but he agreed to go to ours instead. I gave him points for that."

"But you said he was cute, right?" Yvonne started unrolling her sleeping bag, as the girls began staking out places on the family room floor.

Debbie smiled. "I think he is cute, in an intellectual sort of way. He has black glasses and curly hair."

"Debbie, do you think your parents are asleep yet?" Barbra asked, poking her head in the stairway. There hadn't been any sounds of movement from upstairs for a while.

"Probably. Why do you ask? Are you pulling out a six-pack of beer?"

"No. I have a date." Barbra raised her eyebrows. "I'm going out the back door. He is meeting me on the next street over."

"John Anthony is meeting you?" Yvonne asked.

"I didn't say who. Leave the door unlocked so I can get back in."

Debbie looked at Yvonne, shifting her shoulders. Yvonne knew Debbie's parents would call Barbra's parents if they knew.

"It's okay, Barbra. I brought a flashlight," Rosemary offered.

"You can put your sleeping bag right here closest to the door, so you don't have to trip over anyone."

Barbra grabbed her jacket, purse, and the flashlight and slipped out the door to the patio with the stealth of a cat burglar. Debbie stood at the picture window, parting the draperies, and watched the light bob through the back-neighbor's yard. They heard the neighbor's Chihuahua yipping for a short time and saw headlights flicker on the neighbor's street.

"Who is she meeting, Rosemary?" Debbie asked. "You know I could get in trouble for this, especially if something bad happens to her."

"Relax, Debbie. She does this all the time at my house. Tells her mother she is staying at my place, but she almost always sneaks out. Her mother is pretty strict, only lets her go out once a week."

The girls in school all said the same thing about Barbra: no one should be so perfect. Perfect body, perfect smile, perfect hair, perfect grades, perfect voice, and John Anthony Turner, the perfect boyfriend. But sometimes she was the perfect brat.

"You don't know who she's meeting either?" Debbie bit her lower lip.

"She can take care of herself," Joann assured her. "Let's play a game. Do you still have Twister?"

"I brought a game," junior Lila Gates said. "It isn't so much a game as it is a quiz. I got it from my cousin in Omaha. Here, I brought some blank papers and pencils for everyone to write their answers." She passed the papers and pencils around.

Rosemary wrinkled her nose. "This is Friday night. We shouldn't have to take a test."

"Oh, you will like this one, Rosie. Just you wait."

Lila began to read the questions. "You get five points for each one you can answer 'yes' to. Question one: have you ever kissed a boy? Two: have you ever parked or made out with a boy?"

The girls laughed. Oh, it was that kind of test.

Lila went on with the questions. "Have you ever French kissed? Have you ever had a hickey? Have you ever cheated on your boyfriend? Have you ever gone steady?"

Yvonne asked, "So what are they counting as going steady? Wearing his class ring? Wearing his letterman pin? A pearl ring? What if the two people just agree they are going steady?"

Debbie said, "If you think you are going steady, you are."

"Oh, the next question is, 'have you ever been pearled or worn a promise ring?' so I guess they are looking at that separately," Lila said. "So, going on, have you petted above the waist? Below the waist?"

There were some gasps in the room. "This is getting a little personal, don't you think?" Yvonne cleared her throat. "Holy Moly, what is the last question on this list?"

Lila laughed, "Yes, it is very personal. I think it is from *Cosmopolitan*. Maybe you are supposed to be drinking when you answer these. Let me look. Oh, well, the last two questions are 'have you ever had sexual relations?' and 'have you ever been pregnant?' That figures."

"Maybe you should pass the test questions around and everyone can answer for themselves. Then we can just compare the scores," Debbie suggested.

"Okay," Lila agreed. "There are fifteen questions worth five points each, so it is a maximum of seventy-five points."

Rosemary was the first to review the list of questions. "I don't even know what some of these questions mean. What is that one, Yvonne?"

Yvonne looked at the list. "If you don't know what it is, you probably haven't ever done it. Besides, what makes you think I would know what it is if you don't?" She knit her brows.

"Because you are going steady with Dicky Dunn. Everyone knows his reputation."

"What do you mean?" Yvonne flinched and glared at Rosemary.

"Oh, you know. Dicky has been with lots of girls. He told my brother he is trying to have sex with a girl from every high school in town." Rosemary tossed her head. "I am sure that was long before he was dating you."

Yvonne's eyes grew wider as she jumped up and ran into the bathroom at the far end of the basement. Joann followed her and stood outside the locked door.

"Are you okay? Don't pay any attention to Rosie. You know how she likes to gossip. And exaggerate."

Yvonne opened the door and pulled Joann inside, before closing the door again. She wiped tears from her cheeks. "So, you don't think Dick is collecting girls like trophies? You don't think he's been feeding me a bunch of lies about how much he loves me?"

"No, of course not. He hasn't tried to get you to sleep with him, has he?"

Yvonne didn't have to answer when her eyes welled up again.

CHAPTER THREE

Yvonne brushed her hair 100 times until it shined like polished mahogany. She had always protected her shoulder-length hair by using nourishing shampoo and conditioner, and wearing a hat or scarf if she was going to be in the sun very long. Dick told her she looked like one of those Breck girls in the commercials they showed every Sunday night during *Bonanza*.

It was going to be a busy week. She had a date with Dick that evening, which was a Saturday. Then the twirler auditions were Wednesday, and the Junior-Senior Prom was the next Saturday night. Dick insisted they double-date with another guy in his senior class, Ted Rumsfeld. That should be a blast because Ted was taking Yvonne's friend Joann to prom. Yvonne and Joann wanted to go out to dinner at a nice restaurant after prom so they could show off their fancy dresses. Dick had told her some of the guys he knew were having a Purple Passion party after prom, and they might be going to that instead.

Yvonne wasn't sure what a Purple Passion party was, but she had heard there was some sort of punch made with grape juice spiked with rum or vodka. Dick had never expected her to drink alcohol before, so she didn't know why they would start now. But she supposed since he was a senior and it was his last prom, she would let him plan the evening.

She and Debbie were talking about prom almost every night on the phone. They both had the same fabric for their prom dresses and had picked out the pattern together. Debbie's had light blue satin on the bodice, and white lace on the bell sleeves and full skirt, while Yvonne's was a satin floor-length sheath with the same white lace on the bodice. Her dress was cut lower in the back, and Debbie insisted she looked like Jackie Kennedy, especially with her hair swept up in a fancy barrette. Debbie's mother, Bonnie, was an excellent seamstress and had constructed both dresses. They both had appointments to have their hair done at Helene's Salon at noon on Saturday.

That day couldn't come soon enough.

But in the meantime, tonight should be fun too. Dick was taking her out to dinner at King's Restaurant, which was a favorite teen hangout. The burgers and fries were legendary, and they usually had chocolate shakes too. This may be the last time she could eat that sort of thing for a week, as she wanted to be as svelte as possible in her fabulous prom gown. After dinner, Dick said they were going over to his cousin's house. She had never met his cousin, Luke, who was in college. He was about three years older than Dick.

I overreacted at the slumber party, Yvonne thought as she finished brushing her hair. Rosemary was a regular Hedda Hopper, the infamous Hollywood gossip columnist. She wasn't happy unless every other girl was miserable. After all, she acted as though she was such a good friend to Barbra but told terrible tales about her. When it had been time to tally up the scores on that test, to see who had the most sexual experience, Rosemary had insisted it must have been Barbra, although she hadn't even been there when the test was given. Rosie said she answered for both herself and Barbra, and she knew Barbra would've had to answer "yes" to every question except for the pregnancy one.

Debbie had gaped when Rosie implied Barbra wasn't a virgin. But then, she had snuck out of Debbie's slumber party to be with some fellow. It was all silliness. The test was dumb. Her allegations were baseless, about Barbra, about Dick, about anyone.

Dick had been a good boyfriend, after all. Sometimes he flaunted his social status as a senior jock, but his cockiness could be even more alluring than his smoldering good looks. They had been going out for almost nine months, and he'd given her his class ring in December. He bought her a lovely necklace for Christmas, candy for Valentine's Day, and had hinted they were going to a fancy restaurant in Omaha for her birthday in June.

He would be graduating from Capital High soon. In August, he would leave for Ames, Iowa to attend Iowa State University on a football scholarship. She remembered the day when he'd gotten the call from the coach at Iowa State. He had been so excited. He was still that sweet boy.

Dick's cousin, Luke, lived in the southwest part of Lincoln in an older home. She was surprised when Dick parked the car in the driveway, then escorted her to the back door. It was starting to rain as he found a house key under a ceramic turtle near the back stoop and opened the door.

"Don't you want Luke to let us in? We don't want to barge in on him," Yvonne said, taking a step back.

"He knows we're coming. That's why he left the key. Luke won't be home for a while," Dick said jutting out his chin, pulling her by the hand.

"But I thought we were visiting him."

"No, we're visiting his house. It is perfect. He has a nice couch and even a spare bedroom. Which would you prefer?"

Dick swaggered into the living room, turning on lamps and tossing his jacket on a chair. Yvonne sat down on the couch. It had seen better days, but Luke had a blanket over it to make it more presentable. The house smelled musty mingled with the odor of cigarette smoke.

"I don't understand what we are doing here when Luke is gone. He doesn't even have a television in here," Yvonne said. Lightning flashed outside the window and the lights flickered.

"I thought you would appreciate a little privacy, Baby. This is much better than making out in the car. We don't have to worry about the cops driving by and shining their headlights on us. The neighbors aren't going to bother us. We can relax and enjoy ourselves."

Yvonne tried to release the tension in her shoulders and stood up to take off her raincoat. She'd worn a yellow flowered-print shirtwaist dress in anticipation of meeting Dick's cousin. When the ancient furnace rumbled, she felt herself getting warmer, and she had a whiff of the Wind Song cologne she'd dabbed between her

14

breasts when she'd gotten dressed. When she sank back on the couch, Dick crushed his mouth on hers, pushed her to her back, and rolled on top of her.

"Wait! What if Luke comes home?"

"Luke's not coming inside as long as he sees my car in the driveway. He knows the score."

"How? How does he know the score? Have you done this before?" Yvonne pushed Dick back up enough to create some distance.

"Don't be silly, Yvonne. You are the only girl for me. You look so beautiful tonight. Did I forget to tell you? You smell and taste intoxicating. I love you so much, you are driving me crazy." He put his hand behind her head and pulled her back to him and started kissing her again, forcing his tongue between her lips. With his other hand, he began unbuttoning the front of her dress.

"Butterflies, huh?" Dick said kissing his way down her neck. "Suddenly I am a big fan of butterflies."

He was referring to her demi-cup bra with a multi-colored butterfly print. Yvonne had always been tall and slender, and she wasn't as curvaceous as some of her friends. People told her she could be a fashion model or a stewardess. She appreciated the fact that she had a trim behind that looked nice in tight jeans and miniskirts but was afraid any boy would be disappointed she didn't look like the buxom women featured in her brother's hidden stash of *Playboy* magazines. She took a deep breath and held it.

Dick was holding her lips captive again, as he was sliding his hand up her leg. When she stiffened, he stopped abruptly, glancing toward the kitchen. "Do you want some beer? I think Luke keeps some beer in the fridge." He got up and left the room. He came back and set down three cans of Budweiser on the coffee table, still attached to the six-pack ring. Instead of sitting next to her, he went into the back of the house where the bedrooms must have been.

Yvonne pulled the front of her dress together as soon as he left her, not at all sure this was a good idea. What exactly did he have in mind? Was he trying to get her drunk now? Her knees started shaking and she clamped her hands on them. She didn't worry so much when they parked in his car. It had been too cold to stay parked very long, and neither of them was about to take off their clothes when someone could drive by anytime. But this, this was different. It was more intimate, but she could see how easily it could get out of control.

Dick returned to the couch. He had his dark blue oxford shirt untucked and unbuttoned all the way. She'd seen his bare chest before when they went swimming. She'd seen him flex the muscles he'd developed in the football weight room. He held out a flat red foil-wrapped square about two or three inches in size.

"What's that?" Yvonne asked, thinking the wrapper looked like something cough drops came in.

"Ticket to Ride, Baby," Dick said. "I knew I could count on Luke to have supplies." When Yvonne frowned and blinked, he went on, "It's a condom. Luke gets them free at the Student Health Center on campus."

Yvonne continued to stare at him like he was speaking another language.

"It's what? Oooooh. No, we won't need that. Maybe we should leave." Yvonne jumped up as she felt the blush racing all the way down to her butterfly adorned bra and started to button her dress.

"Chill out, Yvonne. You said you love me. Let me show you what love means. We have been leading up to this for months. You don't want to miss the sexual revolution," Dick wrapped his arms around her from behind slipping her dress off one shoulder and unfastening more buttons.

"I told you I'm not ready for that kind of thing. Let's take it slowly. Let's just kiss. Kissing is nice." She arched her neck feeling a warm glow where he was kissing her shoulder now, pulling her strap down.

"We can't just stop at kissing. Guys have needs. Actual physical needs." He nuzzled her exposed neck. "Maybe girls like you are different, but I want more from you. If you can't give it to me, maybe I should look somewhere else."

She pulled away and turned to face him. "What are you saying, Dick? Surely you aren't planning to go out with some other girl who will … cooperate?"

He shrugged.

"But we're going steady. You can't go with someone else."

"Look, I know I am rushing you a little bit. Are you going to be ready for this in a week? I thought prom night would be perfect, but then the Purple Passion party thing came up and I didn't know if we would be alone. When are you going to give in?"

"Stop pressuring me. I don't know when I will be ready to have sex. Maybe it will be years from now. Maybe not until I get married." Yvonne's voice rose, and she pulled her dress back up around her neck and began buttoning it again.

"Married? You want to wait until you get married? I wish I'd known that. I wouldn't have wasted so much time on you. If that is really how you feel, we're done. I can find someone else who isn't such a prude. Girls are always calling me. You're missing your chance."

"You can't be serious. Are you giving me an ultimatum? If I don't have sex with you, you want to break up with me? I thought you loved me."

"I am trying to love you. You're the one saying 'no.'"

"Take me home!" Yvonne put her raincoat back on and headed for the back door. *I can't believe Rosemary was right about him, and I fell for it lock, stock, and barrel.* She heard thundering as she climbed into the passenger seat of the Impala. Angry tears fell in tandem with the raindrops. He didn't emerge from the rear of the house for five minutes, carrying a can of beer.

Dick sat in the driver's seat and looked for a place to set the beer can. He eyed Yvonne briefly, as though he meant to ask her to hold it. Then he shook his head and chugged the rest of it, heaving the empty can out of his window. *He doesn't even see me crying.* She pressed her forehead against the window, trying to put as much distance between them as possible.

CHAPTER FOUR

Yvonne was curled up on Debbie's window seat, with Debbie's Siamese cat, Princess, purring at her feet. "How did I mess this up so completely, Debbie? My timing is terrible."

"You had a fight, that's all. Couples fight. They make up. He's not going to want to miss the prom any more than you do." Debbie smiled faintly and handed her a box of tissues.

"I should have said I would think about it. He said he would've waited a little while. I could have kept things going at least until school ended. But no, I had to go all high and mighty on him and tell him I was holding out for marriage. Why did I say that? Nothing scares a boy more than mentioning marriage. And really, I don't know what I want. But I didn't want to lose Dick. I love Dick."

She'd been crying most of the night before and lapsed into tears again. She'd been afraid to face her parents, her mother in particular, as she would've taken one look at Yvonne's red swollen eyes and begun the third degree. Yvonne couldn't face the questions yet. She was still hoping to salvage her relationship with Dick.

To add insult to injury, she hadn't been able to get his ring off her finger when she got back into his car. She'd forgotten to take it off when she showered before their date, and the yarn had unraveled when it dried. He hadn't asked for his ring back when they got to her driveway. He'd leaned over her after putting the parking brake on. She had thought he meant to embrace her, comfort her, or apologize. Instead, Dick had opened the passenger door from the inside, signaling she could see herself to her door, even though it was pouring rain. She'd been soaked by the time she got inside.

When she'd gotten up to her room, she took the fingernail scissors to the yarn and had been able to remove the ring. By then, she'd begun to hope she wouldn't have to give it back. After a fitful night with little sleep, she had begged off church, telling her mother she didn't feel well, through the locked bathroom door. Her mother had wanted to take her temperature, but she'd managed to convince her she only needed more sleep to ward off a bug.

When her parents didn't return at lunchtime, she'd remembered they were taking her brother out for Sunday dinner. He was a freshman living on the University of Nebraska campus majoring in pre-med. She couldn't have faced Clark either, so it was fortunate for her they'd left her home.

Dick hadn't called. Yvonne had called Debbie after her parents left the house, and Debbie had assured her she'd hear from Dick that morning. But the phone had been silent. She had even picked up the extension in her room to make sure there was a dial tone. The phone had been working fine, but her heart had been broken beyond repair.

"Why don't you just call him?" Debbie suggested.

"I don't think he'd like that," Yvonne said. "I remember when we first started dating, he said I wasn't the type of girl who would call boys. He said he'd liked that about me. Like girls shouldn't be so forward, I guess."

"But you are torturing yourself not knowing what he is thinking. If you call him, maybe you can get together and talk about what has happened. Or if he is still mad, at least you'll know."

"No, I can't."

"Then I'll call him," Debbie said. "He probably won't refuse to talk to me."

"What would you say to him? Your best friend is drowning in her own tears and he needs to fix it? Yeah, that would go over well. No, neither one of us is going to call him. He's eighteen years old. He can call me when he's ready. Maybe after a while, I won't want to talk to him."

Daniel knocked on Debbie's bedroom door then walked right in when no one objected. Debbie and Daniel had about the same coloring, although his blonde hair was darker. They'd looked about as much alike as fraternal twins could when they were preschoolers. If her friend Debbie was beginning to look like a vixen, her brother's looks were emerging as though from a sculptor's soapstone. Yvonne caught herself studying his face whenever she saw him. Sharp angles and possibly whiskers were beginning to form on his face, but the finished product was still hidden and changing day by day. He was still lanky but less clumsy than he'd been even a few months before. And his voice had developed a rich resonance that made her want to listen to the sound regardless of what he was saying.

"Hey, don't just barge in. We could have been undressed in here," Debbie chided him.

"You didn't say not to come in. Besides, I've seen both of you undressed before. No big deal. Uh-oh. What's wrong with Vonnie?"

Yvonne was charmed when he used her childhood nickname, but she hid her reddened eyes and nose behind a tissue.

"Boy trouble," Debbie told him.

"What did Dick Dunn pull now?" Daniel asked.

"We had a big fight. So now I don't know if I am going to prom next weekend."

"I don't know what you ever saw in him to begin with. He's a jackass. You'd be better off going out with pretty much any other boy in school." Daniel snorted.

"It's funny, Danny Boy," Debbie said, "you've never liked any of the boys Yvonne has liked. Even when we were kids."

He shot his twin sister a warning look. "I have never liked any of your boyfriends either."

"That's why I stopped telling you who they are."

"All I'm saying is Rat Fink Dick will probably come around. If not, she's better off without him, prom or no prom," Daniel said grabbing some M&M's out of the dish on Debbie's dresser before he left.

CHAPTER FIVE

Yvonne hadn't heard anything from Dick the rest of the weekend, other than the squeal of his tires laying rubber on Mulder Drive late Sunday night. When she looked out the window, she couldn't tell for certain it was him, but the taillights looked like the Impala's. Was he trying to get her attention? She'd been with him before when he'd done that to show off.

She didn't have any classes with him, since he was a senior, but they were sharing a locker. According to the office records, she shared a locker with Lucy Johnson, who was in her homeroom. But Lucy had given their locker combination to another friend about the time Dick convinced Yvonne to share his locker. His locker was in the "senior hallway" near their classrooms where jocks like Dick acted as if they ruled.

Usually, Yvonne didn't cross paths with Dick at their locker until after third period. After her early morning band class, she hung up her jacket, put her flute case on the floor of the locker, and grabbed her English notebook. When she closed the locker door, he was right behind it, leaning against the adjacent locker. Her heart started pounding, but she couldn't read his expression. *Lord have mercy, he looks like James Dean when he gives me that look.*

He nudged her gently out of the way and opened the locker again.

"Nothin' to say, Baby?" He smirked at her as he pulled his gray sweatshirt over his head, hooking it inside the locker. He smoothed down his green and white striped T-shirt and took a few books from the top shelf, stuffing them into a backpack. He deliberately brushed his forearm again hers when she didn't back up quickly enough.

"We should talk," Yvonne said in a low voice. They were standing too close together according to the school's "No Public Display of Affection" rule.

"You change your mind?" He grinned and raised his eyebrows. Before she had a chance to answer, the first bell rang, and he sauntered off down the hall, greeting his buddies as though nothing unusual was going on.

Yvonne simply stood there, gaping after him. *He is still trying to pressure me. Without even mentioning it, he's using the whole prom date thing as ammunition to get me to cave in.* Angry tears rose in her eyes as she watched him. At the same time, she couldn't help but admire his broad shoulders and lean hips walking away.

She avoided the locker after third period, and she didn't run into him for the rest of the day. *Well, maybe he'll call me tonight.*

If for no other reason, to see if I did change my mind. Maybe we could have some sort of compromise, and we could still go to prom.

There were only two more days of practice for the girls auditioning for twirler and she knew she had to be there after school for that. Dick should have remembered she was doing that too. She tried to keep her mind on the task at hand, but it wasn't easy.

"Okay, we are going to go through the entire routine three times in a row. Then we'll practice the specific twirls we taught you that will be part of the audition. We are going to do it all outside because you can't toss the baton in the air and catch it until you have had to deal with the sun and the wind. I know it is a little chilly today after all the rain this weekend, but you can't let that stop you from doing your best," Debbie was saying as Yvonne caught herself staring into space.

She managed to finish the practice session, letting Debbie do most of the talking. When the girls got into the Volkswagen Bug afterward, Debbie patted her leg.

"Did you get a chance to talk to him at all?"

"I saw him this morning, but I still don't know where things stand. He asked if I'd changed my mind."

"Have you?" Debbie asked. "I mean, if you had to pick someone to be your first, you could do a lot worse."

"Well sure, someday. But he made it pretty clear he ain't waiting around for someday."

Yvonne's telephone was ringing when she walked into her bedroom. She'd asked her parents for a teen line, but they seemed to think it was an unnecessary expense.

"Yvonne? I'm glad I got you," Joann said when Yvonne picked up.

"What's up, Joann? The practice went well. I think we are going to have a good audition on Wednesday if that is what you are calling about. You and Barbra are still coming, aren't you?"

Joann sighed. "I'm not calling about the auditions. I hate to tell you this, but if I were in your shoes, I would want my friend to tell me."

"Tell me what?"

"It's Dick. I guess maybe Rosemary was right. He was making out under the football bleachers with Marcy Bellmore after school."

"Who told you that? Rosie? You said yourself she exaggerates and gossips." Yvonne tried to ignore the lump forming in her throat.

"No. No one told me. I saw him . . . the two of them, myself. I don't think they saw me. They were too busy with each other. When I realized who it was, I turned around and went back the way I came."

"Joann, are you sure it was Dick? I'm sorry, but Marcy Bellmore is always doing something with some guy or another if you listen to the stories."

"He sits in front of me in calculus class. He was wearing a green and white T-shirt today, and khakis. That's what caught my eye in the first place, the striped T-shirt. It's not going to be so pretty after he was rolling around in the dirt."

Yvonne wanted to answer. She wanted to tell Joann she was imagining this. The words stuck in her throat.

"Thank you for calling. I have to go," Yvonne finally managed to say.

She was face down in her pillow when her phone rang again. *I should be crying but I don't think I can process this.* She ignored the ringing phone.

"Yvonne!" her mother called up the stairs. "Debbie is on the phone for you."

Yvonne sighed picking up her extension. "It isn't a good time to talk, Debs."

"No, you have to hear this," Debbie said. "Coach Wilkens caught Dick and Marcy Bellmore going at it under the bleachers after school. Daniel's friend Bill Edwards saw the whole thing while he was waiting for his mom to pick him up by the gym door. Dick might even get suspended."

"It's true then?" Yvonne felt her arms and legs going numb. Like the world had suddenly moved far away from her, and she was merely watching things happen. They'd done *Our Town* as the fall play last year, and now she felt as detached as the narrators had been.

"Do you want me to come over? This is bound to be all over school by now."

A telephone operator interrupted their call, "I have an emergency call for Yvonne Edison from Rosemary Adkins, will you take the call?"

Yvonne couldn't believe Rosemary thought this was an emergency. "Okay, Operator," she answered. Debbie and Yvonne both hung up.

Debbie came through the bedroom door seconds after Yvonne answered Rosie's call.

"Yes, Rosie, I heard something about it. It sounds like there were some witnesses. Yeah, thanks. I'll talk to you tomorrow," Yvonne said and hung up the phone. "Should I leave it off the hook? Do I want to know how many well-meaning friends I have who can't wait to tell me my Prince Charming is a two-timing . . . rat fink, as Daniel called him?"

"Did you break up with him or not?"

"I dunno. I still have his class ring. I thought we would have another chance to discuss our situation. Now, I'm not so sure I want to. Good Golly, I wish we didn't have a date for the prom this weekend."

When Debbie left, Yvonne's mother came in and sat on her bed. Connie Edison was used to the trials of teenagers. Aside from having an older son, she worked as a substitute teacher.

"Something is going on. You left the phone off the hook. You never do that. Are you and Dick having some sort of problem?"

"Oh, Mom," Yvonne covered her mouth with her hand. She couldn't tell her mother everything. She didn't even know where things stood with Dick. "We had an argument. We might have broken up. Then today something happened to him after school and he got in trouble. I don't know what is going on. All I know is that I have this beautiful prom dress I probably won't get to wear." She wiped a tear away. *I am worried more about my prom dress than I am about my prom date. What's wrong with me?*

When she calmed down, her mother left her alone to start her homework. After dinner, Yvonne did the dishes, then slipped out into the backyard and sat on the swing. The rising moon cast a dreamlike glow over the willow tree. Was the willow weeping for her now, like in the Chad and Jeremy song? She heard only a distant owl hooting. It was nearly dark when she spotted him lurking in the shadows.

"Daniel," she said. "What are you doing out here?"

"I saw you from my bedroom window. I wanted to talk."

"If you came to tell me about what happened under the bleachers today—"

"No, I'm guessing you've heard enough about that. You broke up with him, didn't you? You're not still hoping he's taking you to prom?" He moved closer until his face was bathed in the moonlight.

"I dunno. I haven't talked to him since Saturday night."

He cocked his head. "Go to prom with me instead."

"With you? You mean like on a date? You're Debbie's brother. You are like my little brother. It would be too weird."

"Is it because I am a little shorter than you are? It's only an inch or two, and I am probably still growing. I won't be seventeen until August. My cousin grew three inches in his freshman year in college."

"I didn't mean I wouldn't go. You are so sweet to ask me. I am just confused right now." Yvonne raised her feet off the ground and stared at them.

"After everything he did, you still want to go to the prom with Dick, don't you?" Daniel huffed air out his nose and started to walk back to his house.

"Wait. Don't be mad." She pulled herself up turning toward him. "I have to talk to Dick. I did agree to go with him, and I don't want to assume anything. That's not fair. Can I let you know tomorrow?"

Daniel turned around and faced her. She couldn't see his eyes in the darkness, but he nodded. "Yvonne?"

"Yes, Daniel."

"Stop thinking of me like your little brother."

"Okay."

CHAPTER SIX

The rumors were running rampant on Tuesday, even in her early morning band class when they were outside doing marching drills. Since the students were milling around on the field like worker bees, they talked among themselves. The consensus seemed to be that both Dick and Marcy and their parents had to meet with the principal first thing. Several bandmates suggested Dick's father would convince Principal Owen to look the other way since it was only a few weeks until graduation. It was reported Mr. Dunn had met with Principal Owen several times during Dick's high school years.

When Yvonne got to her locker after band, she found a scrawled note from Dick cellophane-taped to the inside. It read: "Yvonne, Meet me at the elementary school playground at 5:15." She put the note in her purse. She didn't see Dick in the senior hallway at all on Tuesday, but she felt countless eyes bombarding her, as though she had the answer to the mystery. She didn't know if Dick was suspended or where he was. He must not be grounded if he planned to meet her later.

It was hard to concentrate on her classes. *What am I going to say to Dick when I see him? Will he even show up? Maybe he was grounded, but he didn't know it when he wrote that note. I have his ring in my purse. I should give it back to him. But what if he apologizes and wants to make it up to me? What really happened with Marcy?*

And then there was Daniel. Dear wonderful Daniel. There had been times when she'd caught him looking at her when she was over at their house. She and Debbie ran around in their babydoll pajamas when they had sleepovers. The last time it happened, a few months ago, Debbie's mother had told them they should either get dressed or wear bathrobes when they left Debbie's room. She said it wasn't proper when they had a sixteen-year-old boy in the household, and he might have friends visiting him too. Yvonne and Debbie had laughed for hours at the idea that Daniel might ever have an inappropriate thought. Most of his buddies were eggheads like he was. But the night before, in the backyard, he'd been looking at her differently, sort of the same way Dick looked at her, as though he was licking his lips like Wile E. Coyote.

And he'd asked her to go to prom with him. Did he tell Debbie about that? Yvonne wanted to tell her, but she supposed she should accept his invitation first. There was the issue of him being shorter than she was. Yvonne had always been tall even though she'd stopped growing at thirteen after she was almost five foot, ten inches tall. She was used to being the tallest girl in her class, even her school much of the time. Debbie and Daniel had been on the shorter end of the spectrum when they were in elementary school. She remembered how Daniel used to say it was Debbie's fault he wasn't taller because he had to share his food with her in the womb. But now Debbie was five foot six and Daniel was maybe five-nine on a good day. Their father was well over six feet tall, so Daniel might be still be growing.

It wouldn't be a problem dancing with Daniel even if he was a little shorter. *Did he even know how to dance?* She tried to remember if he'd gone to the homecoming dance with anyone. She never even imagined Daniel dating anyone. He was just there, part of a package deal. He came with being friends with his twin sister. But she did know him pretty well and would have fun with him.

Yvonne got through her day without any teachers remarking on her wandering mind. She had to concentrate on the last day of practice before the twirler auditions and answer any final questions the girls might have.

When she was riding home with Debbie, she waited to see if she would mention anything about Daniel. But Debbie only wanted to talk about Dick.

"I'm surprised they didn't call you into Principal Owen's office to vouch for Dick, or to find out if you'd been accosted."

"Well thank God that didn't happen. What are you talking

about 'accosted?' I thought they were just necking under the bleachers. They are making kind of a big deal about this. Of course, I'm upset about it, but I don't know why the principal got involved." Yvonne fidgeted with the English book on her lap.

"Marcy told her parents they had sex. Dick denied it. She said he forced himself on her. Didn't anyone tell you about this?"

"What? That sounds crazy. Dick would never force anyone—wait, what time is it?"

"It's a smidge after five if this clock is right. My dad did get the transmission fixed; can't you tell? But if they disconnected the battery, the clock may be off," Debbie said.

"Take me to the elementary school. I can walk home from there. Dick left me a note asking me to meet him."

Debbie slammed on the brakes. "You can't be serious! You expect me to leave you alone with a boy who might be a rapist?"

Yvonne scoffed. "He's not a rapist. I wouldn't believe anything Marcy said. Besides, it's the school playground. It's not very private."

Debbie drove another three blocks to the rendezvous spot. Yvonne spotted Dick perched on the low bar of the jungle gym and got out of the car. She reached back for her book bag and flute case.

Debbie shook her head. "No, you can leave those. I am staying right here. I don't know if you can trust him anymore. You go say what you want to say, then come back."

Yvonne rolled her eyes but closed the door. *I know I am lucky to have a friend who looks out for me, but sometimes she is worse than my parents.* She walked up to the jungle gym as Dick slid to the ground. He ran his fingers through his dark hair.

"Yvonne, listen. I know I screwed things up. I've had to spend the last twenty-four hours apologizing to everyone I know. I don't know what I was thinking when Marcy pulled me under those bleachers. I swear it was her idea. She's the one who took her underwear off. I didn't ever think she'd try to frame me like this. Nothing happened, at least, I didn't do her. I mean, she's already been with most of the guys in school, she's probably got like those diseases or something. Geez, Louise. I don't know how I got here. Maybe if you and I hadn't fought, if you had just been a little more sensitive to what I needed—"

He nearly lost his balance when she slapped him across his face as hard as she could. Before he could make a sound, she turned on her heel and marched back to Debbie's car. She was trembling when she sank to the seat but fumbled in her purse until she found his class ring. She rolled down the window and hurled the ring in his direction. It came to rest in a muddy puddle.

Debbie floored the Volkswagen and fishtailed around the corner on the way home. "Oh my God, oh my God. I can't believe you did that. He's probably had that coming for years. Are you okay?"

Yvonne was still shaking. "I don't know. I have never slapped anyone before. It hurts. It really hurts. I hope I didn't break my twirling hand."

"I guess that means you can go to the prom with my brother."

Yvonne turned and looked at her wide-eyed. "He told you?"

"We're twins. Do you think I didn't figure out he had eyes for my gorgeous best friend? And now we can double date for the prom." Debbie smiled gleefully. Then she looked back at Yvonne. "I'm sorry, I'm sure you are upset about what just happened. But once you get over that creep Dick, you will have fun at prom."

Yvonne wasn't sure she was ever going to have fun again.

CHAPTER SEVEN

They had the twirling auditions in the girls' gymnasium. Most of the intramural games which would've been held there were over for the year. Mr. Humphreys and Mrs. White, the vocal music teacher, were there as sponsors, and they sat at one long table. Joann, Barbra, Yvonne, and Debbie sat at another table pouring over their scoresheets.

They decided to have two girls audition together since coordination was key. The first and second contestants performed together. Then they had the second and third contestants go through the routine again to see if those two were aligned. Then they had the first and third matched up, and so on. If any of the judges weren't sure, they were free to call back any of the contestants to perform with some other partner.

Nancy Evans and Janet Sparks were the first two to do the routine. When Barbra started the reel-to-reel tape recorder playing the music, Janet started four counts too early, and they asked to start again. Barbra had a little trouble finding the right place on the tape, so Mrs. White took over that task.

Yvonne was happy for the distraction. *I can't believe I actually hit Dick. Of course, I was furious. First, he blamed Marcy then me for something that was his fault. But I don't know why I got so . . . violent. At least Debbie will keep it to herself.*

When Nancy and Janet started again, they were both shaking a little. Nancy tapped her foot when the music began, counting the measures. Janet forgot one whole section, so they were off afterward. Both of them looked like they wanted to heave when the song ended.

"It's okay. You're both going to have a chance to do the whole routine at least one more time," Joann assured them.

The judges decided it was better to let Nancy go again with Linda Bridges. They seemed like they worked well together in practice. This time it went smoothly, and Linda even remembered to smile most of the time. Nancy still looked a little green around the gills, but she didn't make any mistakes.

Janet did better the second time when she was partnered up with Susie Neilson, but Susie dropped her baton near the end of the routine. She did a good job picking up where Janet was to complete the song.

Linda's second try was with Mary Barrows. Mary had trouble keeping up, and once she fell behind, her movements became jerky. When Susie and Mary were paired up, it was awkward. They both looked to each other for guidance, but neither of them seemed to know the routine as well as the other contenders.

After the girls had each done the routine at least twice with a partner, they had them all do it together. It was apparent Nancy and Linda knew it the best, and the others watched them. Then they did some freestyle twirls, where all the contestants started doing figure eights, and one of the judges would call out another twirl and they would switch as quickly as they could. They stuck to common twirls they would have to use next season. The last request was for a high toss. They let the girls do this one alone, so they wouldn't have to worry about batons colliding midair.

Mary missed her catch, even after a second try. Janet caught her baton but seemed to forget she was supposed to go into a twirl when she caught it.

Susie gave her baton a mighty heave. It hit one of the gymnasium ceiling braces and came crashing down at an angle. One end hit the table in front of Mr. Humphreys, knocking over the glass of water he had in front of him, spilling it in his lap. The baton bounced off the table hitting him in the forehead, barely missing his eye. His horn-rimmed glasses fell skimming the floor.

He backed away, knocking his chair over and stepping on his glasses.

"Susie! *EEERRR!*" he roared. "You bumbling idiot!" His face was crimson, and his teeth were bared.

Susie backed away shuddering, then raced out of the gym, not even stopping for her book bag, baton, or jacket.

Barbra took one look at his wet trousers and started laughing hysterically. Mr. Humphreys took a step toward Barbra as though to confront her, but Mrs. White laid a hand on his arm and redirected him into picking up the chair and wiping up the spilled water.

Yvonne hesitated briefly, then went after Susie. She found her crumpled against the wall outside the gym.

"Are you okay, Honey?" Yvonne knelt in front of her. "Do you want to continue?"

"He's going to flunk me. I have always gotten good grades in Marching Band, and now he's gonna flunk me. Forget the twirler tryouts. I may not be able to show my face in school after Barbra spreads this around."

"I can talk to Barbra." Yvonne patted Susie's shoulder.

Debbie came up next to Yvonne with Susie's belongings. "I thought you might not want to go back in there right now." Susie grabbed her jacket, bag, and baton and headed down the hall toward the payphone.

Yvonne and Debbie returned to the gym where they found Mr. Humphreys had gotten towels out of the gym office and order had been restored.

Joann asked, "Do the rest of you think you can continue? I guess only Nancy and Linda haven't done their tosses."

Linda spun around after her toss while the baton was in the air. She caught it, but she wobbled when she started doing windmill twirls. Nancy tossed her baton exactly as they had taught her. It wasn't so high she lost control, and she neatly pulled it into a spin upon catching it.

The contestants left the gym for a little while as the judges conferred with the sponsors. When the scores were added, it was unanimous for Nancy and Linda. Mr. Humphreys had his arms crossed and refused to look at Barbra. They debated whether they should post the results on the band room door as they had done in previous years. Yvonne and Debbie lobbied for telling the girls right away, so no one would be anxiously waiting for the results. In the end, they did that.

"Barbra? Can I talk to you?" Yvonne said as they were leaving.

"You're not going to rag on me for laughing, are you? I couldn't help it."

"No, I don't want you repeating the story about Susie. Please don't tell anyone else about her. It was an accident. She is upset enough."

Barbra looked from Yvonne to Joann and then to Debbie. "Fine. But you better warn those other sophomores if you don't want tongues wagging." She strode out of the gym shaking her head.

"I'll bet that girl has never been humiliated in her life," Joann said.

"We should all be so lucky," Debbie said.

CHAPTER EIGHT

Yvonne needed to officially accept Daniel's invitation to be his prom date. She should have called him last night, but she had been too upset over what happened on the playground.

After dinner, she went next door and rang the doorbell. Debbie put her face to one of three stair-step glass panes in the door.

"I need to talk to your brother," Yvonne said.

Debbie's lips curved. "C'mon in." She called up the stairway, "Daniel, better come down, your girlfriend's here."

Yvonne gave her a chastising glare. "Don't even—Oh, Daniel, hi."

Daniel led Yvonne to their back patio.

"Sorry, Debbie has been acting a little weird after I told her we might go to the prom together," he said, motioning for her to take a seat at the picnic table. A few young moths danced on the patio light.

"I guess this might be a little odd for her since we've known each other for so long. But I came over to say I would be happy to go to the prom with you. I appreciate you asking me under the circumstances."

"You said you would let me know yesterday. How do you know I haven't called someone else?"

Yvonne averted her eyes and started to stand. "Well, I suppose you could have—"

He laughed. "I'm just teasing you. Do you want to double with Debbie and Keith? You don't know Keith, but we are in Youth Symphony together. He's an orchestra geek. But I guess I am too." He took her right hand in his. Yvonne winced. "Oh, I forgot. You went all Muhammad Ali on your last beau. Remind me not to piss you off."

Yvonne's ears flushed and her chin dipped. "I wish Debbie hadn't told you. That's not like me at all."

"I know. I know everything about you," Daniel said. "We've been around each other since third grade. I know you aren't the type who gets mad easily. Whatever he said or did, he must have deserved it."

You know what he did. The whole school knows by now. But she wanted to stop thinking about Dick and the mess he created. She wanted to get through the rest of the school year without everyone talking about her.

She went back home to finish her homework. Around nine o'clock the phone rang. At that time of day, her parents assumed it was one of her friends and let her answer.

"Hello, Edison residence," Yvonne said. She could tell someone was on the other end, as though she could feel the electricity coming through the line. "Who's there? I can hear you breathing. Dick, is that you?" The other person snickered then hung up. Before last weekend, he called her almost every night. She didn't know why he would bother if he wasn't going to talk.

Fifteen minutes later, the phone rang again. As soon as she answered, the caller hung up. When the phone rang again after another fifteen minutes, she raced to the kitchen to talk to her parents.

"Dad, would you answer the phone, please? I think we are getting harassment calls." Her father picked up the receiver.

"Harold Edison speaking."

A male voice said, "Your daughter is a real bitch."

Harold hung up the phone and looked at Yvonne. "What's going on, Yvonne?"

Yvonne burst into tears. Whoever was calling had succeeded in making her father scrutinize her like she had just committed a cardinal sin.

Connie went to Yvonne and gathered her in her arms. "This has something to do with Dick, doesn't it, Sweetheart?"

"Oh, Mom. He isn't the guy I thought he was. I gave his ring back to him."

"I heard some gossip this morning at the Ladies' Aid Meeting at church. I know it is wrong to gossip especially in church, but Mrs. Adkins said Rosemary told her a terrible story about Dick and that sweet little Marcy Bellmore. I remember teaching her in Sunday school. Apparently, she accused him of something, then she recanted, then she changed her story. No one knows what to believe anymore. But I'm glad you broke up with him if even part of the story is true," Connie said.

"Your mother and I have talked about this, and you are to stay away from him, no matter what. We don't want you to go out with him again." Yvonne hadn't seen Harold muster up his stern father's face since she was a child.

"I don't think there is much chance of that," Yvonne said. "I clobbered him."

"You what?" Harold said.

"I know you are supposed to turn the other cheek when someone does you wrong, as Jesus said, but I didn't. I slapped the other cheek silly. I don't know what came over me."

Harold turned and coughed to cover his laughter. "It didn't sound like Dick's voice on the phone. He's called here dozens of times. I think I would recognize his voice."

The phone rang again. Yvonne turned toward the clock on the stove. Another fifteen minutes had gone by, it was now nine forty-five.

"Don't answer it this time. Maybe whoever it is will stop if they don't get anyone," Connie said.

The phone continued to ring for five minutes.

"What if they plan to do this all night?" Connie took a towel and wiped off the pan that had been sitting in the dish rack.

"Let's check with the phone company," Harold said. "Maybe there is something they can do." He could see Yvonne jump every time the phone rang. "Honey, do you honestly think Dick is behind this?"

"I don't know if it's him or some of his friends. I remember him telling me he helped T.P. some girl's yard after she broke up with his friend Paul."

Harold reached the night chief operator at Lincoln Telephone Company. He said, "Uh-huh. Okay, we could try that. I would hate for a telephone repairman to show up tomorrow morning thinking our phone isn't working. Yes ma'am. I'll call them first thing tomorrow." Then to Yvonne and Connie, he explained, "She said we could take the phone off the hook, but someone else may try to call us and report the phone out of order. Or if we had a whistle or something that would make a loud noise, we could blow it in the receiver, and try to scare them off. I told her I would call the business office in the morning. I hate to have to change our phone number. If there are threats, she said we could file a police report, and they could put a trap on our line to trace the calls."

They left the phone off the hook after they received more calls at ten, ten-fifteen, and ten-thirty. Even when she could no longer hear the phone, Yvonne had trouble sleeping.

CHAPTER NINE

Dick still wasn't back in school the next day, but Yvonne took matters into her own hands. She stopped in to talk to her guidance counselor, Mrs. Baker.

"I wonder if there are any spare lockers available," Yvonne began, clutching her hands, sitting in the counselor's office.

"Weren't you issued a locker at the beginning of the school year?"

"Yes, but I was sharing a locker with Lucy Johnson. Lucy let another girl use our locker, and I started sharing one with Dick Dunn. He was my boyfriend at the time, but now we are on the outs. I started getting harassing phone calls last night, and well, I think it would be better not to share a locker with him."

"Dick Dunn," Mrs. Baker shook her head. "There's a disappointment to be sure."

"He is coming back to school, isn't he?" Yvonne tried to stop her knee from bouncing. "I mean if not, then I would keep the locker I am using."

"I can't say. I have only heard part of the story. I'm not directly involved with the decision. His father is an attorney, I have been told, and has made some threats if we don't let Dick graduate." When Yvonne's head jerked back and she blinked rapidly, Mrs. Baker added quickly, "Never mind, forget I said anything. Let me see if we have another locker."

She assigned Yvonne a new locker in another hallway. When she was getting her books out of Dick's locker after school, one of Dick's friends, Paul Wesson, came up behind her and stood close.

"Did you get much sleep last night, Yvonne?" he hissed. "I know a bunch of Dick's pals planned to call you to see if what he told us was true." He glanced around the hallway, then put his hands on the lockers on either side of her and brushed himself up against her back trapping her next to the locker.

"What? What did he tell you?" Yvonne tried to push around him, but he was bigger and evidently there to threaten her.

"He said to forget about Marcy Bellmore. If we wanted an easy lay to call you. He said you'd do anything." He ran his hand down the side of her short skirt until he touched her thigh. She shoved his hand back toward him enough to get past him.

Paul laughed. "What's the matter, are you going to slap me too?"

She darted away, heading for the band room to meet Debbie.

What does he want with me? Is Dick going to send all of his friends to harass me?

Paul trailed her down the hall, and soon there were three other boys in Dick's circle of friends who got in step next to Paul. She didn't look back at them, but they were snickering and making catcalls behind her.

Stop it! Just leave me alone. Why can't Dick accept that we are over? Where are all the teachers when you need one?

When she tried to walk faster, they increased their speed and jeers.

"Yvonne Baby! Wait for us, Yvonne! You know you want to!"

Everyone in the halls could hear their sing-song taunting. Yvonne's heart felt like it would burst out of her chest, but she kept moving faster. She rounded the corner to the music classroom alcove, at a dead run. Mr. Humphreys was coming out of the band room and ran into her.

"Yvonne! Stop running. What's going on?" he cried. The four boys slowed down, changed direction, and continued in the main hallway.

Debbie and Daniel were in the band room, along with a few other students. She collapsed on the first elevated platform, gasping. Daniel and Mr. Humphreys converged on her at once. Debbie pushed past them and plopped next to Yvonne, wrapping her arm through her friend's.

"Were those boys chasing you?" Mr. Humphreys asked, squatting down in front of Yvonne and Debbie. His glasses hung crookedly on his nose since they were held together with tape.

Yvonne nodded. *Have to get it together. I'm not going to let those stupid bullies get the best of me. No point in getting Mr. Humphreys involved, he probably doesn't even know them. None of those lame brains plays an instrument.*

Mr. Humphreys looked back toward the door. A bead of perspiration appeared where his hairline receded. "Well, at least they are all graduating next month. They'll be out of your hair soon enough."

"So what, you're not going to report this to Principal Owen, Mr. Humphreys?" Daniel's face tightened. "You're letting them off the hook because they are seniors?"

Mr. Humphreys' eyes darted between the three students. "I didn't get a very good look at them. Yvonne, do you want me to tell Principal Owen about this? You would have to tell him what happened before you got here."

Yvonne shook her head. "No thanks, Mr. Humphreys. I just want this to all go away." She stood and picked up her book bag. "Can we go now, Debbie?"

It was quiet on the ride back to Mulder Drive. When they got to the Adams' house, Debbie motioned her into her room. Daniel stood hesitating in the doorway.

"I know you want to help, Daniel. But I think she needs some girl talk right now."

He nodded, glancing over at Yvonne, who was back on the window seat nuzzling Princess.

CHAPTER TEN

Yvonne took some comfort in knowing the way things had worked out was much better for Debbie. Instead of going to the prom with a boy she barely knew, she now had her best friend and brother by her side as well. She did her best to try to put the turmoil of the past week behind her and enjoy the festivities.

I'll have fun today. I just hope I don't have to lay eyes on Dick.

Debbie and Yvonne had their hair appointments at Helene's. They'd debated for weeks whether to have their hair swept up with hairpins or leave it down in long curls. If they left it down, it seemed like they were wasting their money having a hairdresser fix it. If they had it done in an updo, they were afraid they would look ten years older. When it came time to tell their hairdressers what they wanted, Debbie asked to have her blonde waves swept up, and Yvonne picked something more sedate.

"I think you should look like Brigitte Bardot," Yvonne said, offering one of the many photographs they'd torn out from movie magazines.

"Then I think you should look like Natalie Wood. This picture." Debbie picked out one where Natalie had her long glossy hair in a side part. "Oh, and we brought some fancy hairpins and barrettes with us, in case you think that is a good idea," she said to the stylist. "Yvonne, maybe you should pull part of your hair back behind your ear on one side and hold it with a barrette. Very dramatic."

"Sweetie, I've had about as much drama as I can stand this week. I think I want to go with something simple but amped up. Maximum shine, minimal style. I've got some killer earrings and my mom is lending me a pretty necklace."

They were washed, dried, curled, teased, and sprayed. Two hours after they went in, they had to admit they looked different. They weren't all that sure it was better.

"Your hair does look like the photograph," Yvonne assured Debbie after they were back in Yvonne's room. "And once we get makeup on your eyes, you'll be a dead ringer for Brigitte."

"I dunno," Debbie said inspecting herself in the mirror. "It may be more Marilyn than Brigitte."

"We could do Marilyn makeup instead. Right down to a fake beauty mark. With your figure, you could pull off either one. My hair, on the other hand, is overdone. I don't know why she thought she should use the rat tail comb on me. It is poufy on the top of my head. The photograph of Natalie had her hair perfectly smooth. I'm not trying to look any taller," Yvonne picked up her brush and carefully began taking out the backcombing.

She'd made a few adjustments in her prom attire plans now that she was going with Daniel. She traded in the silver sandals with the rhinestones and two-inch heels for flat ballerina slippers to minimize their height difference. She learned a trick from her mother about being photographed in a floor-length dress. You could bend your knees slightly, and appear an inch or two shorter, and no one would even realize it.

Daniel had made dinner reservations for an hour before the prom started at Tony & Luigi's Italian Restaurant. It was Yvonne's favorite. She didn't know if that was why he chose it, or if it was a coincidence. Keith had driven his car to the Adams' house, then Daniel was driving them all in his parents' Cadillac Coupe de Ville after that.

Keith, Debbie, and Daniel all arrived at the Edison house about five-fifteen. Keith and Daniel had both rented white dinner jackets and black tuxedo pants. Somehow Daniel had managed to come up with a bow tie matching both Debbie and Yvonne's dresses. Yvonne suspected his mother had sewn it out of leftover scraps from their gowns.

When Yvonne came down the hallway, Daniel looked up and smiled broadly.

"That dress is . . . well, I saw the dress when Mom was sewing it, but it looks a lot better with you wearing it. The color with your skin and hair—it looks like art." He squinted like he was picturing a painting.

"You think I look like art?"

"Oh, a masterpiece for sure, not like a Picasso, or some other kooky art." He fumbled opening the plastic box holding her orchid corsage, as his face turned a deeper shade of red. "More like a Rembrandt or a Monet, with their use of color."

"Well, thank you, I think." Yvonne tried to picture what those artists had painted and kept coming up with rotund ladies draped in fabric with some sort of bonnet on their heads. *Note to self: check the World Book Encyclopedia tomorrow for Rembrandt and Monet.*

One advantage of going to prom with the boy next door was that it was easy for the parents to take photos. Harold Edison pulled out a new Polaroid camera for the occasion. Debbie and Daniel's father, Bernard Adams, was using his fancy eight-millimeter movie camera. Neither of them was an experienced photographer. Harold chaired the Agronomy department at the University of Nebraska, and Bernard was a builder.

"This is getting ridiculous," Debbie said. "I'll bet the real Natalie Wood and Marilyn Monroe didn't have to pose for so many pictures."

"I just want to make sure I have two of every shot, so your parents have their own set," Harold told her. Connie was busy stripping the backing off each of the Polaroid photos and laying them out to dry. They had to wait nearly a minute for the image to fully appear, but at least they knew whether the picture came out nicely before it was too late.

Once they got to Tony & Luigi's, Yvonne sank into her plush chair when Daniel held it out for her. She'd only been there with her family. *This place is bubbling over with romance. I feel like a princess.* There were many tables of high school students dressed up for prom, including some of Keith's classmates from

Southeast High School. Daniel seemed more at ease, once he and Keith started joking with each other. The boys dived into the crackers, onion dip, and tiny breadsticks as soon as the waiter brought them.

"Okay, my mom told me you should always start using silverware from the outside and work your way in," Keith said studying the array of forks, knives, and spoons in various shapes and sizes. "What do you think this round spoon is for? Soup?"

"That is for the lemon sorbet." Yvonne's eyes sparkled in anticipation. "It's the palate cleanser they serve after the salad. It is my favorite part of eating here."

"Entremets, as the French would call it." Daniel straightened his posture. "Something sweet and tart to prepare your mouth for the heavy pasta or meat course."

Keith and Debbie both looked at him with big eyes.

"How do you happen to know that, Daniel? You haven't even taken French." Debbie raised her eyebrows. Daniel smiled, then gave Yvonne a side-long look.

"You don't miss a thing, do you?" Yvonne said holding his gaze.

"Nope."

After what they all agreed was a fabulous meal, they arrived at the school cafeteria shortly after the prom had gotten underway. The "Garden of Ecstasy" theme was carried out with hundreds of crepe paper flowers in every color. At the entrance, they even walked over a "lily pond" on a wooden bridge the shop class had made.

"Yvonne and I worked on those flowers over there by the wishing well," Debbie pointed out. The junior prom committee girls had been assigned the task of making most of the decorations.

When they got to the registration table, they had to present their tickets, and Debbie, Daniel, and Yvonne cast their votes for the senior Prom King and Queen. The finalists had been nominated two weeks earlier by the student council.

Yvonne tried not to show any reaction when she spotted Dick Dunn's name on a list of six boys nominated for Prom King. If everything from the past week hadn't happened, she would be there with him tonight. She picked another boy from the list, not one of Dick's cronies. She was pleased to see Barbra Simpson's name on the list of girls and voted for her. Yvonne owed her one, as she'd kept quiet about Susie.

They went to look at the decorations, and Rosemary came up close to Yvonne and whispered in her ear. "Red alert. Dick is here with some dimwit sophomore girl. He's been drinking, along with some of his posse."

Yvonne shook her head and took Daniel's arm. "I couldn't care less," she told Rosemary.

The live combo was loud, making it hard to hear each other. "Let's dance," Daniel said, pulling her onto the floor when they sang "My Girl" by the Temptations, a favorite slow number. "Are you worried I am going to step on your feet?" Daniel teased when she hesitated. "I have danced before you know."

Yvonne pressed her lips together and took a few hesitant steps. She'd never danced with any boy who wasn't taller than her, and she wasn't sure how it would look or feel. He pulled her into a double-clutch and it didn't much matter as they each had their heads on the other's shoulders. *He smells good. Oh my goodness, Daniel is wearing cologne.* She remembered hearing his mother lecturing him a few years ago about showering every day.

He ran his fingers up and down her back. "You sure do look pretty tonight," he said.

"So do you." Yvonne beamed. She never would have imagined she would go on a date with Daniel. He was the bane of her friendship with Debbie when they were children. He often found another neighborhood boy to side with him causing trouble for the girls. But if anyone else tried to pick on either Debbie or Yvonne, he was always there to defend them. Which is why she started thinking of him as a brother. He reminded her of Clark sometimes with his mixture of loyalty and orneriness.

He is right, though. We're getting older and it is time to give him a chance to show me who he is now.

The dancing was fun. Keith and Debbie danced next to them and they tried a few dances some of them hadn't done before. Keith was rather daring, it turned out, and bounced down to the floor to do the splits a few times. Backup dancers did that sometimes on American Bandstand. After a while, they got warm and thirsty. Daniel went to get them some punch and Yvonne stepped outdoors in the courtyard to cool off for a minute.

She'd only gone a few steps when he grabbed her arm, and pulled her around the side of the building, out of sight.

"Hey, Baby, I missed you," Dick said as he pushed her up against the rough brick side of the school building. She was too startled to react when he covered her mouth with his. It felt warm, familiar, and welcome at first. After all, she'd spent months enjoying the way he kissed. Sometimes he was gentle and sweet, but other times he was insistent, without being rough. That's what this kiss was, the kind that meant he was taking charge. Then she snapped back to reality. *I can't be kissing Dick. I broke up with him.* His tongue tasted like whiskey. She pushed him back.

He spoke again before she could, "I see you missed me too." He wiped her lipstick off his mouth. "We should be here together. You look foxy in that dress. Just how I pictured you."

"But we aren't here together. You blew our relationship to smithereens, remember?" She hated that tears were welling up in her eyes. She had to get out of there. She started to walk back toward the courtyard, when he grabbed around her waist from behind, plucking her off the ground.

"Let me go!" Yvonne cried, the tears threatening to ruin her carefully applied mascara. She tried to push his arms away, but he just slid them up toward her breasts.

"What do you have under your fancy gown? Butterflies?"

She managed to break away by elbowing him in the solar plexus. Daniel was standing in front of her. She had no idea how much he had seen or heard of what had happened with Dick.

"Let's get out of here," Yvonne said to Daniel. "I want to go back inside." She slipped her arm through his, but he continued to glare at Dick.

"What did he do to you, Yvonne? I'm not sure we're done here." Daniel looked like he might take Dick on. Dick was bigger, older, and more athletic, and it wouldn't be much of a contest.

Dick smirked, pulling himself up to his full height and smoothing his jacket down.

"No, he isn't worth it," she said. "Please, take me back inside." Daniel looked at her again and nodded.

As soon as they got back into the cafeteria, Debbie met them at the door. "Where were you, Sweetie?" She examined Yvonne's mascara-tracked face and disheveled hair and put her arm around her waist. "Let's go into the girls' room to freshen up."

When they got to the restroom, Yvonne went into one of the stalls as the tears caught up with her. She kept pulling off toilet tissue to wipe her nose and the rivers of mascara running down her face.

"Sweetie, are you okay? Tell me what happened." Debbie's dyed blue shoes appeared on the outside of her stall door.

Yvonne came out of the stall, flushing the toilet. "Dick was outside. He grabbed me before I even saw him. He kissed me like . . . like none of this stuff had happened. Why can't he leave me alone? I don't even know how much Daniel saw, but he was mad too. I didn't want them to start fighting, and get Daniel hurt or in trouble." She stood in front of the mirror at the sink. "Goodness gracious, I look like something the cat dragged in." She got out her comb and makeup pouch and fixed her face.

"You're still in love with Dick, aren't you?" Debbie asked.

"No! Oh, I dunno. How do you turn your feelings off so quickly? I don't want to be." Yvonne grimaced. "I never thought he would treat me like this. He is trying to make it my fault he is acting irresponsibly. I don't need that. But now he's got me feeling sorry for him."

When they left the bathroom, Daniel was waiting outside the door and took her hands.

"Are you sure you're okay? It looked like he was assaulting you. I heard you tell him to let you go. That's how I found you."

"I'm doing better now. Can we get some punch?"

"I wanted to punch him. But I can't do that. I'm a pacifist." Daniel led her over to the refreshment table.

"What's a pacifist? Like a socialist?" Yvonne gulped her punch in one long sip.

He laughed. "A pacifist believes war or any type of violence is wrong. There have been pacifists in the newspapers objecting to the War in Vietnam. If they are drafted, they won't serve in the military, or at least they won't take up arms. I suppose you could be a pacifist and hold a desk job if you were drafted. So far, they haven't initiated a draft for fighting in Vietnam. A socialist believes in shared wealth. Not the same thing at all."

They didn't spot Dick the rest of the evening, and they continued dancing and talking. Yvonne had been afraid the confrontation with Dick would ruin their fun, but it somehow made her feel closer to Daniel as if he could now understand what she'd been going through.

When he pulled the Cadillac into the carport at his house, Daniel waited for Keith and Debbie to get out of the backseat and go up to her front door.

"Aren't we getting out?" Yvonne asked.

"Not yet. I've got to give Keith a little time to say good-night."

"Oh." Yvonne turned to look toward their front door, but her view was obstructed. Had Debbie ever kissed a boy? If she had, she hadn't told Yvonne about it. When she turned back to Daniel, he quickly pressed his mouth over hers. The surprise had her pulse jumping.

When he pulled back, Daniel said, "I guess I should have asked you before I kissed you."

"No . . . I mean it's all right. It was fine. I mean . . . thank you for the evening. It was lovely, the dinner, the dancing…"

"How about the kissing? Was that 'lovely?' Or do we need to practice some more?" He moved in slowly this time, gently touching her lips at first, then putting his hand on her jaw.

"Practicing is good," Yvonne murmured. "Practice, you know makes—"

"Perfect." Daniel kissed her a third time and she felt a familiar warmth. It was nice to know that didn't just happen with Dick. *I should kiss more boys. Well, at least this one more.*

They heard Keith start his car on the street and knew Debbie must have gone inside. Tomorrow the girls would rehash every minute of the evening.

CHAPTER ELEVEN

There were two weeks left of school after prom; only one week for the seniors. Aside from the myriad of semester tests, it always seemed like one of the best times of the year. The weather was warm, and everyone was looking forward to summer. Yvonne felt energized and hopeful again. Seeing Dick in the hall didn't dampen her spirits.

Even the teachers seemed happy things were wrapping up. So she was surprised when she went into the girls' bathroom nearest the music rooms one afternoon and heard someone crying in the stalls. Classes were over for the day, and she expected the bathroom to be deserted.

"Are you okay?" Yvonne asked, not knowing who she was speaking to. She could see saddle shoes and white sox under the stall, but since that was part of the standard Pep Club attire, it didn't help identify the weeping girl.

"Yvonne? Is that you?" a voice said.

It's Barbra, Yvonne guessed. What in the world could she be crying about? She was elected Prom Queen, and she was about to attend college on a scholarship. As usual, the world was at her fingertips.

Barbra emerged from the stall, with red swollen eyes. If she'd been wearing makeup to school, she'd cried it all off. "Can you keep a secret?"

"My lips are sealed, Honey. What's upset you this much?" Yvonne put her arms around Barbra. It wasn't that she didn't like Barbra, it was simply hard not to envy her.

"I found out a few days ago I am pregnant." Barbra dabbed at her eyes with toilet paper.

Yvonne's jaw dropped. She didn't see that coming. So much for the ideal world Barbra was living in. "Oh, my goodness. What are you going to do? Are you getting married?"

"It's such a mess. I told the father. He said he'd pay for the abortion. I could get one in Kansas, I think, if I claim the pregnancy is the result of rape or incest. My mother wants to send me away to live with my aunt in Denver and give the baby up for adoption. I feel like my life is ruined. I was supposed to be going to college in the fall and pledging a sorority. Now I'll probably lose my scholarship."

"Can't you go to college if you are pregnant?"

"I don't know what the point would be. I'd have the baby before the semester ended and would miss classes then. Besides, I can't stay around here. Everyone would know."

"I'm so sorry you're going through this. Is there anything I can do for you?"

"I don't think anyone can do anything to help," Barbra said, tears streaming down her cheeks again. "My father said, 'you've made your bed and now you have to lie in it.' I can't believe how much I have disappointed my parents. They are divorced, you know, but my father was right by my mother's side on this."

"But what about John Anthony? It doesn't seem like he should get off easy when you are taking the brunt of this problem."

Barbra shook her head. "I'd better go home. Thanks for listening, Yvonne. Please keep this to yourself." She left Yvonne standing at the sink, nearly in tears herself.

As fate would have it, the next afternoon, John Anthony came up next to her and started walking with her down the hallway. He was also a junior, and they had a few classes together. Like Dick, he had the broad-shouldered frame of a football player, but his shaggy blonde hair and big brown eyes made him both winsome and masculine. He was arguably the most attractive boy in the school, which is why Barbra latched onto him in the first place. They'd made a stunning couple at prom.

But now, knowing what happened to Barbra, she found him repulsive.

"What do you want, John Anthony?" Yvonne nearly spat out the words.

"I thought you might want to talk. Since we have something in common," he said. "You know, Dick, Barbra."

She turned a scowl on him. "They are both graduating. Big deal. I don't want to discuss either one of them, especially with you." She walked faster to her class and slid into her seat.

She caught him looking at her a couple of times in the classes they shared, and she was glad school was nearly done for the year. *I sure hope he doesn't have me pegged as his next victim, cuz a pretty face is not going to do it for me.*

CHAPTER TWELVE

When school ended, Yvonne expected to see a lot more of Daniel. Dating the boy next door was a little awkward. For one thing, they could see each other every time they came and went. Before, it didn't matter to her what Daniel was up to. Now it was "where's he going, what's he doing, who's he seeing?" She imagined he had the same thoughts about her.

She could see his bedroom window from hers, so she even knew when he got up and went to bed. She heard his classical music blaring from the radio most evenings, and wondered what station played that format. The Edison's and Adams' houses were designed the same way, in mirror images. Debbie and Daniel had adjacent bedrooms on the side of the house facing the Edison's and Yvonne and Clark had matching bedroom spaces facing the Adams' house. Once Connie Edison noticed Bonnie Adams had put Debbie in the bedroom in the back of the house, she had Yvonne take that same room in their house. The back-bedroom windows were farther off the ground since the houses were split levels.

When the children were younger, they made a sport of opening the windows facing each other and trying to throw things through the opposite windows: toys, softballs, oranges, even water balloons, which made a terrible mess. Debbie and Yvonne had even installed a clothesline loop from one window to the other, so they could clip notes to try to communicate, mostly after "lights out." The line was gone now, but sometimes Debbie and Yvonne would talk on their phone extensions in their rooms and look at each other through the windows.

Daniel hardly ever called her on the phone. If he wanted to talk to her, he showed up at her door. She expected him to want to take her places, as Dick had done, to the movies, or out for burgers, or to parties. Daniel seemed to be content to see her when she was visiting Debbie or to come over to her place to play croquet or badminton in the backyard, which often involved at least one of their parents and neighbor kids.

He had a part-time job working at a car wash, and she would see him jump on his bicycle to go there several times a week. Daniel didn't have a car yet. He'd been riding to school with one of his friends or Debbie. Her car insurance rates were cheaper. He also practiced the piano and his French horn regularly, as the Youth Symphony had a few concerts during the summer.

Yvonne couldn't figure out why he didn't want to spend more time with her, though. Wasn't Yvonne his girlfriend? He hadn't tried to kiss her again. They hadn't even had a private place or moment where he could have kissed her after the night of the prom.

She finally confronted Debbie about it, as she didn't think she could ask Daniel.

"I thought your brother liked me after we went to the prom," Yvonne began, as they were eating ice cream cones at Baskin-Robbins Thirty-one Flavors. "But he hasn't asked me to go on another date."

"You know he likes you," Debbie said, rubbing her forehead to calm the brain freeze from the ice cream. "He also likes playing the guitar, piano, and horn. He's working as much as he can so he can buy a car. He said a guy needs a car to take a girl out on dates. I went out with Keith a few times after prom, but I haven't heard from him for two weeks either. Boys are basically idiots."

"Maybe I should go out with someone else."

"Has someone else asked you out?"

"Well, Gary has called me a few times. I would rather go out with Daniel, but he hasn't asked. I think he put me back into the 'friend category' after prom. I hate to say it, but I kinda miss Dick. At least he knew how to make a girl feel special."

Yvonne did go riding around with Gary White, a boy she'd met while she was lifeguarding at the Eastridge neighborhood swimming pool. Gary attended Northeast High School and he liked listening to rock and roll music. He had a stocky build and an abundance of wild bushy brown hair. It was clear, he didn't have a lot of spending cash, but they would go to King's Drive-in to get vanilla Pepsi's. He did have a car, a dented 1960 Buick Riviera. He had to open the passenger door for Yvonne, not out of good manners, but because the door was slightly bent on its hinges and he had to lift it while pulling it open.

She was getting into Gary's car with him one afternoon, when Daniel came flying down the street on his bicycle, and very nearly ran into the mailbox when he was rubbernecking at Yvonne and Gary. Then he overcorrected and slid sideways on his lawn. Yvonne was already seated in the car by the time he landed.

"Are you okay, Man?" Gary called out.

"Yeah," Daniel said, examining his grass-stained Converse All-Stars and scraped leg.

I guess he noticed. Now we'll see if it matters to him. It looked like his pride was hurt more than his body at least.

That night Yvonne opened her bedroom window. The fragrance of mown grass blew in on the breeze and she heard Daniel playing the piano. She didn't hear him often. It sounded angry, as though he was channeling rage or a furious storm. She plopped down on the floor leaning her elbows on the wide sill below the window. She rested her head on her arms tapping her fingers   to the beat.

"Beethoven." Clark stood in her doorway. He was living at home during his summer break from college. "It's one of Beethoven's Piano Sonatas. I forget which one. I took music appreciation last semester. Daniel must be in a bad mood the way he is attacking that. Is he mad at you?"

Yvonne jumped to her feet and glanced toward the window. "Me? Why would he be mad at me?"

"Well, you are hiding in your room, listening to him play the piano, which tells me something is going on. If you want to hear it, you could go over there."

"No. I can't. I mean, it's late and . . . I can hear it from here."

Clark just raised his eyebrows and went to take a shower.

"I have a great idea," Debbie announced around the middle of July. "They are having a Keentime dance at the Antelope Pavilion next Friday night, and we should go. I thought we could take Linda and Nancy too, and make it a twirler outing. I already asked my dad and he said I could borrow the Cadillac."

"That sounds like fun. Just us girls though?" Yvonne asked.

"Yes, just the girls. I don't think Daniel would go if I asked him. He seems to be mad at you."

"What makes you think that?"

"The other day, I said something about you, and he made a sarcastic remark about you hanging around with some cretin from Northeast High School. I asked him if he was jealous and he laughed. It wasn't very convincing though. You should talk to him directly. I don't like being stuck in the middle."

"Hmmm, maybe you're right. I've been waiting for him to make a move, but it's not happening. I like the idea of us girls going to the dance. I'll try to talk to Daniel."

She got her chance the next day when she spotted him throwing the Frisbee in his backyard. Their boxer, Grover, would chase it and manage to pick it up about half of the time. Sometimes Grover would return it to Daniel.

"Daniel, can we talk?" Yvonne said, walking up behind him as he was trying to wrestle the Frisbee out of Grover's mouth.

He looked her up and down and swallowed hard. "What do you want to talk about?"

"I don't know what happened to us. I mean I thought things were going well the night of the prom, but then you seemed to cool it."

"You thought I was cooling it? I have things to do, a job. I have to practice. You started going out with some other guy. What am I supposed to think?"

"I got tired of waiting for you."

"Waiting for me to do what exactly?"

"Ask me on a date. Come over to spend time with me. Kiss me again. Anything."

She was aware that their voices had gotten louder, she glanced around to see if anyone else had heard them. Another boy next door issue: privacy.

He cleared his throat and stared at her.

He has amazing eyes. Why have I never noticed his eyes? Debbie has beautiful blue eyes. I have helped her highlight them. But Daniel's are deeper, more serious, more sensuous somehow. Her heart began to flutter as she stared back, waiting.

"What is it you want from me, Yvonne? It sounds like you want me to act like Dick Dunn, and take you out to nice places, to romance you, to sweet talk you. I know how he operated. I heard enough of you and Debbie on the phone, or in her room. He was trying to get your guard down so you would make out with him, just to see how far he could push it. But he was eighteen. Maybe I am too young for you. I'm not blinded by testosterone pumping through my veins like some of these love-sick fools I see at school."

"What are you trying to say? You don't want to date me?"

"I want to be honest with you. I like you; I always have. But I have to act like myself and keep my personal priorities. I'm not ready to let a girl interfere with that."

When she turned and started to leave, he reached for her arm. "Don't misunderstand. The kissing was nice. The kissing and the dancing. I want to do those again. I don't want to get caught up in anything that may end up destroying our friendship."

Yvonne blinked back her tears. "If you were really my friend, I could tell you how badly I feel because a boy I like only wants to be pals."

"See, this is what I wanted to avoid," Daniel said pulling her into an embrace and fisting one hand in her hair. She clung to him, and it felt comforting like she was hugging one of her family members until it didn't. She felt his body press hard against her before he took her head in his hands. She expected him to kiss her lips, but instead, he kissed her forehead, then let her go.

Don't tell me there's no testosterone pumping now, Buddy. She spun away, almost tripping over Grover in her race to escape. *Debbie is right. Boys are idiots.*

CHAPTER THIRTEEN

The blaring music from the Keentime dance greeted the four girls as soon as they entered Antelope Park. They had the Caddy's windows rolled down and were calling out to everyone they knew as they drove around to find a spot to leave the car. Kids had parked on the grass and the side of the drives. They inspected the famed park bridge for the latest graffiti. Every year kids from one school would adorn it with spray paint claiming their school was superior, and it was often repainted by another school's artists within twenty-four hours. This happened mostly when there were intra-city football games the next night. Yvonne knew Dick had been involved in at least one of these hijinks.

They found a place to park about three blocks away from the dance and piled out of the car. It was the warmest part of the summer, and the girls were all wearing T-shirts, short shorts, and sandals. Yvonne had pulled her hair up in a ponytail, and Debbie was sporting pigtails. Before leaving for the dance, they'd gone up to Yvonne's room and the older two girls helped Linda and Nancy perfect their makeup and perfume.

The pavilion was crowded, and it was warm inside, even with every door propped open. They paid for admittance and got their hands stamped so that they could come and go. A hundred kids were milling around in the park, but extra policemen were working to keep things orderly and trying unsuccessfully to keep the underage kids from lighting up.

"I remember Barbra telling me she liked to come to these dances to meet boys," Debbie shouted, as did everyone else trying to be heard over the noise. "I'm not sure they did much dancing though."

Yvonne hadn't thought about Barbra for weeks. She'd kept Barbra's confidence and hadn't even told Debbie about her pregnancy. Just as she was feeling sorry for Barbra, she caught sight of John Anthony Turner approaching them.

"Hi, John Anthony!" Debbie waved him over. When he walked up to them, Yvonne slipped away into the crowd. "Yvonne? Where are you going?"

"She's mad at me, I think," John Anthony said. "I suppose there are a lot of girls who are blaming me." He caught up with Yvonne, with Debbie on his heels. "Yvonne, hey. I think I know why you keep giving me the evil eye. Is this about Barbra?"

"Yes, Barbra." Yvonne stopped moving and turned on him abruptly. "You remember that girl you knocked up and refused to marry?"

"You've got it wrong," he shouted back, exactly when the band stopped playing to take a break. "I'm not the father. I never even had sex with her." Heads turned toward him when his voice carried over the ringing silence.

Yvonne glared at him. *Is he lying? Is this only part of his act?* She became aware other kids around them were watching. She motioned for him to follow her back outside where there was more space. Debbie kept up with them.

"What are you two talking about? What happened to Barbra?" Debbie said.

John Anthony sighed. "Barbra is pregnant. Everyone assumed I was responsible, but I'm not. You wouldn't believe the hassle I had to go through with her parents, my parents. I'm mad as hell about this, and now the other girls are treating me like I am a pariah."

"If it's not you, who is the father?" Debbie asked.

"She wouldn't tell me. She didn't even tell me she was pregnant. Her father charged over to our house threatening me, scaring my poor little sister half to death. Thank goodness my parents were there. After all the shouting was over, they did believe me at least."

By this time, Nancy had joined them. Linda had been dancing and was talking to some new friends inside.

"Have you heard about Barbra, Nancy?" Debbie said moving closer to her.

"About her giving her baby up for adoption? Yeah, I heard that story." Nancy glanced around as though she was looking for someone.

"But no one seems to know who the father is. Well, Barbra knows. She told me she talked to him about it." Yvonne didn't see any point in keeping the secret now.

"I have my suspicions," John Anthony said.

"I knew she was seeing someone else besides you, John Anthony. Sorry," Nancy said.

"Yvonne, would you dance with me?" John Anthony asked. "Maybe if people see us together, they will at least keep an open mind and not assume I am a sleaze."

Yvonne stared at him for a minute, pursing her lips. Her fingers stroked the gold cross she wore around her neck. He didn't flinch, so she decided he deserved the benefit of the doubt. "Okay," she said. When he led her back to the dance floor, she caught a look of dismay from Debbie, but she would have to deal with her later.

She relaxed and had fun dancing with John Anthony. She still thought he was too handsome for his own good and wondered why he picked her to dance with. The band played a few familiar fast numbers with good beats, and the crowd sang along. When she heard the familiar strains of "Cherish" by the Association, John Anthony pulled her in close. As she laid her head on his shoulder, it reminded her of Dick, and to some extent Daniel too with its lyrics about unspoken love. *I guess John Anthony hasn't had an easy time of it either. Maybe I should at least support him.*

When they were rotating around in a slow dance, she caught sight of Debbie near the sidewall, watching them like a cat outside a mouse hole. For some reason, she looked sad. *I don't know why. Is she upset I accepted the invitation to dance instead of hanging with her? We did come to meet up with boys and dance. Debbie said so herself.* Before the slow dance ended, Debbie had disappeared from view.

Yvonne danced with John Anthony until the band's next break, then she went in search of Debbie. She found Debbie and Nancy talking to three boys she didn't know, just outside the pavilion. Debbie seemed to be flirting with a tall boy with a short Afro haircut. He was dressed in a white shirt with a vest and dress pants. Yvonne's first impression was that he had style. She had to admit she didn't know very many Black kids, there were only a few at their school and none in her class. He and his friends must attend another school. Oh, but that smile. When he flashed a wide grin at Debbie, she knew her friend was being taken in. He had dazzling white teeth and a knockout smile.

She let Debbie and Nancy alone, they seemed to be enjoying themselves. She walked around looking for Linda. She found her in a group of girls, sitting on a bench laughing. One of the girls put her arm around Linda's shoulder and pulled her close as they doubled over in hysterics. *I wonder what is so funny.*

"Yvonne?"

She turned around and found Janet Sparks standing with a tall lean red-haired boy she didn't recognize.

"Yvonne, this is my cousin, Randy Sparks. He recently moved here and is going to be in your class next year," Janet said.

"Nice to meet you, Randy," Yvonne said politely. "You are changing schools your senior year? That must be tough."

"I dunno. Capital High is a bigger school. Class A. It may give me a better chance at a basketball scholarship."

"Basketball huh? Well, from what I've seen, our basketball team could use some help." Yvonne crossed her arms.

"Why don't you dance with me? You can tell me all about who my competition is."

She smirked. "Oh, you mean on the basketball team."

"Maybe." He smiled and took her hand to lead her to the dance floor.

She spent the remainder of the Keentime dance with Randy. John Anthony managed to coax a few other girls to dance, including Linda and Nancy. Debbie stayed outside, apparently talking to the same group of boys. A little later she was dancing with the boy with the knockout smile.

When the dance ended at ten-thirty, the four twirlers met at their prearranged spot on the north side of the pavilion. Once they got into the Cadillac, the bumper-to-bumper traffic snaked like segments of a caterpillar through the park.

"I can't believe all of you danced with John Anthony, except for me. Didn't you remember I had a crush on him, Yvonne?"

"Sure, in eighth grade, Silly. You don't still think you have dibs on him now, do you?"

"Eighth-grade dibs last forever, don't you know that?" Debbie said. "I did meet a very nice boy though. His name is Robert Washington. Not Bob or Rob, it's Robert. His father is a preacher at a Baptist church."

"What would your parents think about you dancing with . . . well, you know," Nancy asked.

"What do you mean, because he's Black? I don't think they'd care. It's not like I am marrying him," Debbie said.

"Well, my Daddy is from Mississippi and I know he'd be mighty upset if I did that," Nancy said.

"I did notice the police officers that were working came over to talk to Robert and his friends several times. I think one of them knew his father. He seemed very sweet though, and kinda shy. He's hardly one of those militant types. He asked if he could call me."

"Sounds like you did well for the night, Debs," Yvonne said.

"Yes, despite your trying to poach John Anthony. Who were you dancing with? I didn't recognize the redhead," Debbie said.

"He just moved here from western Nebraska. Randy Sparks, Janet's cousin. He said he plays basketball. He's going to be in our senior class."

"It looked like you two were getting cozy," Linda said.

"I only met him tonight. But I did give him my number." Yvonne leaned back on the seat and closed her eyes.

"I never give a boy my phone number." Nancy pulled her compact out of her purse smoothing her hair. "I tell them my father's name. He can look in the phone book. That way, he won't lose the number."

CHAPTER FOURTEEN

The rest of the summer flew by quickly. Yvonne and Debbie worked on routines for the upcoming marching band season. Yvonne worked as a lifeguard at the swimming pool four days a week and taught preschoolers how to float. Randy came by the pool most days when she was working. People were looking at them as a couple. Gary had gone to Michigan for three weeks with his family. Another lifeguard told her he'd stopped by the swimming pool one day when she was talking to Randy, but she hadn't seen him. It might have been true because he'd stopped calling her.

By August she was finally over Dick. She only had seen him once after school got out. He was on the opposite side of the Sears' sporting goods department. She didn't think he even saw her. It gave her a twinge of sadness, but it was time to forgive and forget.

Daniel was another story. When Randy started coming over to her house, she thought Daniel might be jealous. Even if he hadn't noticed Randy over at the Edisons, he was bound to find out she was seeing Randy from her conversations with Debbie.

Yvonne and Randy were sitting close together drinking iced tea on the wrought-iron settee on the Edison's patio. Harold and Connie had gone inside after a rousing game of badminton. Randy had his arm on the back of the bench, playing with Yvonne's hair.

Things are about to get romantic. They'd been seeing each other for a few weeks, nearly every day. It was natural things should progress.

Daniel called out as he cut through the yard, "Is the game over? I thought you might need a relief player for badminton." Grover came bounding ahead of him and planted his slobbering mouth in Yvonne's lap.

"Grover!" Yvonne said, "Have some manners!" Grover sat back and wagged his tail. She swatted at the air, glancing at

Daniel. "Randy, this is the loveable Grover. Shake, Grove."

The dog offered a paw, and Randy shook it smiling.

"And Daniel. He lives next door with Grover. Daniel Adams, Randy Sparks. Randy is going to be in our class at school." The scowl she gave Daniel was frosty. *What are you doing here?*

Daniel shook Randy's hand too, then sat in the chair across from them. Yvonne's eyes widened as she nodded and jerked her head toward Daniel's house. Daniel kept his eyes on Randy.

"I just finished listening to the Cardinals game. Gibson was on fire!" Daniel said.

"Oh Geez, that was tonight? Get outta here! Are you a Cardinals fan? I watched a game earlier this summer at Busch Stadium with my dad and uncles. They're going all the way this year!"

It was like they were both speaking another language, talking about RBI, batting averages, at-bats, strikeouts, ERAs, home runs. She knew what some of it meant, but why did they care? It was yawn, baseball. And more baseball. Then when she thought they were winding down, they'd start analyzing another player's record for the season.

I may as well go inside and watch Peyton Place. Daniel doesn't even notice the dirty looks I am giving him.

After an hour, Daniel got up to leave. When Randy started to go with him, Yvonne stood crossing her arms and narrowing her eyes at both of them.

Randy turned back saying, "I'll be right back, Yvonne." The daggers in her eyes stopped him short. He looked back at Daniel.

"Yeah, she's pissed off." Daniel lowered his voice. "And I have to warn you, she's got a nasty right hook." A slow smile spread across his face as he signaled to the dog to follow him home.

"What's wrong?" Randy asked.

Yvonne flounced back to the metal bench, and Randy quickly joined her.

"I take it you aren't a baseball fan?"

She glared at him. "I thought you were here to see me. We finally had some time alone and then he barges in and wants to talk baseball. I have no interest in or knowledge about baseball. Maybe you should just go on a date with him!"

"Well, you're prettier." Her icy expression was unchanged. "Maybe I will go out with Daniel. We could be friends. Tell me, what would you like to talk about?"

She hoped Daniel might be too busy to bother them when he spent his earnings on a 1962 Plymouth Fury hardtop. He bought it from his uncle's used car lot in Omaha. Debbie had gotten the Bug from her uncle too. Daniel spent the next few weekends tinkering with the Fury in the driveway. On the second Saturday afternoon, Yvonne caught Randy detouring over to see what Daniel was doing instead of ringing her doorbell.

She supposed he needed to make friends with other guys since he was new in town, but she didn't appreciate it horning in on her date time. At first, she didn't think Randy and Daniel would have much in common, but it turned out Randy was a serious student too, not to the point of being a total dweeb, but he'd been first in his class at his former school. The next thing she knew Daniel was going over to Randy's house to play a board game called Fight in the Skies.

She had to tell Randy how she felt. "I think it is nice you and

Daniel have become friends, but sometimes it seems like you are spending time with him when you said you were coming over to see me," Yvonne told him one evening after they'd been late for a surprise birthday party because he'd stopped to discuss the new carburetor Daniel was installing.

"I like Daniel. Is that a problem? He told me he took you to the prom last year, so the two of you must get along," Randy said.

"What else did he tell you about me?"

"That you'd been friends since childhood, you were his sister's best pal. You dated some jerk last year who graduated. A jerk who cheated on you. And then you slugged him."

"I didn't slug him. I slapped him. For some reason, Daniel found that funny. But I don't go around attacking people, just so you know."

"The way he talked about you, I would have said he was in love with you. But he kept saying you were just friends."

Yvonne arched her eyebrows. "Huh. Yeah, that's right. We're just friends."

"Good, cuz we decided we should go on a double date."

"What? Who is Daniel going to go out with?"

"I don't know. He's going to let me know. He said we should all go to King's."

Andrea Mitchum was the girl he chose for their double date. She wasn't sure how she felt about Daniel going out with someone she considered one of her friends, although they weren't close. Andrea was a year younger and played the flute in the orchestra. Daniel was one of the few who played in both band and orchestra.

When the night came to go on the date, the plans changed. Randy told her they were going to the Starview Drive-in Movie Theater. Yvonne liked the idea.

Starlight. Moonlight. Romantic movie. All of this is custom designed for a first kiss. And maybe more than one.

She'd gone to the drive-in theater with Dick several times the previous summer and didn't even remember what movies had been playing. The drive-in featured second-run movies most people had seen, or movies bad enough no one wanted to see. Yvonne thought the advantage of that was when your parents quizzed you on the content of the movie, you already knew the plot, or if it was one of the turkeys, you could invent something, and they wouldn't know the difference.

Everyone knew teenagers went to drive-in movies to neck, and she supposed the proprietors didn't mind, as long as they sold enough popcorn and Pepsi. When Randy came to pick her up that evening, she was surprised when he said Daniel was driving his car, and they were relegated to the back seat. Daniel's car was a two-door, so they had to climb around the front seat to get in, not ideal for two people with long legs. Then they had to wait in the warm car while Daniel went inside Andrea's house to get her and visit with her parents. Yvonne's pancake makeup and eye shadow streamed slowly off her face in the heat and her deodorant went on strike. They hadn't even made it to the destination yet. She didn't even want to think about how much her date was sweating.

"Do they have drive-in theaters where you lived before, Randy?" she asked, more out of boredom than anything else.

"They didn't even have a regular theater within fifty miles of where I lived," he said. "This movie is about four years old, I think, but I have never seen it."

Daniel and Andrea made it to the car, and they headed to the drive-in. Once they found a good spot to park, and Daniel added the speaker to his car window, they settled in to watch the animated shorts that preceded the movie. Almost immediately, Daniel put his arm around Andrea's shoulder, and she leaned against him.

Yvonne gaped. Her face seemed to lose feeling. They barely knew each other. Randy pretended not to notice them.

"Is that a concession stand down there?" Randy asked.

"Yeah, they have popcorn, hot dogs, candy, and pop," Yvonne forced herself to focus on Randy.

"Does anyone else want something to eat?" he asked. When no one spoke up, he went to the concession stand himself. In about ten minutes he returned with various treats.

"You should have come with me, Yvonne. They had a big variety," Randy said, pushing his way into the back seat. "I got popcorn, licorice, and a couple of Pepsis. Oh, and here was the strangest thing I found. Dill pickles. They sell whole dill pickles!" Daniel started laughing, then Andrea joined in.

Yvonne furrowed her brow and looked at Randy, who was holding up a six-inch-long dill pickle. "You're seriously going to eat that?" It not only smelled like dill and vinegar, but she also caught a whiff of garlic.

"Why wouldn't I? They're delicious. Here, have a bite." He put the pickle up to her mouth. Daniel had turned around to see her reaction and started laughing harder.

The smell made her eyes water. "I think only pregnant women eat dill pickles."

Randy laughed and took a big bite. "That's not true, my grandmother cans them all the time on the farm."

This isn't going the way I expected. I'm not sure I would want to kiss anyone after they ate that thing. Then the movie started. It turned out to be a war epic, apparently, a similar theme to the Fight in the Skies game, starring Lee Marvin and Steve McQueen. *This has to be the worst movie Steve McQueen ever made.* But Randy and Daniel seemed to enjoy it, whooping and hollering when the fighter planes shot down the enemy.

The second movie of the double feature was a spy thriller she'd seen a couple of years earlier, and she hadn't appreciated it the first time. Even Daniel appeared to have gotten bored, as he pulled Andrea closer and then they scooted down into the seat so only the tops of their heads were visible from the back seat.

Randy seemed oblivious to this. By this time, he'd consumed all of the food he'd bought and wormed his way back out of the car to find the restroom. Yvonne began counting how many blocks she would have to walk to get home from there.

When Randy climbed back in beside her, she decided to be more direct. "Do you know why people go to the drive-in, Randy?"

"Well, I heard that dad over there in the station wagon tell his kids to lay down on the sleeping bag, so for him, it was a way to get his kids to sleep. But I guess it is cheaper than a regular movie."

She pointed to the front seat, where Daniel and Andrea's heads had now disappeared.

Randy shook his head. "I think they're missing the movie."

And you're missing the point.

"You think this is supposed to be romantic, is that it?" He grinned. "Come here." He pulled her into his lap, positioning her so she had an unobstructed view over the front seat to see the movie screen. "Is this better?"

Yvonne sighed. Maybe a little bit. She decided to pay some attention to the show, although the audio had started to crackle in and out from the speaker. "Look out, here comes the part where someone shoots a bullet through his top hat." Then she affected a phony British accent, and added, "Egads, I'll have to have my butler send this out for repairs!"

"You've seen this movie before?" Randy asked.

"Yes, it's pitiful." She went back to impersonating the hero in the movie, "Take that, you nasty Russian spy doll!" as the hero sprayed some sort of gas out of a canister.

Randy laughed and took up her game, raising the pitch of his voice and affecting a bad Russian accent, "You Brits are all alike, all steam and no substance!" as the Russian female spy shot at the hero again.

They went back and forth like this, with Yvonne making up silly dialogue for the suave British spy and Randy making up even sillier lines for the glamorous Russian villain pursuing him. Daniel and Andrea sat back up and played along. Soon they were adopting the parts of additional characters as they appeared. Often they missed their cues when they were laughing too hard.

When they were leaving the drive-in, Randy said, "Now I get why drive-in movies are fun. You're all pretty good at this game."

Yvonne had to snicker. *Is he really that naïve?*

CHAPTER FIFTEEN

It was nice starting school with a boyfriend. *Lucky me, last year I was dating a football player and this year a basketball player.* It was too early for Randy to try out for the team. But it turned out, his family moved to Lincoln when his father got a job as a history teacher and assistant basketball coach at Capital High, so she didn't know how he could miss.

All the coaches took an interest in Randy. Even though he was six foot, three inches tall, he declined to play football. The cross-country coach convinced him his sport wouldn't be likely to injure him and it would be good off-season training for all the running on the basketball court.

Between his meets and the band performing at all of the football games, and the Saturday band contests, Yvonne didn't see much of Randy outside of school. But they managed to share a locker, right next to the one she'd shared with Dick Dunn last year. Although he still hadn't tried to kiss her, Randy did hold her hand in the hallway when they weren't loaded down with books. She hoped that would send a signal to the other girls this new guy was taken.

Homecoming was approaching quickly. The twirlers had an ambitious show planned, including twirling hoops, flags, and fire batons. The fire batons were the riskiest. Aside from the obvious risks of being burned or dropping a lit baton onto the grass field, there was a good chance of rain on any given Friday night in October. But that is what made it special.

"We're not going to toss the fire batons. Principal Owen forbade it. But Mr. Humphreys got him to agree we can twirl two at a time. We are going to need to practice with the unlit batons as they are heavier than regular batons," Yvonne explained to Debbie, Linda and Nancy. She and Debbie gave Linda and Nancy a chance to design the routine for the hoops, and Debbie created the routine for the flags, while Yvonne did the routine for the fire.

Yvonne was quite surprised when the homecoming royalty finalists were listed in the morning announcements over the intercom. She and Randy had been nominated by the student council. Unlike the prom royalty, where only the attendees voted, everyone in the school got to vote for the Homecoming King and Queen in their homeroom class.

"You might get chosen," Debbie assured her later. "I know you always think it will be a cheerleader or one of the class officers, but a lot of kids know who you are. You can thank ol' Dick Dunn for that in part, but the kids I have talked to are glad to see you with someone like Randy."

"Don't be silly, Debbie. I'm not particularly popular. I am

surprised Randy was nominated too. Maybe they felt sorry for him having to start a new school as a senior."

"I dunno. Randy is friendly. I see him horsing around with the jocks in the lunchroom in fourth period."

"Well, he could be friendlier, if you ask me." When Debbie raised her eyebrows, she backtracked. "Never mind, forget I said anything."

She was still waiting for that first kiss. What was it with boys? They came on too strong or not at all. She decided if he didn't try to kiss her by the homecoming dance, she would have to make the first move herself.

In previous years, the school had the homecoming football game on Friday night, then everyone had to rush home, change their clothes, and come back for the homecoming dance which didn't start until about ten o'clock and went until midnight. The school administration determined this was potentially dangerous after some of the students got into a car accident returning to school. So this year, for the first time, the homecoming dance was going to be held on Saturday night from eight to eleven.

Yvonne was relieved to hear this, as she was already worrying herself sick about the fire baton performance. The twirlers practiced a couple of times with the batons lit, but it seemed like they had trouble keeping synchronized, as they were all a little worried about getting burned.

"Just pretend there are flowers on the ends of the batons, not fire. Flowers are pretty and they won't hurt anyone. Lots of pretty orange flowers," Debbie had suggested. They all made jokes about the flowers on their batons, and it did seem to relax them. By the end of the last practice, they were mastering all of the routines. They made a plan to all go to King's after the football game and have fun even if everything didn't go smoothly.

When it came time for the band to go out to the field for the pre-game performance, it was sprinkling, and Mr. Humphreys said there had been some lightning. If there was too much lightning, they could even call off the football game. Yvonne's heart sank. All that practice, and we might have to postpone it all. The pre-game show was canceled.

Fortunately, it only sprinkled for about ten minutes, and the lightning stopped. The football players and the fans got a little wet, and the bleachers were soaked. The twirlers had raincoats and ponchos they put over their heads. Because of the fire twirling, they all had their hair pulled into tight buns, except Linda whose hairstyle was short. They had sequin headbands on to reflect the firelight. By the time halftime came, the rain had stopped and there was at most a slight mist in the air.

Right before the band took the field, playing "Light My Fire" by the Doors. Mr. Humphreys and his student teacher lit all sixteen ends of the batons, and the twirlers launched the routine. Because Yvonne knew it would take a few minutes to light everything, the opening sequence was staggered, so she was performing alone for eight counts, then Linda joined her for eight counts, then Nancy, and Debbie was the last. The crowd roared its approval and Yvonne caught sight of Daniel on the sidelines with his parents' movie camera. She was thankful when they got through it, and no one even made a mistake. They tossed the fire batons in a metal barrel filled with water and grabbed the hoops to perform the next song.

Nancy dropped her hoop once but picked right back up where the others were. They even tossed the hoops in the air without any problems. The flag routine went as planned for the most part, but Debbie forgot where she was for a beat or two, even though it was her routine. Overall, considering how much harder this performance was, they did very well. And the fans showed their appreciation with cheers and applause.

"Oh my God, I was soooo nervous. I have never had such stage fright at a performance," Debbie admitted when they were crammed into a booth at King's. "But I'll bet I'll remember this as the best show we ever did." The tantalizing smell of freshly fried potatoes and onion rings filled their senses as the waitress handed out their food.

"I saw Bill Edwards taking photos of us for the school paper. And that sports photographer, you've seen his name in the *Lincoln Journal* . . . Hank Barber, he took some pictures of us too. Or at least of me. I smiled right at him." Linda flashed her pearly whites.

"I am just glad it is over!" Nancy said.

"I hear ya, Sister," Yvonne agreed. "Toast to the fabulous twirlers of Capital High." They all clinked their vanilla Pepsi glasses.

"Now all we have to worry about is tomorrow night!" Debbie said.

"Are you excited about going to Homecoming with Robert, Debbie?" Nancy asked.

"I can't wait. And his homecoming at Lincoln High is next weekend so we get to do it twice."

"Wow. Are you wearing the same dress to both?" Linda asked.

"No, I am wearing a red dress to our homecoming tomorrow, but I am wearing a dressy blue sweater and skirt to his homecoming. I think it will look okay; it looks like a dress."

Linda and Nancy were excited about their dates as well. Nancy had gotten rid of her old-style glasses and was now wearing contacts most of the time. When her eyes were tired, like they were now, she wore wire rims similar to John Lennon's. She was going to homecoming with Peter Thompson, who sat right next to her in the band and played the saxophone. Linda was going with John Anthony Turner. They'd dated off and on since the night of the Keentime Dance in July.

Yvonne had found a gold velveteen dress on sale in the summer for homecoming. It was a new kind of fabric that was both stretchy and soft. She wondered if it was too clingy, but her mother hadn't vetoed it, and it wasn't as short as some of her dresses. She often had trouble finding clothes that were long enough.

"Okay Debs, open your eyes, I have the dress on," Yvonne said. In her mother's three-inch stilettoes she sauntered into the hallway outside Debbie's room where there was a full-length mirror mounted on the wall. Yvonne tugged at the hem when the dress rode up as she took a step.

"I think it is dazzling, Dahh-ling. Give me your best runway walk," Debbie said in an affected voice.

Yvonne strutted down the hall and back into Debbie's bedroom, swinging her hips and comically wiggling her eyebrows. She posed like a model with one hip slung out. "What do you think? Ready for the catwalk?"

Debbie walked up to her pulling the hem down a couple of inches, as it was creeping up into the danger zone. "You're going to have to be careful this doesn't ride up so high."

Daniel appeared in Debbie's open doorway staring. His lips parted slowly.

Debbie laughed. "See, that is the kind of reaction you want from Randy," she said turning back to Yvonne.

Yvonne squirmed. *I didn't think he was home. Why is he looking at my legs like that? Why do I like him looking at my legs like that?*

Their eyes held briefly. Before she could speak, he slipped back into his room.

CHAPTER SIXTEEN

She hadn't danced with Randy since that first night at Keentime. She swore he'd gotten even taller, although she was wearing those two-inch high sandals she'd bought for prom. It felt odd to look up to someone she was dancing with. Maybe she'd gotten used to Daniel. He had grown too. She noticed he was eye-to-eye to her now.

Daniel took Andrea to the homecoming dance. Yvonne supposed they were an item now. They hadn't had another double date, and Debbie hadn't said much about Daniel's dating life. He was letting a girl influence his priorities now. It was just a different girl.

When the combo took a break, she and Randy went out into the courtyard. She had a flashback to what had happened with Dick when he had grabbed her out there and shuddered.

"Are you cold?" Randy asked. He leaned against the building and pulled her into his arms. He was wearing a sports jacket, shirt, tie, and dress pants. She leaned up against him feeling warmth radiate from his body. She tugged down the skirt of her dress so it wouldn't ride up.

He stroked her hair. "You know, I'd kiss you right here, but I don't want you to freak out."

"Why would I freak out?" Other couples were cuddling and kissing around the courtyard. There was path lighting illuminating the area, but it was dark in the shadows.

"Well . . . Daniel told me you had a bad experience with that old boyfriend. He made it sound like he tried to force you . . . anyway, he said he didn't think you would want to kiss anyone again. At least not until you are out of high school."

She reared back on him. "Daniel said what? Are you kidding me? He knows that isn't true! Why would he—" *This must be*

Daniel's idea of a joke. He's trying to ruin my love life.

She grabbed Randy's lapels and pulled him into a kiss so quickly they bumped noses. He laughed and tilted his head and kissed her again. She was still steaming at Daniel but enjoyed the way Randy was lifting her while wrapping his arms around her.

Debbie and Robert were among the couples in the courtyard. They were necking across the way, when one of the chaperones, Mr. Evans, walked up to them.

"You. Boy. Stop that. Let her go," Mr. Evans said to Robert sharply.

"What'sa matter?" Robert said. "We're just kissin'. Everyone out here is kissin', look around."

"Yes, but you can't do that," the chaperone insisted. "All of you, come back inside. This is a school event and school rules apply."

The other couples started to return to the cafeteria. Yvonne rushed over to Debbie and Robert. "What was that all about?" she asked Debbie.

"He has been scowling at us all night. He doesn't approve, you can tell. That's one of the reasons we ducked out here, to get away from his dirty looks. He isn't the only one either, some of the boys have been making rude remarks." Debbie's voice shook.

"Better not react when people treat ya rudely," Robert said. "Don't give 'em an excuse to make it worse. Ya get mad, dey call ya a troublemaker, even when dey started it."

"I'm sorry that happened, Man. Most of the kids here are decent," Randy said. "A few of them called me Farmer Boy and Cheeto-head when I first set foot, but now they're cool. I noticed you had some pretty slick dance moves earlier. Would you mind giving me some pointers?"

Robert looked at him briefly then glanced at Yvonne, before

looking back to Randy, as though he was trying to gauge his sincerity. "Ya serious now?" The band was playing some Motown music, right up Robert's alley. "Okay, Randy, I can teach ya some moves, but dere's one thing ya might as well accept right up front."

"What's that?"

"White boy can't dance."

Randy laughed. He couldn't stop laughing, and soon Robert, Debbie, and Yvonne were laughing too. But then Robert demonstrated some fancy footwork and Randy tried to mimic him, with some success. Robert seemed to have a certain grace, in the way he moved his hips, knees, and feet, which was hard to imitate. Other couples soon gathered around and also tried to do the steps Robert was teaching.

"Whatchew all doing here? This ain't no damn dance class!" Robert said, but the twinkle in his eye told them he was teasing. The band noticed what was going on and continued to play more Rhythm and Blues.

"Look what he did," Debbie said, slipping her arm through Yvonne's as they stood back watching.

"I know, Robert is an amazing dancer," Yvonne said.

"No, I meant Randy," Debbie nodded toward him. "He took a bad situation where Robert was being targeted and turned it into a positive thing. Like, look at this guy. He's a great dancer. Let's learn from him. You ought to hang on to Randy. He's got character."

"By the way, I'm going to kill your brother."

"What did dear Daniel do now?"

"Randy finally told me Daniel warned him not to try to kiss me. That something Dick had done had scarred me for life, and I might freak out if someone tried to kiss me."

Debbie had trouble talking she was laughing so hard. "And all this time, that's why he didn't try to kiss you? The drive-in? How hilarious. I'm sorry I'm laughing but that's absolutely something Daniel would pull. He's just jealous."

"Jealous? No, he's just infuriating."

Neither Yvonne nor Randy were selected as the Homecoming King or Queen, but they had to pose for photographs as attendants. The rest of the evening went much better. Randy kissed her goodnight at the door as though it was the most natural thing in the world. When she went up to her room, she looked out her window several times, waiting for Debbie to turn her light on in her room. Then she planned to call her to discuss the end of the evening. She waited for about an hour but didn't see Debbie's light, so she went to bed.

Her parents allowed her to miss church the next morning knowing she'd been out late, and she was enjoying sleeping in. The phone woke her up. Debbie sounded frantic and said she'd be right over. Yvonne only had time to grab her robe before she barged through her door.

"I don't know what to do, Yvonne. This is way beyond my experience." Debbie began pacing in front of the bed.

"Calm down, Honey, and tell me what you are talking about."

"Robert was taking me home last night, and there was a cop car behind us. They pulled him over, right down there on Randolph. He wasn't speeding, he wasn't doing anything wrong."

"Why did they stop him?"

"They didn't say. But one officer came to his side of the car, and his partner came to my side and they shone their flashlights in on us, blinding us. They told him to get out of the car. Didn't ask for a license or registration, just 'get out.' I was scared by then. The cop on my side told me to scoot back across the seat closer to the door. He said, 'What are you doing, Missy, riding around with a coon?' Robert had already told me not to say anything to them, so I kept my mouth shut. I couldn't believe someone would say that in Lincoln, Nebraska. Especially a policeman.

"I couldn't hear what they said to Robert, except for something about him being dressed like a pimp. The cop on my side went back around and stood too close to Robert. It looked like they were trying to make him strike out or talk back to them, and if he did, they probably would have arrested him or hit him. One of them had that Billy club thing out and pushed it up to Robert's neck. I was in shock. I wanted to scream at them that they were way off base, he was a nice law-abiding kid, not hurting anyone." She sat next to Yvonne on the bed, twisting a lock of hair around her finger.

"Finally, I guess they had their kicks. They asked where he was going in this neighborhood. He told him he was taking me home and told them where I lived. They let him get back into the car, and they followed us to my place. But I could see on his face how upset he was. When he pulled into the driveway, he told me to get out of the car, and don't look back, to go into the house as quickly as I could. I felt like I was throwing him to the wolves or something. I hated it. Then he apologized I had to see that. He apologized! He wasn't the one who should have apologized. I felt like I should apologize for the crazy racist White police force. But it wasn't my fault either. I started to cry and did what he asked me to. But now I am wondering if I should tell my parents and ask them to report those cops."

Yvonne listened in stunned silence. She had no idea this could happen in this day and age. What happened to the Civil Rights Act? The ink was still damp on that and the cops thought they could pick on Black teenagers? Why? She had a new admiration for Robert and his self-control. But why should he have to control himself? She'd read about the race riots in Omaha when George Wallace had come to town to speak. There had been riots in lots of cities in the past few years, including Detroit, and Newark. Yvonne felt like they were immune here. Maybe she was wrong.

"Tell your parents, Debbie. They will know what to do. Have you talked to Robert since he left you?"

"No. I am afraid something happened to him. I hope he just went to church this morning, and that is why he hasn't called."

Yvonne didn't see Debbie again for the rest of the weekend. On Monday, she still looked upset in band class. After school, when they were working on their routine for the next show, Debbie finally opened up.

"Robert called me after lunch yesterday. He said the cops tailed him all the way home, but then left him be. I took your advice. Told my parents what happened as you suggested," There was an unmistakable hard edge in her voice. "They decided I shouldn't go out with Robert anymore. They don't want me sucked into some dangerous situation. They don't care about Robert's rights being trampled on. They don't want their precious little girl to risk anything, to stand up for what is right. I told them his father was a minister, for goodness sake. His family is certainly not radical. They don't care. They don't want me to get hurt. But I am hurt. I love Robert. I don't want to stop seeing him." When the tears overwhelmed her, she dashed to the girls' restroom in the music wing.

Yvonne followed her into the bathroom and remembered how she'd found Barbra crying in the same place last spring. She stopped to wonder if Barbra had gone to Denver or if she had the abortion. She never did hear who the father was.

But now it was Debbie who needed sympathy. "Isn't there a chance they will change their minds? They might be over-reacting to what happened last night." Debbie didn't answer, she just kept crying.

She finally came out and looked at Yvonne in the mirror. "I

shouldn't have told them. Big mistake. I wish I hadn't listened to you."

Yvonne did a double take. "You aren't blaming me? I didn't expect them to tell you to break up with him. But surely you knew that dating a Black boy might have some risks."

"Dating anyone has risks. What do you mean?"

"There are still a lot of people who don't think anyone should date outside their own race. You have encountered a few of those recently. People get ugly about this. I just don't think you should be surprised. You've seen what has happened on the news. Racism is wrong, but that doesn't mean it isn't all around."

"I thought you would back me on this, Yvonne. It's so easy for you. You don't even notice all the boys falling for you. Robert is the first real boyfriend I've had. The first boy I believed loved me for myself. And maybe because we knew we'd have detractors, it made it more special. If he was willing to put up with people criticizing us, then he must really care. And now it's all falling apart through no fault of mine or his." Debbie walked out of the bathroom, grabbed her belongings, and went to her car. By the time Yvonne followed her out the band room door, the Volkswagen Bug shot out of the parking lot.

"There goes my ride," she said aloud. She still couldn't figure out why any of this was her fault. She liked Robert. She did support their relationship. But she wasn't blind.

CHAPTER SEVENTEEN

Yvonne tried to be there to support Debbie. Naturally, she would be upset if she was forced to break up with Robert. Debbie had listened to her when she broke up with Dick, after all, but

Debbie continued to be cool to her. They had no choice but to work together on the upcoming twirler show, but often Debbie asked Linda or Nancy to inform Yvonne of something, to avoid talking
to her.

"I feel bad Debbie is missing the Lincoln High homecoming this weekend. I know how much she wanted to go with Robert," Yvonne said while she and Linda were working on one segment of the next routine together.

"Oh, she's going. At least that's what she said."

"But I thought her parents forbid—"

"She's going with Robert's friend, Lester Gibbons. Lester's the president of the chess club, and probably happy to have a date arranged for him if he even wants a date," Linda chuckled. "And according to Debbie, he is about as white as a boy could be."

"Why would Debbie want to go to the Lincoln High homecoming at all, if she can't go with Robert?" Yvonne asked Linda.

"It seems obvious. She'll meet up with Robert after they get there."

"But Debbie isn't going to ditch poor Lester, surely. She wouldn't do that."

"She didn't tell me that part. The fewer people who know the better. I'd guess Lester is being paid, or maybe Robert is taking some other girl, and then they'll switch at the dance. All I know is Lester is the beard," Linda said.

Several Saturday nights later, Yvonne and Randy went to see the movie *Romeo and Juliet* at the Cooper Lincoln. It had only been out a few weeks, and the theater was crowded. It was the perfect date movie. Even more so, for a couple like Debbie and Robert, whose love had been forbidden. And then she spotted them, sitting in the balcony. Yvonne tried not to stare and didn't think they even saw her.

The next afternoon, Debbie knocked on Yvonne's bedroom door.

"Your mom let me in. You must not have told her you are mad at me," Debbie began.

"I'm not mad at you. You're the one who thinks I wanted to break up you and Robert when nothing could be further from the truth."

"I saw you last night. You saw us. Are you going to tell anyone?" Debbie crossed her arms.

"No way. But don't you think it's time you let me in on your little scheme?"

Debbie sighed. "I guess that's what best friends are for."

Yvonne held her arms open for a hug. "Come here, you silly chick. Tell me what's happening."

Debbie embraced her friend then they both plopped on the bed. "I hardly know where to start. Robert had this idea to have one or two of his friends come pick me up, then I would either meet him at the venue or get in his car at some public place. We did want to avoid the hassle we had with the cops after homecoming, but his friends aren't always there to take me home. We talked about asking Randy to take me home when he was taking you home last night, but we didn't want to break up your romantic night."

Yvonne rolled her eyes. "It was kind of a drag. Randy said the movie was boring. Shakespeare, you know, makes it a little hard to understand. The story did make me think of you and what happened with your parents."

"At least he is kissing you now, right?"

"Well, yes, he kisses me goodnight. But that seems to be the only time. And the thing is, he doesn't seem . . . eager to kiss me, like Dick was. It's more like a ritual."

"Yvonne, you are never satisfied! You don't want boys to pressure you for sex and you don't want them to be gentlemen. At least you have a boyfriend who can come to your door."

She laughed. "I guess you're right. Are you taking Robert to Linda's holiday party next Saturday?"

"I don't know. I mean, I'm not worried about Linda, but I don't know if I can trust the other guests to keep quiet about Robert."

"What does Daniel say about your secret rendezvous?"

"I haven't told him. I didn't want him to have to lie to our parents."

"Uh-oh. You know he's bound to find out. Especially if you go places together like the most popular movie in town."

"I know. What can I do? It's love." Debbie bracketed both cheeks with her hands in mock dismay.

CHAPTER EIGHTEEN

Linda Bridges had a massive family room for entertaining in her basement. It was an older home in the nearby Piedmont neighborhood built in a time when understated elegance put form over function. Most of her classmates referred to it as a mansion, with its pillared countenance, and ivy-strewn balcony.

"We could re-enact the Romeo and Juliet thing right here," Randy said, gesturing to the balcony overlooking the grand entrance.

"Would you like to?" Yvonne asked with a twinkle in her

eye.

"Not the death part. Too young to die." He smiled back.

Linda had invited about fifteen kids from the junior and senior classes, mostly band members. Because Daniel was invited, Debbie didn't bring Robert. Linda provided burgers, hot dogs, and lots of snacks, and soft drinks. But it was clear after her parents went back upstairs that the main event was to play "Spin the Bottle."

Yvonne had played once before when they were about twelve, and the boys in the group all protested. She guessed this crowd might be more interested.

Linda pulled out a large empty wine bottle and asked everyone to sit on the floor in a circle, alternating boys and girls if possible.

"If the spin lands on you, the spinner has to kiss you. If a girl is spinning and she ends up on a girl, she can spin again, same with a boy-on-boy combination. Unless he or she wants to kiss the same-sex person. It is the spinner's choice."

There was a lot of chortling in response to this. The boys seem to think they wanted to see girls kissing. Yvonne wondered why they didn't figure out it meant less kissing for them.

John Anthony spun the bottle first. It stopped pointing to Nancy. She offered him her cheek, and he shrugged and complied. Nancy spun the bottle and it pointed to Debbie. She blushed and had to go again. The second time it pointed to Peter Thompson, whom she'd been dating since homecoming. He didn't wait for her to try to minimize the kissing when she leaned toward him, he took her face with both hands and her mouth with his. This brought cheers from the rest of the group. Nancy's face turned crimson.

Peter spun the bottle and got Daniel. His second spin netted Debbie.

"You don't have to—" Debbie started to tell him not to repeat what he'd done to Nancy, but he ignored her and kissed her in the same forceful way.

"My father taught me to never do things halfway," he teased.

Debbie seemed to have a little trouble getting her bearings, but when she spun, it pointed to Randy. With a smile aimed at Yvonne, she wrapped her arms around his neck and kissed him quickly on the lips. Randy spun and got Linda. Yvonne had never watched him kiss anyone, so she was amused. He deliberately moved in very slowly and when Linda got tired of waiting, she kissed him gently and laughed.

Linda spun and got Yvonne. Everyone waited for her to spin again. She was seated next to Randy, and Yvonne was on the other side of him. Instead, Linda flung herself past Randy and knocked Yvonne over, and kissed her on the mouth before Yvonne knew what was happening. Randy could have saved her, but he burst out laughing.

"Holy crap, Linda! What are you doing?" Yvonne tried to sit back up and gain her composure. She hadn't expected that at all.

Everyone else was laughing at her. Except for Daniel. He looked uncomfortable.

"Spinner's choice, Yvonne. Your turn." Linda grinned triumphantly.

"Did we agree to play this dumb game?" Yvonne said. She sighed and decided she'd better be a good sport. Yvonne spun the bottle and it pointed to Daniel. She hadn't kissed him since prom. But there were plenty of times she'd wanted to. Or she wanted him to kiss her. *I might never have a better chance than this. And the truth is, I don't care if Randy or Andrea are sitting right there.*

He was across the circle, so she had to crawl into the center. He met her halfway. It was like he read her mind. They both got on their knees and wrapped their arms around each other like they weren't playing a game. Maybe she was just trying to show everyone she didn't want to kiss a girl; she would rather kiss a boy any day. That's how she rationalized it later, she was making a point. But at the moment, it felt right. Like something she'd wanted to do for a long, long time. She tried to let him go after a second or two, but he hung in there longer. There were hoots and hollers from most of the guests, but Randy and Andrea just stared.

The game went on awhile. Yvonne could sense Randy was upset; he didn't look at her. But Debbie did and mouthed "Wow" when she thought Randy wasn't watching. She didn't look at Andrea, but she and Daniel left after a few minutes.

"What else did you have in mind, Linda, strip poker?" Randy said sarcastically.

Linda flashed her signature grin. "No, I thought we'd turn the record player on and dance."

She got out some records, and let other kids pick some of their favorites.

"Let's go," Randy said to Yvonne. He grabbed their coats from another room and handed hers to her.

"Well, I don't know. You want to leave already?" She looked at Debbie. She didn't like leaving her when she knew why she was there stag.

"Yeah. I'm leaving. You coming or not?"

Yvonne felt the chill before he even opened the Bridges' front door.

As soon as they were in Randy's car and he started the engine he said, "Do you want to tell me what that was all about? Or maybe I should clue you in and save time."

"What are you talking about?"

"You and Daniel."

"Oh, it was a game. You were playing. You kissed Linda."

"Yeah, and she kissed you too. But she was joking around. I was joking around. You and Daniel, not joking. You're in love with him, and he's obviously got it bad for you too."

"No!"

"Deny it all you want. I know what I saw." Randy forgot the car was already running and turned the key again. He snarled when the engine did. He let Yvonne out on her driveway and didn't speak to her again for days.

CHAPTER NINETEEN

October 24, 1979
Lincoln, Nebraska

Outside her dining room picture window, the first maple leaves were changing their wardrobe from bright green to amber and crimson. A fat brown squirrel scurried down a tree with his cheeks bulging. *He is preparing for the hard times. Summer is over.*

Maybe the summer of my life is over too. Life had always been good, maybe too good. Maybe this is the price I have to pay for all of the wonderful things that happened in the past. I was the lucky one back then, back in high school. No, I was the sensible one who didn't let a boyfriend dictate what I was going to do. I thought I would have plenty of time to have children when I was ready. Turns out, I didn't.

The sound of the front door closing snapped her back to the present.

"What's wrong?" Yvonne said to her husband when he walked

in and put his briefcase down. "I know that look: it's bad news."

"I'm going out of town next week. I have to go to Minneapolis to take some depositions. I'll be gone for three days, maybe four."

"Next week? Did you check the calendar?"

"I don't need to check the damn calendar. This is work, Yvonne. What am I supposed to tell my boss? Sorry, I can't go to Minneapolis next week because it is right in the middle of the designated days I have to have sex with my wife? That won't fly."

Tears stung her eyes. He was right. She had no idea this was going to be so hard on both of them. She pulled the calendar off the wall.

"So what days are you talking about? The twenty-eighth through the thirty-first? Exactly when I will be ovulating."

He threw up his hands and walked into the living room to fix himself a drink.

None of this had seemed unreasonable when her fertility specialist, Dr. William Schott, was explaining it to them the day after Easter.

"You've been taking your temperature every morning, it looks like," Dr. Schott had said. "Based on this, we can pinpoint your ovulation timeframe. You should keep taking your temperature for twelve months to give us more data. But here, I have listed the days you should be having intercourse. I suggest writing this on a calendar where you will both see it. It is important to wait about forty-eight hours in between to maximize the sperm count. The days circled in green are the most important. Those are the days you're most likely to conceive. But in case things are off a day or two, the adjacent days are also included."

Since then, they'd been trying to stick to the schedule. At first, it was a running joke. One of them would remind the other they had a sex date that night. But after several months without results, it became more of an obligation.

She joined him in the living room. "Don't drink too much. You know what Dr. Schott said."

"Oh my God. Do we have to do everything on Dr. Schott's timetable? We can't even have sex for three days, according to the holy calendar. This booze will be long gone by then. Besides, how do we know if this is even going to work? He said he thought it was likely there was something else at play here. You might need surgery or hormones or something. This stupid schedule he has us on may be a waste of time."

"Yes, but this is the least invasive. You know doctors always like to start with something easy, whether it works or not. I suppose we might as well forget it for this month since you're not going to be here." She couldn't stop the tears rolling down her face.

He put his arms around her and leaned his face on hers, wiping her tears away with his thumbs. "You're not trying to make me feel guilty, are you?" She shook her head. "We'll get through this, Yvonne. We'll have a baby somehow, someday. We just have to be patient."

He poured her a glass of wine and she curled up on the new sofa, facing the fireplace. Their miniature schnauzer, Prosecutor, jumped up next to her, nestling against her thigh.

He splashed more scotch on the ice in his highball glass. "I was thinking maybe we should go on a trip before spring. Somewhere warm like Jamaica or the Bahamas. I don't think you need a passport for the Caribbean." He looked out the window at the falling leaves and sighed. "It might be good for us to relax and not worry about this for a little bit. Doesn't that sound nice?"

"Do you think looking at beautiful scenery is going to make this problem go away?" Yvonne rested her head on the back of the sofa. "If I get a lovely suntan in the middle of winter, I'll forget I am . . . barren?"

"You're not barren, for Pete's sake. Are we living in Biblical times? We simply haven't solved the mystery yet."

"Well, we solved your half of the mystery. All you had to do was jack off in a specimen cup and you came out with more than a passing grade." Yvonne shook her head.

"You think this is easy for me or that I want to see you go through this? The disappointment every month. This whole routine is crazy. I can still remember when we enjoyed ourselves in the bedroom. When do we get that back?"

"Well, we won't know anything more for a few months, not until we keep this schedule for a year." She set her wine glass down on the coffee table. "If I have to have those hormone pills or even worse, the shots, it could cost a lot of money. Our health insurance won't cover it. I don't know if taking an extravagant vacation makes sense until we know what we are dealing with."

"Well, I know one thing we are dealing with: stress. And it isn't helping either of us," he said, pressing the cold glass against his forehead.

Yvonne sighed. "Can I have another glass of wine?"

CHAPTER TWENTY

December 28, 1968
Lincoln, Nebraska

"What's your problem, Vonnie?" Clark asked. "You've been moping around here all day. Didn't we just have a nice

Christmas?" He threw a pillow at her across the couch, where she was sprawled watching *Get Smart* on television.

"I guess I'm bored. Randy is out of town at a basketball tournament. He hasn't even given me a Christmas present yet. I don't know if he even got me one. Debbie went to her grandparents for Christmas. It seems like everyone is busy. Not me, I'm sitting home on a Saturday night with my dreary big brother." She smirked and threw the pillow back at him.

Her brother shook his head. Clark was about six feet two and finally filling out. He'd always been tall and skinny like Yvonne, but she could see how he was starting to look like their dad, or at least what Harold looked like in his wedding pictures. Angular, and solid. He was too busy studying to lift weights, but he did his share of jogging, she supposed. His wire-rimmed glasses gave him the look of a scholar.

"And just when I was going to ask if you wanted to go to a party with me," he fired back. "I suppose I could go alone."

"Party? What party?" Yvonne leaned forward putting her feet on the floor.

"A guy I went to high school with, Jimmy Means. He put the word out he is having a party at his house. He lives over on Eastridge Drive somewhere. I think his parents may have left him there this weekend. It's supposed to be for kids who graduated from Capital High, but you can tag along. You'll graduate in a few months. You can always walk home if you aren't having fun."

"Give me ten minutes."

Clark looked up the address in the phone book. He was right, it was about five or six blocks from their house. When she got into his car, he said, "You need to know there will probably be some booze there. Beer I am guessing. All Jimmy can afford. You should not drink any even if someone offers it to you. I might have some beer though. I'm almost twenty."

"Oh, I don't like beer. Dad let me taste some once."

"Good. And don't stick with me. There might be some girls I want to talk to."

Since Yvonne knew there would be older kids at the party, she'd put on more makeup than usual, and a nice sweater and jeans with her boots. Even if she wasn't going to drink, she could pass for nineteen at least. One advantage to being tall.

There were probably forty or fifty teenagers at the house, some of them were milling in the carport. Kids were sliding on the snow-slicked driveway and breaking icicles from the eaves to stir their drinks. Once inside, Clark introduced Yvonne to Jimmy, who seemed to be blitzed already. She then wandered off on her own, trying to follow Clark's directives.

She should have known. Why hadn't she even considered it? Standing in front of the fireplace, big as life, was Dick Dunn. He was entertaining a group of boys with some college story, gesturing wildly while trying not to spill his cup of beer. When he glanced in her direction, he stopped talking and stood there grinning at her.

She gave him a frosty stare and strolled up to the group.

"Hello, Dick. What's happening?"

"Will you all excuse me? It's time for a little reunion," Dick said to his audience and steered her into the dining room.

"What in the world are you doing here, Baby? Are all your little friends playing with their Christmas toys tonight?"

"Clark brought me. I was bored," She batted her eyelashes and combed fingers through her hair.

"Ah, Clark. Yeah, it's been a long time since I've seen your big brother. So, are you going steady with anyone new?" He picked up her left hand. "No ring."

"No. I mean I am dating someone on the basketball team. At least I think we are still dating. He's been busy, you know, with basketball."

"He must not be paying enough attention to you if you are roaming around on a Saturday night."

Her lips curled. "You always knew how to flirt, Dick. I guess that must come in handy at Iowa State."

"I do all right. But you and I have some unfinished business."

"We do? I guess I remember things differently." She was having fun joking with him. It would be nice to put all of those bad memories aside, now that time had passed.

"Let's see if we can find someplace not quite so crowded." The house was full of laughter and pounding rock music, and the smell of beer and cigarette smoke. She did think it would be nice to take a little break from the noise at least. He put his arm around her waist and guided her down the hallway. There were kids gathered in several bedrooms with open doors. At the end of the hall was the parents' bedroom. There was a big handwritten sign taped to the closed door that said "No Admittance. Stay Out of This Room." Dick gave her a sidelong mischievous grin when the doorknob turned.

He locked the door behind them, pinning her wrists against the door.

"I don't think Jimmy wants anyone in here," Yvonne said.

"Signs like that are for people with no imagination, and I have imagined doing this to you many times," he said, leaning his forearms on the door beside her head and kissing her until she was gasping for air.

She knew it was a mistake, but sometimes you had to go with the flow. Get your groove on. She knew what Dick was capable of now. She wasn't quite as innocent as she'd been last spring. And if she hadn't missed Dick, she missed the way he was attracted to her. No one since had made her feel desirable. Randy had been acting more distant since Linda's party. Daniel acted as though their kiss hadn't even happened. If Dick was too aggressive, at least he knew what he was doing. He never denied his feelings, he put them right out there, raw and unapologetic. Tonight she wanted what he was offering.

In one swift move, he pushed her sweater up and her blue jeans down, and ran his hands up and down her torso, making her pulse race.

"You're so damn beautiful, I can't stand it, Baby. Let's get on the bed."

Yvonne fought to clear her head. "We can't get on their bed. Jimmy would have a fit if he knew someone was in here."

"Jimmy is three sheets to the wind. He won't even know who was in here." He picked her up, carried her to the large bed, and pulled her sweater over her head. He ran his hands over her hip bones, sliding her bikini panties down.

"Wait." She couldn't think. She couldn't breathe.

"I've already waited forever, Yvonne. You're seventeen now. I remember you said we'd do it when you were seventeen."

"I don't think that was exactly what I said." She felt like she was floating in warm honey. What was it she'd told him about her seventeenth birthday? "I need to use the bathroom first. I'll be back." She put her sweater back on and tugged up her jeans.

"Okay, but hurry. I'll get undressed." When she closed the door behind her, he was doing exactly that.

Miraculously, there was no one in the bathroom across the hall. She looked in the mirror. *Do I really want to do this? Do I want Dick to be my first? Why can't I think clearly?* After she used the bathroom, she opened the door and ran smack into John Anthony Turner.

"Oh, John Anthony. I didn't know you were here," she said. She couldn't go back into that bedroom with the big sign on the door while he was watching.

"I'm glad I ran into you, Yvonne. I saw you come in, and I wanted to warn you. Dick Dunn is here." He took hold of her arm and pulled her a few steps down the hall.

"Oh, don't worry about me and Dick. We're okay now."

"I don't know if anyone ever told you the whole story about Dick and Barbra."

"What do you mean? What about Dick and Barbra?"

"Dick was the father of her baby. She'd been sneaking out to see him while I was dating her. He wanted her to have an abortion, but she decided to go to Colorado and give the baby up for adoption. She finally admitted the whole thing to me last week after she got back."

Yvonne's jaw dropped. "Dick? Dick and Barbra? He . . . he was the one?" She jerked her eyes back toward the bedroom door.

Like a bull through the gate, she pushed past John Anthony, through the other rooms, looking for her brother. She found him in the kitchen, drinking beer and joking with a girl she didn't know.

She was starting to cry, which got his attention. "Clark, you have to do something for me." She grabbed his sleeve and pulled him to the bedroom hallway. John Anthony was nowhere in sight. "Go into the room with the sign that says, 'No Admittance.' Tell Dick I won't be coming back."

Clark blinked slowly then his eyes went wild. He marched up to the door and burst through it. She'd never heard her brother swear before, but she guessed Dick got the message. When Clark came back down the hall, his face was flushed, and his veins in his neck bulged like a weightlifter's. He grabbed her arm roughly and practically dragged her out of the house. She wasn't even sure he was going to stop for their coats.

When they got back into his car, Clark slammed his palms on the steering wheel. "Jesus Christ, Yvonne! I can't even talk to you right now!"

Yvonne could only sob and thank her lucky stars that she had been spared.

CHAPTER TWENTY-ONE

January 20, 1969

Connie Edison hadn't been a substitute teacher at Capital High School while her children were in attendance there. Yvonne wondered how her mother managed to be assigned classes in all of the other high schools. But after the semester break, her mother took an assignment at Capital High for a teacher who had broken her leg.

"I felt sorry for Mrs. French falling on the ice over the Christmas holidays. I think they had someone else covering for her for a week, but they asked me to fill in for the next month. I know you won't want your mother invading your privacy, but we'll both have to deal with it," Connie told Yvonne as they drove to school the first day of the second semester. "I should be done by one-thirty or so. You'll need to keep riding home with Debbie or call me for a ride when you are ready to leave."

Four days later, Connie came to Yvonne's room after dinner.

Yvonne was reading her English assignment. "What's going on, Mom?"

"Honeybun, how are things between you and Randy?"

"I'm not sure. I haven't talked to him much. He spends most of his free time practicing for basketball."

"How are things between Randy and Daniel? I thought they were good friends." Connie cupped her elbow in her hand and ran a finger across her lips.

"I think they are good friends, why do you ask?" Yvonne knitted her brows.

"Something is going on. Maybe I shouldn't mention it to you, but any of the kids might."

"You are pussyfooting around something. What are you talking about?"

"They are both in my third-period civics class. On Monday, Randy said something to Daniel that I didn't hear, but Daniel said something rather rudely back to him. I don't know what exactly. It might have been, 'get off my case.' That's what caught my attention. Then I noticed dirty looks passing between them throughout the class. They sit across from each other, so it was hard to miss.

"We were discussing the government's obligations and I asked Randy, 'what do you think the responsibility of government is to the people it governs?'

"He said something like, 'government needs to be honest. Like if a politician promises to repair the potholes in the street, he should take care of it when elected. So you can trust him.'

"Then I asked Daniel if he thought politicians had to follow those ideas that they campaigned on or did they need to compromise with other officials to achieve anything?

"Well, he hadn't even been paying attention. He asked me to

repeat the question. Then he answered that 'they have to be flexible and work within the government system.'

"Then Randy said, 'so it is okay if they lie?'"

"Before I could say anything, Daniel snapped back that officials can change their minds just like anyone else. Then he made some odd remark about girls. Something like, 'don't girls have any say in this?'"

"They both looked at me and turned red. I called on some other kids to try to get the discussion back on track." Connie watched Yvonne's face.

Yvonne jerked her head back. "That doesn't sound like either of them. They are at the top of our class."

"That's what I thought. Today I was walking down the hall leaving for the day. I heard a noise like someone bumped into a locker. It was Daniel. I saw him hit a locker like he fell or was pushed, but I didn't see what happened. Randy was walking away, and Daniel yelled something after him. I saw other kids turn to look at them. It seemed like Randy must have pushed him. I didn't do anything about it because I hadn't seen it all, and it seemed to be over. Why would they be fighting?"

"I have no idea," Yvonne answered. Maybe it had something to do with her. She had heard from Debbie that Andrea had broken up with Daniel, but that they were back together again. Things had seemed a little off since Linda's party. She'd have to ask Debbie if she knew anything about it.

CHAPTER TWENTY-TWO

February 5, 1980

"Infertility has become a common concern in the field of gynecology. In your parents' generation, only one in ten married couples had difficulty bearing children. Today that figure is one in six," Dr. Schott told Yvonne and her husband. "It looks like it has been a year since you first came in. Do you have your temperature calendars with you?"

Yvonne handed him the calendar where she recorded her temperature every morning, and each time they had sexual relations for an entire year. The doctor studied the charts in silence for a few minutes.

"You said that you have been trying to conceive for how long?" he asked.

Yvonne swallowed. "Almost two years now. It had been almost a year when I came in to see you the first time, and we have been doing the calendar thing for a year. Right after we moved into the new house." Her husband nodded solemnly.

They'd found their dream house only a month after they started looking. It had a big backyard, three bedrooms, and a basement. They'd decorated and imagined what it would be like with children. And every month when she wasn't pregnant, the dream house had seemed less comforting. Like it was mocking them. *We could have stayed in an apartment and saved our money.* After nine months, they'd gotten a dog. At least the dog could enjoy the backyard.

"The first thing to do is run some more tests," the doctor continued. "Check with my nurse and she will set up the appointments. You both must realize this is nobody's fault. The worst thing a couple can do is to blame themselves or each other. It is hard enough to follow through with some of the treatments without fighting among yourselves or feeling guilty."

Of course, you feel guilty. It is supposed to be the easiest thing in the world to get pregnant. It happens all the time to people who don't want to get pregnant. Especially to high school girls who don't want to get pregnant.

It was already grating on her nerves. All of her co-workers and friends seemed to think they could comment on her childless state. She had lost count of how many women had assured her that getting pregnant was easy, you merely had to have a glass of wine and relax, and it will happen naturally. As though her mounting anxiety was the problem. It was easy to see how couples got divorced over this situation. It was getting harder to see how any endured.

CHAPTER TWENTY-THREE

February 13, 1969

"I think I am going to have to break up with Randy," Yvonne told Debbie, as they were giving each other manicures in Yvonne's bedroom. Debbie was putting the final topcoat on Yvonne's Red-Hot Mama nail polish. Yvonne rubbed her itchy nose with her wrist.

"I thought you liked Randy. Hold still. You don't want to muss it."

"I like him. I don't think I love him. I don't think he loves me either. We're mostly good friends and it has gotten a little sad. I've hardly seen him since the basketball season started. Now basketball he loves. I mean he calls me; we have gone out a few times this year, but it hasn't been the same. We went to a movie last weekend and he fell asleep in the theater."

"But just wait until after the Sweetheart Dance tomorrow night."

"I will. Don't worry. You still think you and Robert can go

together?"

"Daniel won't be there. He's going on a ski weekend with some guys from Y-Teens. I think the coast is clear since Peter Thompson will be the one picking me up."

"And Peter is meeting Nancy at the dance? Won't her parents wonder why he isn't picking her up?"

"Well, I think the plan is he picks me up first, then I have to wait in the car while he goes in to get Nancy. I hope it isn't too cold."

"Do you and Robert ever have any time alone? It seems like these elaborate schemes don't give you much privacy. It is too bad he can't simply come over and hang out."

"We've had some time alone. Since his father's a minister, Robert has a key to the church, and he also has a key to the minister's manse. That's a house across the street from the church where the minister and his family usually live, but this one was too small for the Washington family. Robert has five brothers and sisters, and the house only has three bedrooms. The church rented out the house and that helps pay for the rent on the Washingtons' place. Or maybe they have a mortgage, I'm not sure. But right now, that house is empty. The church is doing renovations between renters. We have gone there a few times. We go in the back, so the neighbors won't see us."

"Wow. I had no idea. That sounds like a Dick Dunn move. He hasn't tried anything, has he?" Yvonne was surprised Debbie hadn't mentioned this before.

Debbie smiled but she didn't meet Yvonne's gaze. "Well, I don't know exactly what you would call it, but he keeps a sleeping bag in the trunk of his car. There is no furniture in the house, except for one worn-out couch. And they are replacing the furnace, but we use the space heater the renovation crew leaves there."

"Are you saying what I think you're saying? Have you had

106

sex with him?"

"No, but things have gotten pretty close. I think I'm a little chicken. Robert said he doesn't want to rush me. He is so sweet; I can hardly believe it sometimes." Debbie pressed her lips together tightly.

Wait a minute. It sounds like he's taking you to an abandoned house his father's church owns, and you're getting naked in a sleeping bag using a space heater. I'm not sure sweet is the word I'd use.

It sounded like Robert's moves weren't confined to the dance floor. Not to mention the fact neither set of parents knew they were even dating. But Debbie was clearly in love with him.

The Sweetheart Dance was a fundraiser for one of the school clubs and was held in the Cornhusker Hotel Ballroom downtown, so that made it special. And this year it was held on Valentine's Day and you couldn't beat that for romance.

Randy showed up at her door with six red roses. Roses were more expensive around Valentine's Day. He hadn't been able to work a part-time job with his basketball schedule so he must have dipped into his savings. *Maybe we'll be able to work this thing out after all.*

They were dancing to a ballad when Debbie and Robert came in with Nancy and Peter on their heels. Debbie and Robert looked happy as he pulled her onto the dance floor. Nancy didn't.

"Is there something wrong with Nance?" Yvonne asked when Debbie got near them.

"She doesn't approve. You know that 'my Daddy's from Mississippi' routine. I guess she didn't realize Peter was picking me up first, so now she's mad at him too."

"That's her problem, not yours," Yvonne said.

"I don't think we are staying long anyway," Debbie winked.

"Oh, we can dance a couple of songs at least. I wanna see if ol' Randy here has gotten any better at the Watusi," Robert said.

"Not much," Randy admitted.

The band switched to something faster and the others enjoyed watching Robert execute some new dance moves. When they tried to imitate him, they had to laugh at their own shortcomings.

After about thirty minutes, Yvonne and Randy sat down at a table to rest. Debbie and Robert were heading to the coatroom.

"Where are they going?" Randy asked as Nancy and Peter sat down next to them at the table.

"I think Debbie and Robert are leaving," Yvonne said. She wondered if they were heading to romance in the manse.

"I can't believe the way she is acting." Nancy crinkled her nose.

"Why do you care, Nancy?" Randy said, crossing his arms.

"I don't care who she is dating. He seems nice enough. What I don't like is she is sneaking around after her parents told her she couldn't date him. And now she is dragging Peter into her lie, and by association, me."

"Lighten up. Haven't you ever lied to your parents, Nance?" Randy leaned toward her.

"Never."

Randy laughed, "Then it is about time you started, Doll."

When the evening was over, Yvonne and Randy parked in her driveway.

"Thank you again for the roses, Randy. No one has ever brought me flowers. It was very sweet," Yvonne said.

"It's nothing. I figured Valentine's Day, flowers, it's traditional."

"It's not nothing. You can be sweet. You are often sweet to my friends, like tonight with Nancy. You made a point but also a joke at the same time, trying to calm her down. But I don't know about us. It seems like things aren't great between us, apart from the roses."

"You hurt my feelings, Yvonne. And you never apologized either. Are you just expecting me to forget about it?"

"I hurt . . . oh, you mean when I kissed Daniel? That was months ago. It was supposed to be funny. But I guess if I hurt you, it wasn't very funny. I am sorry, I didn't mean to upset you."

"This seems a little convenient. You know what I think? You were waiting to see if Daniel dumped Andrea and wanted to start something with you. That didn't happen, so now you are sorry. Sorry you messed things up with a guy who cared about you, over a guy who will always be more like a brother."

"What do you want me to say? I blew it, I guess."

"I want you to tell me the truth. Are you in love with Daniel?"

She met his eyes, hugging her purse in front of her. "No. I don't think so."

"Are you in love with me?"

She flinched. *That's not fair. He's never said he loves me.*

"You'd better get out of the car," Randy said, looking back down the street. "It's almost your curfew time." The muscles in his jaw clenched.

She got out of the car. He pulled out of the driveway and didn't look back. *Happy Valentine's Day.*

CHAPTER TWENTY-FOUR

April 21, 1980

"Debbie, I am so glad you were home. I don't know how much more of this I can take. It seems like I am going to the doctor or some kind of specialist all of the time. They are starting to complain about my absences at work," Yvonne propped herself up in her bed, trying to juggle the phone that was normally on the bedside table.

"What has Dr. Schott been telling you? Chantelle, stop it! Hang on, Yvonne. Chantelle is terrorizing the cat." Yvonne could hear Debbie set the phone down. A cat yowled, a child whined, a door closed.

She missed Debbie, seeing her every day as they did in school. Oh, they'd had a few ups and downs since then, but they still were nearly as close as they had been as children, even when they didn't talk for weeks at a time. Debbie had moved to Columbia, South Carolina about seven years ago, and had three children now: two sons and a daughter. Yvonne had only been out to visit her twice. It was a beautiful place to live.

"Okay, I'm back. I sent her out to the backyard so we should have some peace. Too bad preschool is only half days. Where were we?" Debbie was slightly out of breath.

"I don't know where this is going. It seems like we started with a conservative approach where I was taking my temperature and the doctor gave us a schedule of when we should be having sex. It didn't seem to do any good. Then we had to have sex right before the doctor's appointment and they did some sort of postcoital extraction to determine if the sperm were getting to my cervix. I guess they were. Dr. Schott did an endometrial biopsy, where he scraped the lining of my uterus. That was so painful, I wanted to forget the whole thing. If that wasn't bad enough, two weeks later, he did another horrible exam where they injected dye into my uterus, then x-rayed it. Excruciating, and I had to try to lie on the table without moving. After a few weeks, we switched doctors. Just the thought of going back to Dr. Schott made me sick. Now we are seeing a Dr. Mayer."

"So, have they told you what the problem is?"

"Not really, but they have given us a lot of possibilities and I guess we have to eliminate them one by one. This new doctor thinks I may have endometriosis affecting my ovaries. Or maybe it has something to do with my appendix bursting three years ago. I could have gotten inflammation which causes scar tissue ... I don't know. I am supposed to have a laparoscopy. To look for scar tissue."

"I have a girlfriend here who has endometriosis. She has a lot of pain, that's what sent her to the doctor. Do you have pain, you know, where your ovaries might be?" Debbie asked.

"No, just the usual menstrual cramps. They have asked me that more than once."

"You know a woman in England gave birth to a test-tube baby. Maybe you could do that."

"I know you're kidding, but they did mention artificial insemination as an option. Like they do with livestock, for goodness sake." Yvonne switched the phone to her other ear.

"Why would they do that when you have a husband?"

"Well, I guess if they determine I can't conceive a baby, we could use a surrogate. So that would be putting his sperm inside another woman who would carry the baby to term. It wouldn't be my baby, but it would at least be his."

"Really? I've never heard of that."

"I guess it is rather new. It's only permitted in certain states so far, but it makes more sense to me than adoption. It is very expensive of course, the doctor bills, and then you may have to pay all of the expenses for the surrogate mother, including her doctor and hospital bills. I don't know where they find a woman who would be willing to be pregnant for someone else. I mean if she is unmarried, people would be shocked she was pregnant. If she is married, her husband probably won't go along with it. Then there is the whole risk that she might want to keep the baby, who would be as much hers as the father's."

"I could do it for you."

Yvonne sighed, "I love you, Debbie, but there is no way you could do that."

"Sure, I could! It was easy for me to have babies. We aren't having any more. I could have a cute little tow-headed baby for once. Just what you ordered."

"Think about it. No doctor in his right mind would impregnate you with my husband's sperm. It could be a DNA disaster."

Debbie paused. "Oh. I see. Well, you should have thought about this before you married my twin brother."

CHAPTER TWENTY-FIVE

May 14, 1969

Yvonne and Debbie didn't have to do as much to prepare for the twirler auditions this year, it was Linda and Nancy's responsibility now. Their main job was to serve as judges. They did help prepare the contestants for the auditions in the three weeks prior to the tryouts.

"I'm a little worried about Linda," Nancy told Yvonne on the third afternoon of after-school practices. She seems to have some sort of flu bug she can't get rid of. Almost every day she is in the bathroom puking. I hope she doesn't have one of those eating problems."

"What do you mean, 'eating problems'? Does she have trouble swallowing?"

"I know a girl from our church who refused to eat. When her parents forced her to eat, she would go into the bathroom and vomit. They said she had an eating problem. I guess it is a real disease." Nancy nodded.

Debbie overheard what Nancy said, and chimed in, "Linda is already so thin, she can't afford not to eat."

Just then Linda emerged from the nearby bathroom. The girls who were practicing for the auditions were leaving, so only the four current twirlers remained to put things away.

"Why are you all looking at me like that?" Linda scanned their faces.

Yvonne spoke up, "You seem to be ill. We are wondering if you are all right."

Linda took a deep breath. "I may as well tell you. I'm pregnant."

Debbie's hand flew to her mouth and Nancy went pale. Yvonne's mind instantly went back to when Barbra had told her nearly a year ago she was pregnant. What was this, a twirler curse? Who was the father? The only guy she knew Linda had dated was . . . of course, John Anthony Turner. That was just too much of a coincidence.

Nancy's eyes were full of tears. "How do you know you're pregnant? Are you sure?"

"I have the signs. I missed my last period. I have been puking for a week or more, and I don't seem to have a fever or any other flu symptoms. I went to Planned Parenthood, but they told me to come back in two weeks if I still think I am P.G."

"I didn't even know you were dating anyone seriously," Debbie said.

"I know. I haven't brought him to school functions. His name is Tom Case. He graduated from high school last year. We've been dating since January. I plan to bring him to prom." Linda ran her fingers up and down the placket of her blouse between the top two buttons. "You know how impatient these older guys are. Well, at least you know, Yvonne. You were with Dick Dunn."

Was she was never going to live that down, even the part that wasn't true? "I dated Dick, but I didn't sleep with him."

Linda snorted. "That's not what he told everyone."

"You don't act very upset about this, Linda. Are you getting married? What did your parents say?" Nancy cried.

"Well, I suppose I'll be upset about it when I have to tell my parents." Yvonne caught a glimpse of Linda's vulnerability. She was putting up a brave front, but the façade was cracking. Yvonne took Linda in her arms.

"Yvonne, stop. You are going to make me cry!" Linda said as her eyes welled up.

"Sweetie, this is just the kind of thing you should cry about. Quit trying to be so damn tough all the time. Don't you know pregnant women are always crying, even the ones who are older and married?"

Linda did dissolve into tears then and the other girls joined in a group hug.

"I don't know what I should do. I can't marry Tom. I don't even want him to know. He's in college. He'd have to drop out and get a job. I'm supposed to finish high school. Nancy and I were supposed to be in charge of the twirlers next year. I simply want it to go away."

"Babies don't just go away. They tend to grow." Debbie put her hand on Linda's midsection.

"You need to tell your parents, Linda. They will know what to do. Tell them how you feel about it," Yvonne said.

Debbie rolled her eyes at Yvonne. "That's always your solution. Tell your parents. How do you know what Linda's parents will do?"

Yvonne was taken aback, but then remembered that Debbie had blamed her when she told her parents about Robert and his run-in with the police officers. "I don't. But they are her parents. They're grown-ups."

Linda didn't say any more about her possible pregnancy in the coming days. They conducted the twirler auditions and two more promising sophomores were chosen to replace Yvonne and Debbie.

Debbie was quiet as she drove Yvonne home in the Volkswagen after auditions.

"It feels a little weird that we have just picked our twirler replacements. I guess I didn't expect that. Maybe it feels weird that we are finishing high school," Yvonne said studying her friend.

"*Umm-hmm*," Debbie murmured.

"Is there something wrong, Debs?"

"I think maybe Linda did have a stomach bug. My stomach's been kind of queasy too. I hope I feel better by next weekend for prom."

"Maybe you are pregnant too," Yvonne laughed.

Debbie gave her a cool glare. "Don't even joke about it."

Yvonne's mouth went dry. *She doesn't mean . . . Debbie and Robert haven't gone that far surely. She'd tell me. Wouldn't she?*

Yvonne had just gotten out of the shower and back to her room around nine o'clock when the phone rang.

"Yvonne! A miracle happened. I can't believe it," Debbie was bubbling over like a bottle of champagne. "My parents agreed to let me go to the prom with Robert!"

"What? How did that happen?"

"I told them I'd talked to Robert on the phone, and he told me he hadn't been hassled by the cops since Homecoming. I said he wanted to take me to prom, and I wanted to go with him. They said they guessed one night wouldn't hurt if he hadn't had any more trouble. As long as Daniel was there to keep an eye on things. Oh, and they said I should drive the Cadillac instead of Robert driving. Can you believe it?"

"That is amazing. But you didn't tell them you and Robert had been going out all year?"

"No, are you out of your tree? That would have ruined the deal. But once they get used to this, maybe they will let me see him sometimes."

"You said Daniel was going to prom? I thought he and Andrea broke up again."

"Oh, they did, months ago. I think he is going stag with some other guys."

"You can go to prom without a date? Since when? Maybe I should have done that."

"Oh, you know you'll have fun with Gary White. You haven't been with him since last summer so you should have a lot to talk about."

"I don't recall Gary being a big talker. Mostly he liked to drive around and play the radio loudly. But I didn't know who else to go to the prom with. It was nice of him to agree to go."

"So, we should drive together, then you won't have to worry about that car of his with the defective door. Linda is still having her party before the prom, isn't she? At least the boys won't have to pay for a fancy dinner."

Debbie and Yvonne had bought prom dresses this year. Bonnie Adams had started working at a local department store, Hovland-Swanson, and she got an employee discount. They were able to buy both dresses at fifteen percent off. Yvonne knew Debbie had intended to go with Robert all along, but at least now her parents were aware of it.

CHAPTER TWENTY-SIX

Whenever Yvonne thought about going to the prom with Gary, she caught herself biting her nails. *What am I worried about? We ended things on a good note. I talked to him in October, maybe again in February. He told me to call him if I stopped dating Randy, so I did. It's that we haven't seen each other since last summer. What could go wrong? Maybe he can't dance. I should have asked him if he could dance.*

She almost didn't recognize him. When she came down the hall in her dark pink gown with a tulle overlay, he was talking to her parents in the living room. She had worried he would feel uncomfortable wearing a dinner jacket, but he wore one in a deep jewel green hue with a muted paisley design. He looked like he could be in a combo with that outfit. His previously shaggy brown hair was now cut short, and he looked like he'd lost weight. Daniel had made fun of Gary's prominent forehead and bushy brows, but the shorter haircut minimized those.

"Gary? My gosh, look at you," Yvonne gushed. She couldn't help it.

"I think that's my line. You look very pretty, Yvonne. I got you a corsage. It's just a white rose, I didn't know what color you'd be wearing." He smiled broadly.

She was still in shock. This isn't going to be embarrassing, after all, showing up with him. They posed for a round of photographs then went next door to meet Debbie and Robert. Daniel was leaving himself, and he scrutinized Gary as though he was trying to place him. He jumped in his car before Yvonne could formally introduce them.

Debbie was bouncing off the walls. She beamed every time she gazed at Robert chatting with her parents. He looked debonair in a white dinner jacket and pale-yellow ruffled shirt. Robert seemed to have gained a little weight, looking manlier. He reminded Yvonne of Eddie Kendricks of the Temptations, the one the girls seemed to adore on *American Bandstand* and *Shindig*. Robert's Afro had gotten longer, or bigger. Debbie wore her blonde hair down this year. It was well past her shoulders. She wore a yellow sleeveless empire waist dress that coordinated with what Robert wore. Debbie had lost a few pounds and the dress was flattering.

They met Linda's boyfriend, Tom Case, at her house. He was good looking but seemed older than nineteen. Yvonne would have described him as rugged, someone who looks like he would rather be hunting or fishing than wearing a tux. He didn't strike her as Linda's type. It turned out it wasn't a large party, only about ten couples, but there was an elaborate spread of food on the deck by the swimming pool. They even had "mocktails" to drink, made with punch and ginger ale, and garnished with fruit.

Yvonne found a minute alone with Linda in the mini kitchen.

"Are you feeling any better, Linda?" she asked.

"I think the worst has passed. I'm not blowing chunks

anymore. I did get a test done at the clinic."

"False alarm?" Yvonne whispered.

"No, I was right. But mum's the word tonight." She made a gesture of zipping her lips.

Yvonne went back to join Gary. *I don't know how long she thinks this is going to be a secret.*

When they checked in at the prom, they had a chance to vote for the prom king and queen candidates. The student council had nominated a dozen girls and boys for each this year. Last year it had only been half of that. She was surprised her name was on the list, but even more shocked that Daniel's was.

Maybe I shouldn't be so amazed, I guess he was elected class vice-president. And she supposed she would even call Daniel handsome now. He'd grown at least two inches, and like Gary, he was starting to look like a man and not a boy, more angular if not muscular. And he still had those knock-you-on-your-ass eyes. He hadn't given her one of those heart-stopping looks in a while, but he could have gotten a date for the prom if he'd tried.

She knew her chances for prom queen were pretty much nil, especially when she considered Barbra had won last year and she was a twirler. Her popularity probably tanked afterward when everyone learned she was pregnant. She voted for herself and Daniel, figuring at least they would each get one vote.

Gary wasn't the best dancer, but he at least tried, and she gave him credit for not giving up. Robert and Debbie seemed to be lost in a world of their own and Robert didn't even attempt to give Gary any dance pointers. At one point, Robert was chatting in a corner with Randy. Randy had brought one of the Junior Varsity cheerleaders, Lauren James, as his date, but it didn't look like he was paying a lot of attention to her. *That seems familiar.*

About halfway through the evening, it was time to crown the king and queen. The president of the student council, Ed Perkins, stood at the microphone in front of the band, signaling the drummer to play a drum roll.

"First of all, congratulations to all of the seniors who were finalists for king and queen. We gave you more candidates this year, to spread this honor around. However, it did make it a little more difficult to determine a clear winner in the voting. For 1969, the prom king is Daniel Adams."

Everyone cheered as Daniel joined Ed on the stage. Yvonne and Debbie stood side by side applauding and whooping. Daniel looked uncomfortable, glancing at the crowd until he focused in on Yvonne. Then he gave her one of those looks she'd been missing as if she was the only one in the room. Ed placed a papier mâché crown on Daniel's head, a baroque creation from the art club.

"King Daniel, we have a little problem, and those of us who were asked to count the votes decided you get to solve it. We have a tie vote for the prom queen, so you will get to pick the winner."

"Oh shit," Daniel muttered about the time Ed shoved the microphone in his direction. The crowd laughed. The teacher chaperone next to Ed rolled his eyes.

Ed continued, "Both of these lovely ladies got twenty-one votes, but we're not going to let you have both of them. So you get to be the tie-breaker between Mitzi Mason and Yvonne Edison." Daniel looked stricken, and once again locked eyes with Yvonne.

Mitzi was the head varsity cheerleader, a cute little blonde with a vivacious personality. Everyone liked her, except for perhaps those who were jealous.

She was exactly someone you would expect to be a prom queen. I must be getting the protest votes, from kids who don't want the obvious choice. But poor Daniel, what is he going to do? For most of his school life, he's been one of the fringe kids, the smart kid who didn't worry about who liked him. Will he boost his popularity by choosing Mitzi?

Yet how could he not pick me? He barely knows Mitzi, except in passing. We've been close for ten years. Debbie would never forgive him if he didn't pick her best friend.

"Uh-hmmm," Daniel cleared his throat as the color rose to his face. "I guess I'll say Mitzi."

Mitzi made her way to the stage amid a lot of cheering from the crowd. Daniel looked at Yvonne again, who was too stunned to react. He mouthed, "Sorry," before he was caught up in Mitzi's crowning.

Debbie's voice echoed as though she was at the bottom of a well. "I'm going to kill him when he gets home. I'll wait until he's asleep and find some diabolical way to slowly suck the life out of him."

Yvonne froze in place, then felt the heat rushing to her cheeks as she turned and rushed out into the courtyard, trying to sort out what she was feeling. Gary followed her and reached for her hand. She flinched.

"Where are you going? Are you mad? Talk to me. Isn't that your neighbor, Debbie's brother? You must have thought he'd pick you."

"No," she shook her head sharply. Her stomach felt rock hard. "It doesn't matter. He could have just flipped a coin. Actually, he should have flipped a coin, or Ed should have. I'm embarrassed I guess."

"Then come back inside. You don't want anyone to think you're a sore loser."

She studied him. *Who knew Gary had that much depth? Or any depth at all?* She took his hand and went back in to watch Daniel dancing slowly with Mitzi. As she watched them, she began to wonder if this was why she'd wanted Daniel to pick her. She wanted to dance with him again, to feel his arms around her. Mitzi didn't care, she had a steady beau. A couple of times, he glanced at her standing there watching, but then he quickly looked away.

After the royalty dance was over, the couple was whisked away for photographs. In a few minutes, Yvonne was asked to be in a group shot and had to stand on the other side of Daniel, who had Mitzi on his arm. She couldn't remember when it had been so hard to force a smile, but she did it.

When the photographer was finished, Daniel leaned in and said in a low voice, "Meet me out in the gym hallway in ten minutes." Yvonne just met his eyes then walked away, joining Gary in the line for punch.

What could he possibly have to say to me? She hadn't intended to go, but by chance, Gary excused himself to use the restroom. She might as well take advantage of it. The gymnasium hallway wasn't directly connected to the pathway most prom-goers would be using to get to the cafeteria. It wasn't blocked off, but it wasn't in use.

Daniel was standing near the closed double doors of the gymnasium. She strode up to him and stood facing him.

"What?" she said.

He locked eyes with her for a moment then he grabbed her upper arms and pulled her up into a kiss. This wasn't the kind of encounter that would ever be permitted in the school corridor. Her initial shock quickly turned to wonder as her heart seemed to throb in her throat. Her mind went blissfully numb as he kept tasting, teasing, and brushing at her lips and she felt like her blood had started simmering. *God, I like kissing him, why don't I get to do this more?* She freed her arms and wrapped them around his neck and his hands slid to her waist. After what seemed like minutes, he pulled his mouth back. They were both breathing hard.

"I've wanted to do that for a long time," Daniel said, moving his hands onto either side of her face.

"What stopped you?"

"Sometimes I don't think you even notice other people around you. Can you really be that dense?"

"I don't know what you mean."

His gaze drifted back to the hallway leading to the prom. "Randy stopped me for one thing. He was my friend and he accused me of trying to steal his girlfriend. Then there was Andrea. I guess I screwed that up. And now I see the Neanderthal is back from last summer."

"What? Oh, you mean Gary. I had to find someone to take me to prom. It's not like I had many choices."

"See? I just don't think you get it." He stroked her cheek with the back of his hand. "Boys are straining their necks to get a look at you walking down the hall. You could have had any boy in our school take you to prom if you'd given them the time of day. Don't you know how beautiful you are? Aren't there any mirrors in your house? Why do you think you got so many votes for prom queen?"

"I dunno, I guess I have some friends." She looked upwards impishly. "Twenty-one friends."

"You don't have friends, you have admirers. If you want them to be friends, you have to pay more attention, to look them in the eyes and see what's going on."

Her brows narrowed. "So, you think I'm shallow. Beautiful and shallow. Gee thanks."

"Not shallow. Oblivious. Do you want to know why I picked Mitzi for prom queen?"

"Not really. Okay, tell me."

"I knew I could dance with Mitzi without feeling anything. I was afraid if I danced with you, if I got to put my arms around you again, everyone in the room would see how I felt about you." He laughed, "Everyone except for you, of course. You would miss all of the signs."

"Then just tell me. How do you feel about me?"

"I love you. What do you think?"

"I think I love you too. But I need to be sure." When she slid her arms around him again, he pulled her back into a kiss.

One of the chaperones stood in the hallway and coughed intentionally. "You kids know this hallway is off-limits. You'd better get back to the prom."

Yvonne backed away from Daniel, but she was floating on exhilaration.

"You'd better go find your date. He's probably looking for you," Daniel said. She smiled into those intense blue eyes, turned, and headed back to the cafeteria. He walked over to chat with the chaperone.

He doesn't want anyone to see us together tonight. Probably for the best. But what is he going to do tomorrow?

CHAPTER TWENTY-SEVEN

Daniel sat in his car in the school parking lot. He'd left the prom after his encounter with Yvonne. He had to admit, it had been quite a night. His mind was racing. Ed Perkins had given him a heads-up he was going to be on the list of senior finalists for prom king, but he never imagined he would win. He'd considered not going to prom at all. It wouldn't be as much fun as last year when he'd gone with Yvonne. And he had enjoyed going with his sister and his friend Keith. Then everything had fizzled between him and Yvonne afterward.

He knew she was used to dating an older guy with a car. Someone who was a big man on campus, so to speak. He didn't much like Dick Dunn, but he respected his style. Or he did until

Dick was caught with his pants down under the bleachers, figuratively if not literally. He knew Yvonne had just agreed to go to the prom with him last year because she needed a last-minute substitute.

I tried to tell her last summer how I felt about her. I barely had time for myself, let alone a girlfriend. I was lucky to even find that lousy carwash job, but at least it gave me some spending cash. By the time I had some, she had started dating someone else. I thought she'd get it when I bought a car. You need a car to take a girl out. Hell, the only time she was ever in my car was with Randy.

He felt a little guilty about Randy. It wasn't like him to try to sabotage some other guy's relationship. But he was there first. Randy may not have known it, but he was the one horning in.

How long have I been in love with Yvonne? I suppose since eighth grade when girls stopped being such a pain in the butt. I think I looked up and saw her differently for the first time. Vonnie was no longer the beanpole kid with a mouthful of braces and studious black glasses. All grown up. And drop-dead gorgeous.

She didn't seem to notice or understand how irresistible she was. How it was impossible to tear his eyes away when she'd been running around his house in pink babydoll pajamas. How she knocked the breath out of him when she'd been swinging her hips around modeling that slinky homecoming dress.

He could see other boys pining over her too. Not just Dick, Randy, and Gary. He couldn't blame them. He could stare at her face and her long graceful neck for hours. The way her hair swayed when she walked or danced. And those never-ending legs made his own grow weak.

Did she think it was easy for boys? They always had to make the first move and what if they blew it? What if it wasn't welcomed? He wasn't gonna go around kissing someone unless . . . she wanted him to. Apparently, she'd wanted him to. She didn't object. No, she'd kissed him back. Enthusiastically.

Tonight, she should have been mad as hell at him. He'd had the power to make her prom queen and he hadn't done it. He'd forgotten to even apologize for that. But she'd listened to him. For once, she'd listened and understood what he'd been trying to say for years. He couldn't believe his luck. She said she loved him too. Who'd a thunk it?

He wasn't going to blow his chance this time. Maybe he'd been afraid to act on his impulses last summer. But it was time to find out how to get Yvonne to fulfill his fantasies. He'd come to understand Yvonne needed a lot of attention. Maybe she didn't need a fancy car or expensive dates, but she did expect a boy to dote on her. He could do that if that's what it took. He'd have to.

On Sunday afternoon he called her on the phone, and they went for a walk around the neighborhood, holding hands and talking about the last two weeks of school. On Monday morning, he showed up at her locker and walked her to her first-period class. They had two classes together in the afternoon, and he met up with her again after school. For the first time since he started driving himself to school a few months ago, she rode home with him and not his sister.

"I've never ridden in your car, Daniel. Oh, um . . . not in front at least. This is nice. It's a nice car, and you keep it real clean." Yvonne combed her fingers through her hair, tucking one side behind her ear.

"You can sit over here, a little closer," he said.

"I wouldn't want to interfere with your driving." She gave him a sidelong look but scooted toward him.

He put his arm around her shoulders and pulled her next to him. "I only need one arm to drive. By the way, did I tell you I got a Merit Scholarship?"

"A Merit Scholarship? Isn't that like the Holy Grail? Free tuition to any college? I remember Clark was a finalist when he was a senior."

"Yes, it should cover my tuition at college as long as I keep my grades up." He had to give her credit for never treating him like he was too studious.

"Oh, yeah, that's right. I'm sure Debbie told me you were planning to go to the University of . . . Kansas, was it?"

"Yes, in Lawrence, Kansas. It's about four hours from here."

"Huh. I got a scholarship from the newspaper. It is nice, but only for one hundred dollars. I get a break on tuition since my dad works for the university. My grandparents are paying for my dorm room. I should be okay if I get a job."

He caught her furrowing her brow.

"What? What's the matter?"

"We aren't going to have much time together, are we? You're moving to Kansas."

"We've got all summer, Yvonne. Let's just enjoy it."

CHAPTER TWENTY-EIGHT

The Saturday after the prom, Connie Edison woke her husband and daughter with pancakes for breakfast. "It is a perfect day to get some of those spring-cleaning chores done," she announced. "Harold, get out the big extension ladder to clean the gutters and the outside of the second-story windows. Yvonne and I will wash the interior windows. Then you can start working on your room, Yvonne."

Yvonne rolled her eyes. "This was supposed to be a perfect day to do whatever I wanted. Nothing on the calendar and very little homework left."

But even her mother's chore list was not enough to dampen her spirits. Things had been going very well with Daniel. Last night they'd gone on a real date and it was the first time they'd ever parked and made out. *That car of his has a lot of room in it. I'm not even worried about Daniel trying to take advantage of me. In fact, I might have to take advantage of him.* She laughed out loud.

She cleaned out her closet first, packing up her winter clothes. Around mid-afternoon, she was wiping down her open bedroom window when she heard voices from next door. The lights were all off in Debbie's and Daniel's bedrooms. Grover was barking, and he rarely barked. She went back to her cleaning. There were more raised voices, including what sounded like Debbie and Bernard Adams shouting. She couldn't make out what they were saying and she wasn't sure she wanted to know. It felt like she was eavesdropping. She closed the window and didn't hear anything more for about an hour. Robert's car was parked on the street in front of the Adams' house.

Later she was putting clean sheets on her bed when she heard a door slam. She turned toward the window in time to see Daniel storm out of the house and get into his car in the driveway. He backed out much too fast and tore off up the street.

I wonder where he is going in such a hurry. Was he mad? What happened?

A little while later, Debbie and Robert came out of the house and stood on the driveway. It looked like Debbie was crying as she put her head on Robert's shoulder. He put his arms around her with one hand on the back of her head. Yvonne couldn't help focusing on that. His right hand, the color of maple syrup, glistening in the sunlight, over Debbie's lovely pale blonde hair. He was stroking her hair, comforting her.

I wish I had a photograph of this, I can see there is a story. But I am still trying to figure out what the story is. Debbie nodded her head in response to something Robert said, and they returned to the house.

Yvonne went back to her bed-making chore, but a few minutes later, their doorbell rang. She went to the stairway and heard her mother talking to Debbie so she bounded down the stairs.

Debbie and Robert stood on their front porch one arm around the other. Debbie had a small overnight bag with her.

Robert addressed Yvonne as soon as she came into view, "Hey, Yvonne. I was gonna axe your mother if Debbie can stay here tonight."

Yvonne frowned in confusion. "Absolutely she can spend the night, she's spent lots of nights here. It's okay, isn't it, Mom?" She turned to Connie.

"What is this all about, Debbie?" Connie asked.

Debbie burst into tears. Robert looked down as he dug the toe of his shoe into the cement on the front porch. "We had a disagreement with her parents. Ev'ryone jus' needs to cool off. I'd take her home wid me, but our house's crowded. She knew you had a spare bedroom if Clark ain't here."

Yvonne motioned Debbie to come in and put her arms around her.

"Is everything okay, Robert? Are you okay?" Yvonne asked him. *He doesn't look okay at all. I have never seen him look so glum.*

"Tryin' to make sure Debbie's okay before I leave. I'll be back tomorrow morning to check on her."

Yvonne and her mother exchanged looks. "We'll look after

her," Connie said, and Robert turned and headed toward his car.

"Yvonne, what's going on?" Connie asked.

"I don't know, Mom. I've been cleaning. I guess there was some sort of fight."

"Would it be all right if I don't tell you about it tonight? I don't think I can go through it again today," Debbie whimpered.

"Debbie, you didn't do anything illegal, did you?" Connie asked. "Or immoral?" Her gaze shifted back to where Robert's car had been parked.

Debbie started crying harder, and Yvonne started herding her up the stairs. "Mom!" Yvonne said, "You know Debbie would never do anything like that. Let her alone."

When they got to Yvonne's room, Debbie sat down on the bed and Yvonne stood waiting. The smell of ammonia from the window cleaner and laundry soap permeated the air.

"I don't want to talk about it right now. My life is falling apart, and I can't even think straight. Do you want me to sleep here or in Clark's room? I'm not sure I'll be able to sleep, but I should try."

Yvonne knelt in front of her and looked into her eyes, with her hands on Debbie's knees.

"Daniel told me I don't pay enough attention to the other people around me. Have I missed something important going on with you, Debs?"

"It's not your fault. I didn't tell you." Debbie wiped her tears with the back of her hand. "I didn't tell Daniel either. He is so mad at me. I don't think I can face one more person yelling at me."

Yvonne continued to look at Debbie, waiting for more.

"Really, can I just go to bed? I don't want to talk about it tonight."

"Of course. Sleep in my bed, I changed the sheets a little while ago. I'll go sleep in Clark's room tonight, but we haven't had any dinner. Don't you want anything to eat?" Debbie shook her head and started taking a nightgown out of her overnight case.

Yvonne went to the dining room to eat pizza with her parents.

"You don't know what is going on with Debbie and her parents?" Harold asked her.

"No, she doesn't want to talk about it. All I know is they are upset with her, and Daniel is upset with her. I think she'll tell me more after she has had some sleep."

"It must be about that boy. What's his name, Robert?" Connie said. "Bonnie told me they wouldn't let her go out with him because the cops were hassling him about driving in a White neighborhood and going out with a White girl. But they let her go to the prom with him. Maybe something else happened."

"Her parents don't know she has been dating him all year," Yvonne said.

"What do you mean, they don't know?" Harold leaned toward Yvonne.

Yvonne tried to keep her voice from shaking. *Maybe this was a bad idea telling my parents but it's time to be truthful.* "Robert is a perfectly nice guy, but since her parents told Debbie she couldn't date him, some other boys have picked her up for dates, then she and Robert met up."

"And she thought this was okay? To deceive her parents like that?" Connie let out her breath.

Yvonne looked down at her plate of half-eaten pizza. "I don't know. I guess." She blinked back her tears. "She said she was in love with him."

"I think we may need to go over and talk to Bonnie and

Bernard," Harold said.

"No, Daddy. Not tonight, please. Can we try to stay out of it, just for tonight? Maybe if I see Daniel in the driveway, I can ask him."

"All right, Young Lady. But whatever you learn from Daniel or Debbie, if it has anything to do with you or with her staying with us, you need to tell us."

Yvonne nodded. She couldn't eat much more after that. It was a beautiful night, so she went out in the backyard and sat on the swing watching the moon. *What was going on with Debbie? Did she tell her parents she'd been dating Robert on the sly? Did they try to prevent her from dating him again?* After it got darker, she heard a car drive up and a door slam. She walked between the houses and spotted Daniel coming home. He saw her in the porch light and walked up to her.

"Did you know about this?" He huffed out his breath and crossed his arms.

"I still don't think I know about it. Debbie is sleeping in my bed but she wouldn't talk."

Daniel motioned for Yvonne to follow him to his backyard where he sat on the picnic table and put his feet on the seat. He covered his eyes with his hands.

"She's pregnant."

Yvonne gasped. "No! No, no, no, no. Are you sure?"

He looked up. "She said she went to a clinic. I guess they do some sort of test. I don't know, this is not something I figured I had to learn about when I was seventeen. I can't believe she would do anything so stupid. We haven't even graduated from high school for Christ's sake."

Yvonne sat down on the seat next to his feet. She felt like her head was going to explode. *How could Debbie have done this?*

Well, she didn't do it alone, there was Robert after all. How could either one of them have been so careless? It must have been that house she talked about. The sleeping bag, the space heater. Oh no. Hadn't she learned anything from Linda or Barbra?

"I feel sick. I can't believe this is happening," she said.

"That makes two of us. I have been driving around for hours but I can't figure out a way to undo this. I had to get out of there. I was afraid I was going to attack Robert and that would make things worse. I am surprised my father showed any restraint."

Yvonne slid her legs around so that she was facing the tabletop and put her head on her crossed arms. "I think I heard your dad yelling."

"Oh, he did that. Everybody was yelling. This is the worst thing that has ever happened to my family," he sighed. "And get this; Debbie thinks they are getting married." He put his hand on Yvonne's shoulder and rubbed it.

"What?"

"Married at seventeen. She is delusional. My dad is like 'No Way Jose.' She's supposed to start nursing school in the fall."

"I'm so sorry, Daniel. I knew this could happen I guess, but I thought they would use their heads. I mean at some point you simply have to put the brakes on."

"I don't know what you mean. How could you have known this could happen? She was pretending to date other guys. It turns out she has been sneaking around to be with Robert. Or at least she said it was Robert's baby. I don't know what is real anymore."

"I did know she was sneaking around. I am surprised no one told you." Yvonne covered her mouth with her hand.

"What? What does that mean?"

"She went to the Sweetheart Dance with him. A bunch of

kids saw them, I saw them at *Romeo & Juliet* when I was with Randy. I told her someone would spill the beans to you. Peter picked her up once and Nancy was mad about it. I thought she might tell you."

"Are you serious? You knew about her seeing Robert when our parents forbade it and you didn't say anything? If not to my parents, how could you not tell me?"

"It wasn't my place to tell you or anyone else."

Daniel's brows folded. "But don't you see? If you had, she might not be pregnant. Maybe if this had come out sooner it wouldn't have gotten this far."

"And she never would have forgiven me. You told me I don't have friends. You're wrong. I do know how to be a friend and part of it is keeping their secrets."

"I'd better go inside. I am still too angry to be rational. I don't want to say something I'll regret. This is a huge mess but it isn't your mess. That wasn't fair. I'll see you tomorrow." Daniel pushed off the table and went into the back of his house. Yvonne stared at the door closing behind him and let tears spill down her cheeks. She felt like her heart was slowing down as if time was standing still.

Daniel and his parents must feel ten times worse. I can't imagine what Debbie is going through. She's going to have a baby.

CHAPTER TWENTY-NINE

The next morning, she heard Debbie in the bathroom. *What do I say to her? This is not the self-respecting girl I have known since we were eight. I mean, she sympathized with me when Dick was pressuring me to go all the way. I want to scream at her. I want to scream at the top of my lungs. But her family has done that to her already, even her own twin brother. She needs a friend, someone to listen to her. I hope I can do that.*

She was in the bathroom for quite a long time, so Yvonne got up and knocked on the door.

"Are you okay, Debs?" Yvonne said.

Debbie opened the door, wiping her mouth. "Do you happen to have an extra toothbrush?" The smell of vomit explained her request.

Yvonne went to the linen closet next to the bathroom and fished out a toothbrush in a plastic box. Connie kept spare supplies of most necessities. Clark had a habit of coming home and crashing without preparation. Debbie brushed her teeth and Yvonne used the bathroom before following Debbie back to her bedroom. She sat down on the bed next to Debbie.

"Daniel told me," Yvonne began, glancing down before meeting her friend's eyes. "How far along are you?"

Debbie startled, then studied Yvonne's face. "About two-and-a-half months, I guess. You aren't mad at me?"

Yvonne sighed and stood, walking around the room. "I was mad last night then I was sick about it. Now I guess I am just baffled. Didn't you realize this could happen? Why didn't you stop him? Or use some sort of birth control?"

Debbie stiffened. "I know it looks like we were foolish. It's not like he forced himself on me. He asked if it was okay, if I wanted to do it even. I was a little scared, but I did want to get closer to him. We shared something that we haven't shared with anyone else. I guess I thought I wasn't very likely to get pregnant, but if I did it would solve one problem."

Yvonne arched her brows and crossed her arms. "How does this solve anything?"

"Remember this happened before my parents even knew I was seeing Robert. I didn't think they would agree to let me see him again. But if I was pregnant, they would have to accept him. This makes him like family already."

Yvonne shook her head trying to clear the cobwebs. "Do you have a plan?"

Debbie beamed, "Robert asked me to marry him."

"You're still seventeen. How old is Robert?"

"Um, I guess he is eighteen. His birthday is in October."

"You would both need the consent of your parents to get married. Do you have it?"

"Well, no. My parents are dead set against it. So are Robert's but he thinks they will come around."

"And what if they don't? I had this discussion with Linda already. She told me in Nebraska you have to be nineteen to be married without parental consent. The baby will be here long before you are nineteen. In Kansas and Iowa, it is only eighteen. That's why teenagers get married in Marysville. You'd still have to wait until your eighteenth birthday in August."

"You are sounding very judgmental, Yvonne. What is it you think I should do?"

"I think you should have kept your pants on, but I know it is too late for that now. If I were in your shoes, I would put the baby up for adoption." When Debbie put her hands over her ears, Yvonne rolled her eyes. "Of course, I'm not the one in love with Robert."

"I'm going to marry him, Yvonne. No matter who stands in our way. I want you to be my maid of honor."

"Debbie, have you thought about what you could give a baby? Robert was planning to go to college, wasn't he? You said he wanted to study mechanical engineering. You should go to nursing college. Afterward, you can have lots of babies."

"I'm not going to negotiate about the life or the raising of my baby. You are sounding like my parents. It's my baby. Robert and I want to have our baby."

"But what about your life, Debbie? It's just starting too."

"I had to compromise that as soon as I got pregnant. We'll make it work." Debbie pulled her clothes out of the overnight bag and started to change out of her nightgown. Yvonne had seen her undressed many times over the years, but her bare belly now made her think about what was growing inside.

Yvonne put on a sleeveless dress to go to church. "I'll have to get back to you on the maid of honor thing. Naturally, I hoped to be a part of your wedding. I figured it would not be so soon. Do you want to eat some breakfast here? You must be hungry."

Debbie shrugged. "I could eat something. I usually only throw up once in the morning. Then I'd better go back home and face
the music."

CHAPTER THIRTY

The seniors had three more days of classes. Daniel had been giving Yvonne a ride home from school. On Tuesday he had to meet with the speech teacher and the principal after school so they could go over his commencement speech. Daniel was class valedictorian and Randy was salutatorian, so they both had to give speeches. Yvonne was happy to be in the top ten percent of her graduating class.

Since she'd agreed to wait for him, she wandered down to the band room and found Linda practicing some twirls by herself.

"Linda, I am glad I caught you. Do you have a few minutes to talk?" Yvonne said.

"Sure. But let's go outside. Anyone could come in here." She left her baton on a chair.

When they were outdoors, they walked along the path toward the football field. "How are you feeling?" Yvonne asked.

"I am doing okay. I told my parents. They freaked out, but now they are calmer. My mom said she'd take me to a doctor in Overland Park, Kansas, in a few weeks. I'm not going to tell Tom."

"Are you sure he doesn't deserve a say in this?"

She sighed and looked down at the field. "My dad thinks so, but I don't want to mess up his life. He'd want to do the right thing, to marry me, I know that much about him. But I don't know him well enough to decide to spend my life with him. I am still growing up. Maybe I'll have a baby later. Maybe I will even have one with Tom."

Yvonne stopped walking, forcing Linda to look at her. "Can I help you in some way? I may not have chosen what you are choosing, but I can see it will be hard to do. Do you want me to go with you?"

Linda raised her eyebrows and rounded her eyes. "You would do that for me? It's not like we are going to stop and shop for clothes on the way, you know. This won't be a pleasant trip. but it would help me if I didn't have to talk to my mother. I feel bad enough I upset my parents. You wouldn't mind?"

Yvonne put her arms around Linda. "I'm in. If I were in your shoes, I would want someone to hold my hand. And not my mother. That would be even harder. Just call me and tell me when."

They walked back to the band room and found Daniel looking for Yvonne. She went to meet him, then turned to look back at Linda. Yvonne made a zipper motion across her mouth, and Linda mimicked the motion.

"What was that all about?" Daniel asked, slipping an arm around Yvonne as they headed for the parking lot.

"Just girl stuff. How'd your speech go?"

CHAPTER THIRTY-ONE

May 4, 1980

Daniel looked at his watch. Running late was sometimes unavoidable when he had to appear in court. Even a continuance hearing could run long. He jumped out of his Ford Mustang and bounded up the steps of the doctor's office building. Only a few minutes past two. Yvonne shouldn't be too upset. But both of them seemed to get upset over the smallest things these days.

He raced into Dr. Mayer's waiting room, as Yvonne was standing up to be taken back to meet with the doctor. *She looks nervous. Of course, she's nervous, we're about to find out the results of the laparoscopy she had done last week.* He'd taken off work for that too, but at least she seemed to recover quickly, with some mild cramping.

Dr. Henry Mayer got right to the point. "As we suspected, Yvonne, there was some scar tissue and inflammation. It appears you have endometriosis. There are adhesions on your ovaries and outside your uterus."

"What does that mean? Is that why she isn't getting

pregnant?" Daniel asked.

"Yes, that is most likely the cause of your infertility. The best course of treatment is a drug called Danocrine. You must take it twice a day by mouth. What it does is put your body into menopause."

Yvonne shook her head. "Menopause? At my age?" She rubbed her ear.

"Both pregnancy and menopause will shrink the endometriosis. Since you can't get pregnant due to endometriosis, we have to convince your body it is in menopause. And you will stop having periods, you'll have hot flashes, mood swings, and all the other symptoms of menopause. There are also some serious side effects of this drug so we will only keep you on it for eight or nine months."

"This sounds crazy," Yvonne squinted at the doctor. "Going into menopause will help me get pregnant?"

"Yes, it should after you are done with the course of treatment. But I caution you, you don't want to take a chance of actually getting pregnant while taking this drug. It can cause severe birth defects. You will have to be sure to use a condom, or a diaphragm to avoid that when you have intercourse."

"Wait a minute," Daniel said. "We are trying to have a baby, and you are telling us to use birth control?" He jumped up like he was arguing in front of a judge, gesturing to bring home his point. "So even though we've been trying to conceive for two years, now you think you have identified the problem. And we're supposed to put this whole thing on hold for another nine months and then, if it works, start all over again. If this is the solution, why didn't you start with this? Why didn't you do this laparoscopy a long time ago? This is unbelievable. Freaking unbelievable."

He felt the pressure rising in his neck and face. His gaze jerked back to Yvonne before he strode out of the room. He didn't stop until he was back on the steps in the front of the building. He felt like taking a swing at someone, someone wearing a white coat. Swearing under his breath, he paced along the front of the building, raking his hands through his hair.

Holy shit, who do these doctors think they are? Treating these poor women like science experiments. Doesn't he realize how hard this is on her? I shouldn't have left Yvonne there. She won't know where I went.

After about five minutes, she showed up at the entrance and spotted him.

"That was very rude. I can't believe you just walked out." She pulled her sunglasses and car keys out of her bag.

"Where did this guy get his degree, Quackville University? I'm going to start looking at medical malpractice lawsuits. I'll bet he's been sued more than once. And this drug. It has to be pretty powerful if it can put a twenty-nine-year-old healthy woman into menopause. Who knows what it might do to you? I don't think you should take it. This may be where I draw the line."

She burst into tears.

"Damnit, Yvonne. You can't do that."

"No." She pounded her finger into his chest. "You can't do that. You can't draw a line after everything I have had to go through to get to this point. When you go through all those painful tests, and embarrassing exams, and waiting and hoping while your heart is breaking—"

He put his arms around her, kissing her hair, and let her cry. "Okay, okay. Don't cry, Honey. We'll look into it further."

I'll check up on this doctor and this drug. How far do we have to go to have a baby? There has to be a better way.

Three nights later, he came home to a candlelit table and the smell of beef stew simmering on the stove.

"Well, this looks nice. Is it a special occasion? Are we having company? I didn't forget an important anniversary, did I?" he asked giving her a quick kiss.

"No, no company," she smiled, "but we are celebrating." She put some warm rolls on the table and a bowl of salad. "Do you want some wine or something to drink?"

"I want to know what we're celebrating. Did you get a raise at work?" He sat at his usual place at the table and put his napkin in his lap.

"The doctor's office called today." She appeared to be studying his face, as she sat next to him.

"Tell me they changed their minds about the dangerous drug they wanted you to take."

She laughed, "Actually that is true. They no longer want me to take the drug."

"Great." He sensed more to the story. "Why?"

"They take blood and urine pretty much every time I go in there. But the other day, they had to do a pregnancy test before they could prescribe that drug."

He searched her face for what he thought she was trying to tell him. "Are you saying—"

She shrugged. "Pregnant."

He jumped up, pulling her to her feet, and swung her around in a hug.

"I can't believe it. How could this be? What did they say? How do you feel? You'd better sit down." He knew he was babbling but couldn't seem to stop.

Yvonne put her hand on her belly. "I feel fine, wonderful actually. I am a little bit in shock. I guess one of those little swimmers got through the obstacle course."

He helped her sit at the table again and started to sit.

"Oh, the stew. I have to get that." She pushed her chair back.

"I'll get it. Let me wait on you tonight." As he went back to the stove, he took a big breath. Their streak of bad luck seemed to have been broken. *Now, all we have to worry about is parenthood. Tomorrow. We can worry about parenthood tomorrow.*

CHAPTER THIRTY-TWO

June 17, 1969

Yvonne debated whether to tell her parents she'd agreed to accompany Linda on the trip to Kansas to have an abortion. It had been hard enough telling them Debbie was pregnant. They hardly knew Linda, although she thought they knew her parents. Linda had an older sister in Clark's class, so they'd seen them at school functions. But if she didn't tell them the truth about Linda, she was going to have to come up with an elaborate lie to explain why she'd be gone all day. It was about a four-hour trip each way, and she didn't know how long Linda would need to be at the clinic.

"Mom, I need to tell you something. You know sometimes it is important you support a friend, even if you don't quite agree with them or understand what they are thinking." She poured herself some orange juice and a glass of milk and put them on the kitchen table.

"You're talking about being Debbie's maid of honor," Connie said, sipping her coffee.

"No, well actually, this is sort of the same thing. But this is another friend, Linda Bridges. She's going to be a senior next year. She's a twirler. Been over here."

"Oh, yes. Cute girl with that pixie haircut."

"I told her I would go with her and her mother today to Overland Park, Kansas. She's having an abortion." She looked down at her glass of milk, feeling the weight of her mother's gaze.

"Linda is pregnant too?" Connie shifted in her chair and looked out at the bird feeder. "Poor girl. She must be terrified."

Yvonne blinked and found her mother's eyes, surprised she heard sympathy. "I think she is. That's why I want to help her, to be there to give her emotional support. She hasn't even told the boy she is dating. She doesn't want him to know. I told her I thought that was wrong, but it is up to her."

Connie nodded. "Is there anyone going along for her mother? I can't think of her name right now. Mary maybe. Mary Jo, I think that's it."

"I don't know, I didn't ask. I suppose the fewer people who know the better."

"I guess I'll ask her then. When are they picking you up?"

"In about an hour. I have to take a shower."

"Two of your friends are pregnant. One of your friends from last year, Barbra, was also pregnant. What about you?"

"I'm not pregnant!" Heat was quickly searing Yvonne's face.

Connie sighed, "But are you avoiding it? Have you been sleeping with your boyfriends?"

Yvonne splayed her hand over her chest, "M-mom, why would you think that?"

Connie continued, "Have you ever—"

"No! Never. My friends may have let their hormones push their common sense out the window, but I haven't. I mean, I have kissed boys, I have made out with boys. I know what the attraction is, but I don't want to be in their situation."

"Good." Connie nodded. "Before you change your mind, you should get a prescription for birth control pills."

"Mom!"

"I'm just saying, better to be safe than sorry. I'll go get dressed and see if Mary Jo wants my company today."

Linda's mother was pleasantly surprised by Connie's offer to accompany them on the trip. She had a roomy Oldsmobile, and Connie sat in the front with Mary Jo Bridges, while the girls moved to the backseat. Yvonne realized she'd only seen Linda's mother when she was the perfect hostess. This whole ordeal must have shattered the wholesome image she had of her family.

The mothers were engaged in a steady stream of small talk. They talked about their husbands, their other children, fashion, the upcoming moon shot, and the hippies in California.

Yvonne reached over and put her hand on Linda's shoulder. She'd never seen her look so pale and small. Normally Linda's larger-than-life personality bubbled out of her, but today she scanned the scenery outside and rubbed her crossed arms as if she was chilled.

"How are you doing?" Yvonne said quietly.

"I just have to get through today, then I'll be okay." She sniffed. "It was nice of you and your mother to come along."

"You'll never guess what my mom told me this morning." Yvonne leaned over toward Linda.

"What?"

"She wants me to go on birth control pills!"

"It's a little late, isn't it?" It was the first time she'd seen Linda smile that day.

"No! You still don't believe me about Dick, do you? I'm still a virgin!" Yvonne glanced toward the front seat, trying to ensure they weren't being heard.

"A virgin, really? Want some pointers?" Linda raised her eyebrows. They both started to laugh. That got the mothers' attention. Yvonne marveled that Linda was able to laugh about anything.

A few minutes later, Connie diverted from the small talk. "If you don't mind my asking, Mary Jo, why are you going to Kansas to take care of this? Can't a local doctor help her, or at least one in Omaha, maybe at the medical school?"

Mary Jo stiffened but she didn't shy away from the question. "I looked into it. It isn't allowed in Nebraska. Kansas is one of the closest places. We could have decided to spend the night, but she wanted to make the trip as quickly as possible. Even in Kansas, we may have to concoct a story about rape or incest to comply with their rules. We'll see what they say when we get there. They told us to come early to complete the paperwork."

"My sister had an abortion," Connie said.

"What?" Yvonne said.

"My sister became pregnant when she was almost forty. She didn't think she could have any more children, so she stopped using birth control. Her last child was ten when she got pregnant again. I guess they had a reason to believe the fetus had some sort of abnormality. I don't know the whole story. She told us at the time she'd lost the baby. But a year later, she told me they had to abort it. I think her health may have been at risk too, maybe that was why she could have her regular obstetrician do it. It's never easy."

"You didn't tell me that before, Mom," Yvonne said.

"You were twelve, it wasn't something for you to think about."

Yvonne thought about what her mother had said that morning. What they were doing right now. *I am eighteen. At least my mother thinks I am old enough to know about things like this. I didn't know how good I had it when I was twelve.*

It took longer at the clinic than expected. No one was allowed to go into the procedure room with Linda. They said they had a staff person there to comfort her. After the procedure, they monitored her for a bit to make sure she didn't have a fever or other complications. On the way home, they got some McDonald's hamburgers and milkshakes, but Linda didn't want to eat anything. She said she was afraid she couldn't keep it down.

On the long ride home, Linda's head drooped. They'd given her a sedative.

"Why don't you lie down, Linda?" her mother said.

"Here, put your head in my lap," Yvonne offered. Linda curled up with her head on Yvonne's lap. Her mother had brought a blanket, and they put it over Linda's arms and legs. Yvonne thought Linda had fallen asleep until she heard her weeping. She stroked her hair and her arm, trying to comfort her. Simon and Garfunkel were singing about that bridge over troubled waters on the radio. Yvonne leaned her head on the window and hoped her friend would be able to get over it.

CHAPTER THIRTY-THREE

Daniel had told her they would have the whole summer to

enjoy each other's company. The reality was most of their conversations centered on Debbie and Robert. It took a few weeks before Bonnie and Bernard Adams accepted that they weren't going to talk their daughter out of getting married or having the baby. They even had a meeting with Robert's parents. While his minister father strongly disapproved, there wasn't much Robert's parents could do to dissuade them either.

"I don't know what happened to my parents," Daniel complained when they were driving around watching fireworks on July Fourth. "They were so opposed to this whole thing, and now it is like my mom caught baby fever. I guess they have gotten used to the idea this child will be of a mixed-race. I have heard it can be very tough on a kid. But now my parents are planning to let Debbie and Robert live with them and turn my bedroom into a nursery."

"You're losing your bedroom? What about when you come home from college?"

"I guess they are assuming I won't. If I have to put up with a screaming baby, maybe I won't want to."

"You won't want to see me?" Yvonne crossed her arms.

"Sure I will. My dad says they will convert a space in the basement for my bedroom. It might be better once they get it done. Oooh, look at that one!" Daniel pointed to a big chrysanthemum effect lighting up the sky. They had found a place to park atop a hill and leaned back on the seat next to each other. They watched in silence for a few minutes.

"Yvonne. I want to ask you something. And maybe I have no right to ask you this." Daniel kept his eyes on the sky when she turned to watch him. "But I've heard the rumors."

"I don't know what you mean."

"Well, Barbra Simpson was pregnant. Linda Bridges was pregnant. And now Debbie." He sighed. "It made me wonder about you and Dick Dunn."

"What about me and Dick Dunn?"

"You know, I'm sorry. I shouldn't have mentioned it."

"I still don't think you have mentioned it." Her eyes rounded. "You want to know if I had sex with Dick?"

He turned back to her blinking. "Well . . .um."

"No." Yvonne furrowed her brow. "I'm not sure why you think it has anything to do with you, but I had to tell him 'no' on more than one occasion. He at least took 'no' for an answer. And then he dumped me right before prom."

Daniel smiled straightening his shoulders. "His loss was my gain. Then what about Randy?"

"Randy?"

"You were dating Randy while Debbie was dating Robert."

"You think Randy and I . . ." Yvonne laughed. "No way. As a matter of fact, you told him something crazy that made him afraid to even kiss me for months."

Daniel chuckled and scratched his cheek. "You mean that worked?" Yvonne pushed away from the seat to face him.

"What did you tell him?"

"I don't remember exactly. I saw Dick grabbing at you and you elbowed him in the chest at the prom. I think I told Randy you didn't like to be manhandled."

"I think you told him I didn't want to be kissed."

"Well, maybe that was part of it. Geez, I didn't want him coming on to you."

"Why not? You certainly weren't."

He put his hands on either side of her head, running them through her hair. "My mistake." He kissed her softly then.

"We haven't talked about this. Are we going to be able to date each other after you go off to Kansas?"

He looked away again, watching the fireworks. "I don't know. I think we can see each other sometimes, but it won't be the same. You'll find some other guy who is going to school here in Lincoln and I might find someone at K.U. I think we should be free to do that."

Yvonne scowled and brought her bare legs up to her chest, wrapping her arms around them. Her sandals lay in a heap on the floor of the car. "So, what you are saying," she said, fighting back tears, "is we are going to break up when you leave."

He looked back at her. "I don't like that idea either. It seems like we finally got it right. But I don't see how we can keep our relationship going, and one of us or both of us is bound to get hurt."

"Don't you think breaking up is going to mean we get hurt?"

He caught the light of the fireworks reflecting off her face, revealing the tears running down her cheeks. "Don't cry. We both knew this was coming."

"Maybe I just didn't want to think about it."

"Then you shouldn't have brought it up." He scooted over closer to her, putting her legs in his lap, and wrapping his arms around her. "It's not happening yet though. There is still time for us." She forgot everything else when he pulled her into a kiss.

There is something very romantic about making out against the backdrop of fireworks. If only our love wasn't fading away like the last burned-out tendrils.

CHAPTER THIRTY-FOUR

Yvonne was sweating, and she'd just taken a shower. She stood in front of the window air conditioner in her parents' bedroom with her bathrobe open to the cool air. How was she going to put on her taffeta dress without dying of heatstroke?

Debbie and Robert had decided to get married after Debbie's eighteenth birthday on August 3, 1969, so the Saturday after that was selected. There had been record high temperatures for the past two weeks, and the high was supposed to be 102 degrees at six o'clock when they planned to have the wedding reception at nearby Bethany Park. At least the church was air-conditioned. The wedding would take place at five o'clock at Northern Baptist Church where Robert's father served as pastor.

Debbie and Yvonne had gone on a shopping spree with their mothers to pick out a wedding gown for Debbie and a bridesmaid dress for Yvonne. They had to go to Omaha to find a salon where you could buy a dress without ordering it.

"I think this is the one I want," Debbie pronounced pivoting around in front of the three-way mirror. She was wearing a poufy white satin gown with long sleeves and an open lace overlay. It had a scoop neckline which would at least be a little cooler in the summer.

"Do you happen to have this gown in ivory?" Bonnie asked the salesclerk.

"Why would I want ivory?" Debbie asked. "I would rather have white, Mom."

"Well, you know what they say about wearing white on your wedding day, Dear. You'll be almost five months along by then."

Yvonne looked at her own mother, who was raising her eyebrows. Tradition dictated only virgin brides wear white. That was another popular topic in the Ann Landers and Abigail Van

Buren advice columns. In the end, they couldn't get the style Debbie wanted in ivory in time so she took the white.

Yvonne had convinced Debbie to let her pick a beautiful sleeveless dress in lavender taffeta. It was on sale, probably because the color was unusual. The design might not look very good on some girls, but on Yvonne, with her long legs and slim figure, it looked like it was made for her. It had a full floor-length skirt and came up to Yvonne's neck. She decided she was wearing her hair up in a bun, to keep cooler.

She thought she was going to be hot until Daniel and his father came out of their house, both decked out in black tuxedos. They already looked like they were melting.

It's Debbie's day, she kept reminding herself as she stuck a washcloth and hand towel into her bag along with extra makeup, a comb, and hairpins. When she and her parents got to the church, Yvonne was directed into a small room off the narthex. Debbie and her mother were already there, trying to keep cool in front of a small fan.

"It's so hot in here. I thought there was air-conditioning," Yvonne said.

Bonnie said, "Only in the sanctuary, it turns out, and in one of the big rooms downstairs they use for fellowship."

Debbie's face was red and blotched because of the heat. Her flaxen hair was a mass of curls cascading onto her shoulders topped by a three-tiered veil. Yvonne took out the washcloth and found the ladies' room. She came back to Debbie with a wet washcloth to put around her neck and décolletage. She wet the hand towel as well and took turns putting it to her face and letting Bonnie use it. Fortunately, there wasn't much of a delay in getting the wedding underway. Bonnie left to be escorted down to the front pew.

Robert's brother Truman, who was an usher, came to tell her they were starting the processional. She took one last look at her best friend, as tears welled up.

"I can't believe you are getting married, Debs. But I know you and Robert will be happy. You both know how to fight for what you want and now you're getting it." She gave Debbie a hug, and they did air kisses as they'd seen on television. "We don't want to mess up all of that fancy lipstick we used."

Yvonne snatched up her rose and carnation bouquet and followed Truman. She felt everyone's eyes on her as she made her solo journey down the long aisle. The music from the organ wafted through the sanctuary like a rising cloud. She saw Robert standing next to Reverend Washington along with his older brother, Donald. She could see Daniel and Truman still seating some last-minute guests. She marveled at how well the guests were dressed. There was a mixture of Black and White faces, but more people on Robert's side since his father was the minister of this church. She'd never been an attendant in a wedding and the whole thing felt surreal. But at least she felt a little cool air descending on her shoulders. *Thank you, Jesus.*

She took her place in front of the church as Debbie and her father started down the aisle. Debbie looked as joyous as she'd ever seen her. Her face was no longer red, she was nearly pale. She didn't necessarily look pregnant, but definitely like she'd gained weight. The dress fit her a month ago but was now a little too tight.

Her father handed her off to Robert, and Reverend Washington began the wedding ceremony. He was about halfway through his message about love everlasting when Debbie began swaying a little. Debbie had both hands on her bouquet. Robert looked at Debbie and then at Yvonne, as he put a hand on Debbie's elbow. Yvonne reached out to Debbie as she started falling backward. Donald jumped in when he saw what was happening, and between the three of them, they kept her from hitting her head when she sank to the floor.

Debbie's father then rushed up to her, and they laid her on

her back. She was out cold by then. The congregants gasped as if on cue. Yvonne picked up the cascade bouquet which had fallen out of Debbie's hands.

Luckily, Donald had medical training and he checked her pulse and breathing and pronounced it normal. He told them to elevate her feet slightly above her heart. In a few minutes, Debbie opened her eyes to find Robert, Reverend Washington, Donald, Yvonne, and her father looking down at her.

"I'd say this is going to be a wedding to remember," Reverend Washington said. Everyone else laughed as they helped Debbie into a sitting position on the floor.

Yvonne crouched down next to her. "Are you feeling better, Honey? What happened?"

"I just got dizzy, and then I remember starting to fall. That must have been a surprise to everyone." She turned and looked out at all of the guests sitting in the pews. "I guess that added to the drama." She smiled and tried to stand up holding onto Robert.

He knelt next to her on the opposite side. "Don' try to get up so fast. You feel any more light-headedness? Any pain anywhere?" His eyes fell on her abdomen.

"No, I'm fine. I think. We should continue. Can we?" Robert, Donald, and Bernard all helped her back to her feet slowly. Yvonne offered her the bouquet when she appeared to be stable. The rest of the ceremony went smoothly, but Yvonne got the sense Reverend Washington was skipping a few sections of his notes to speed
things along.

When the wedding party gathered at the back of the church to receive the guests, Daniel brought Debbie a large glass of ice water. "Drink this down, I think you may have been dehydrated and overheated."

She seemed better once she drank the water. After the

receiving line, the wedding party posed for photographs. The photographer had intended to do some of them at the park, but because of the heat, he thought it was wise to take as many as he could in the air-conditioned sanctuary.

Debbie dropped into the front pew next to Yvonne after the photographs were finished. "We'd better get to the park, but I am afraid I might get over-heated again."

"Sweetie, I realized the lace on your sleeves is sewn separately from the satin underneath," Bonnie said. "We might be able to remove the undersleeve, and then you would have just the open lacework. Air would flow through that. It might be cooler."

Yvonne went with Debbie and Bonnie to the room they were in before the ceremony. Before long, Debbie had the dress and veil off and Bonnie was cutting off the interior sleeves.

Yvonne looked to see what hair supplies she had with her. "Debbie, what if we put your hair up for the park? It would be cooler and show off your shoulders and even a little cleavage."

Debbie gathered her hair up in her hands. "Yes, do it. Please."

Yvonne fashioned a cross between a French twist and a chignon, keeping it loose to show off the curls the hairdresser had fashioned that morning.

"I wish you both had come up with these ideas earlier!" Debbie said. "Maybe I wouldn't have gotten so warm."

Even though it was hot at the park, they were at least in a shelter that provided shade. Daniel and Donald had gone to every grocery store in a ten-mile radius buying bags of ice. After everyone had their fill of punch, iced coffee, tea, and cake, they tossed ice cubes at each other for fun. This wedding was more entertaining than Yvonne had expected.

She sat next to Daniel on a picnic table after most of the guests had gone.

"You look very handsome in a tuxedo." She batted her eyes at him. When it appeared no one was watching them, she planted a quick kiss on his lips.

"You'd better take a picture then. I'm never wearing one again. I feel like it is all plastered to my body with sweat."

"I know what you mean. I wanted to unzip this dress halfway down my back and pull this high neckline down."

"Why don't you let me help you?" He started unzipping the back zipper.

"Stop now. We're at a wedding, remember?"

"Maybe we can sneak out. I know a place where we can cool off. Do a little skinny-dipping."

She turned on him with wide eyes. He'd never suggested anything like that before. She held his gaze for a few more seconds. "Let's go!"

His eyebrows shot up just before he leaped to his feet. He grabbed her hand and they bid everyone a hasty goodbye.

By the time he rushed her into his car, she was laughing so hard tears ran down her face. "We're not actually going skinny-dipping, are we?"

"You already agreed to it, you can't back out now."

He had a little trouble finding the spot on the rural pond that he wanted, as it grew darker. When they parked, he pulled a flashlight out of the glove compartment. Yvonne still wasn't convinced he meant to go through with it, but she followed him down a path through the bushes toward the pond.

"Have you been here before?" she asked.

"Yeah, a friend of our family owns it. He lives up on the hill. We've been here fishing. Keep your voice down, we don't want them to come and investigate." He stopped close to the water and took off his shoes and socks. "Do you want me to unzip your dress?"

She stared at him in the enveloping twilight. Fortunately, the moon provided some light and it seemed like the stars were brighter out away from the city lights. He moved behind her and unzipped her dress. It slid it off her body and he ran his hands over her skin as the dress dropped. She turned back around to him and kissed him, and he stroked her bare back. The cool air on her skin was a welcome relief and contrasted with the heat generating from his fingers and mouth. Then she pushed him gently away and stepped out of her dress, and shoes.

"Last one in is a rotten egg!" Yvonne cried as she peeled off her panties, unhooked her bra, and left her clothes all in a heap on the ground. Before he had a chance to gawk at her, she was plunging into the water.

"Aaaah! It's cold!" She sputtered out water when she spoke.

Daniel shed his tuxedo as fast as he could, but there were cufflinks, cummerbunds, and other little formalwear obstacles slowing him down. He stumbled into the pond in her direction, barely avoiding half-submerged branches in the water. The moon reflected on the water's surface, giving it a magical mirror effect.

"I can't believe we're doing this, Yvonne."

"Trespassing?"

"No, naked."

"Oh yeah. It feels nice though."

He pulled her to her feet wrapping her in his arms. "This feels even nicer."

The water was about waist high when they stood up. When he kissed her longingly, she wondered why she hadn't gotten those birth control pills as her mother had suggested. Well, she wasn't going to have sex in a dirty old pond anyway. Who knew what kind of parasites were living in it? She knew his hands were roaming her body, but when she felt something brush past her leg, she jumped.

"What was that?" she cried looking down at the water.

"What's the matter?"

"Something hit my leg. Are there fish in here?"

"Of course. This is a fishing pond. They stock walleye and catfish, I think. Some of those get pretty big. I've seen turtles, and beavers here. There might be some snakes."

"Snakes?" She whirled away and splashed toward the shore.

"Come back! I was only joking about the snakes," he pleaded.

"No, there's something big in there. I felt it. I don't want to be fish bait, especially when I can't see them. How do you know there aren't sharks or jellyfish?"

He waded back to the shore to find her nearly dressed again. "I guarantee there are no sharks or jellyfish in a freshwater farm pond." He turned on the flashlight to sort through his pile of discarded clothes and pulled on his shorts and trousers. He wadded up the rest of his clothing and carried it back to the car. Yvonne took the flashlight and led the way up the path.

They got back into the car, as Daniel found his shirt and shoes and put them on. He started the car but kept the headlights off until they'd turned a corner.

"Well that was a first," Yvonne said.

"Skinny-dipping?"

"No, naked."

CHAPTER THIRTY-FIVE

Yvonne walked around Four Star Drugstore, pretending to look at gifts and greeting cards when she wanted to bolt out the door. She hugged herself mostly to keep her hands from shaking. *I shouldn't have come here, too many people I know shop here.* A glance at the pharmacist assured her he was working earnestly.

"Yvonne?"

Oh no. The last person who can find me here. She looked up into Daniel's face, cringing.

"I didn't know you were heading here. My dad's sick at home, but still thinks he needs his smokes. He figured since I am eighteen now, I can buy them."

"You can't be here now. You must leave before anyone sees you. Or sees us together." Yvonne pulled her long hair toward her face, as though it could curtain her.

"What? What's gotten into you? It isn't a secret we are dating."

"Shhhh. Don't say that here. Go outside until I leave." She made shooing motions with her hands, while he frowned and shook his head.

"Yvonne Edison, prescription is ready," the pharmacist called over a loudspeaker.

Daniel squinted at her, as she was still motioning for him to leave. He went outside and stood in front of the drugstore.

Yvonne charged the prescription to her parents' account and walked outside. Daniel stood right by the door, but she hurried to get into the driver's side of her father's Pontiac. He got in on the passenger side.

"Do you mind telling me what that was all about?"

Yvonne sighed. She opened the prescription sack and pulled out a plastic disc container and handed it to him.

His expression was blank. "What is this?"

She rolled her eyes. "Birth control pills."

He almost dropped the disc in his haste to give it back to her. "I'm leaving in a week and you're getting birth control pills?" He watched her press her lips together. "Oh. Or I'm not leaving for a week and you're getting birth control pills?"

She put the disc back into the sack and put it in her purse. She pulled out her sunglasses and put them on. "My mother said it was better to be safe than sorry."

"Your mother knows about this?" He leaned toward her wide-eyed and pulled her shades down to see her eyes. She nodded. "Oh my God. That probably means my mother knows about it."

"I was trying to keep the whole neighborhood from knowing about it! Then you showed up."

He started laughing and glanced back toward the store. "To buy cigarettes. You know cuz that's what people do after . . . have a cigarette."

Yvonne snapped, "I don't plan on smoking or doing, you know. I am being prepared. I may not even take them until I think I need them. Please just go get your cigarettes, this has already been humiliating enough."

He put his hand on the door handle. His tone got more serious. "I think you have to take them before you need them. That is how you are prepared. I guess it's smart. But I don't want to think about you being prepared for some other guy you'll meet in college." He started to open the door, then stopped. "I know I'm leaving next week, but I don't think we're done." He looked back at her. She'd pushed her sunglasses up into her hair. "If this is the real deal, it will still be there later, after college, at Christmas time.

I don't know when. I just don't think we're done."

"Don't make me start crying yet. That's scheduled for the day you leave."

"You shouldn't have to cry at all. Have fun." He looked at her bag where she'd put the pills. "If it is meant to be . . ." He took her hand and kissed it, then got out of her car and went into the drugstore.

CHAPTER THIRTY-SIX

May 26, 1980

Yvonne didn't feel normal when she got up on Memorial Day. She was happy she no longer had to take her temperature every morning, but she felt queasy. *I suppose that goes along with being pregnant. Just a little bit pregnant. About five or six weeks pregnant. A long way to go.*

They'd invited her parents, Daniel's parents, Clark and his wife, Annette, and their four-year-old son, Matthew, to come over for a Memorial Day barbecue. It might be too early to tell people she was pregnant, but everyone in their families knew how long they'd been trying, and they were bound to be thrilled.

They were keeping the dinner plans simple: hamburgers and hot dogs on the charcoal grill, potato salad, Jell-O, lemonade and iced tea, and cake and ice cream for dessert. The Jell-O and cake were already made. She had to peel ten pounds of potatoes to get started. Daniel had gone into the office for a couple of hours to get some paperwork off his desk. He'd missed some work with all of her procedures and he probably wanted to catch up.

She felt the first odd twinge around noon. The potatoes were boiling, Prosecutor was running around the backyard, but she felt something like a cramp. Like a mild menstrual cramp. *That's funny. I won't be having cramps for a long time.* When she used the bathroom, there was a little blood on the tissue. Not much, but she hadn't seen any before. She decided to lie down until Daniel returned.

"Yvonne? Holy smokes. Are you trying to burn these potatoes? It smells like they are scorching. Where are you?" The sounds of Daniel banging pots around in the kitchen and opening the patio door stirred her from dozing.

"C'mon Boy, where's Mommy?"

He came into the bedroom where she was curled into a fetal position on the bed.

"Something's wrong," Yvonne said.

"What do you mean? Did you forget about the potatoes? And the dog?"

"No, something's wrong with me, I feel like I have cramps. They are getting worse."

He took off his shoes and laid down next to her. Prosecutor jumped up and nestled at his feet. She tried to straighten out her legs to pull her husband closer, then winced.

She blew out her breath. "Ooooh, it hurts." She stroked her belly. He placed his hand over hers. "Would you get me a heating pad?"

He frowned. "Did you call the doctor?"

"It's a holiday, the doctor won't be there."

"That's why God invented answering services. Do you want me to call?"

"No, not yet."

"Do you want me to cancel everything tonight?"

"I don't know yet. Let's wait. Did I ruin the potatoes?"

He got out the heating pad from the linen closet. "I never noticed how neatly you folded and stacked all of the towels and sheets by color. You probably won't have time for that if there are children running around. If . . ." He stopped to take a deep breath.

He gave her the heating pad and a towel to protect herself from the heat. He plugged it in by the bed and said, "I'll go see if I can salvage the potatoes. Maybe I can cut off the burned parts."

"Hmmm. The recipe is on the counter if you feel ambitious."

After about twenty minutes, he came back into the bedroom, with a drink in his hand. "Feeling any better?" She shook her head. "I think the potato salad is rescued. There is just less of it."

He took a long swallow from his highball glass. "We have both read a lot of books and magazine articles about fertility and pregnancy. Hell, we should be experts by now. This doesn't bode well. Are you bleeding?"

She sat up and reached out to him to help her get up. "I think I should go check." She walked into the bathroom gingerly. When she pulled her shorts down, they were soaked with blood, before she even removed her panties.

Daniel stood in the doorway. "I'm calling the doctor's office."

"No," she cried and reached her hand out for his as she sat on the toilet. She felt the life tumbling out of her, and she started sobbing hysterically. "I'm losing it, I can feel it," she managed between her sobs. He knelt on the floor and let her lean her forehead on his shoulder. She normally wouldn't have wanted him to see her like this, but this was about both of them. It was his baby too. Women shouldn't have to endure this alone.

He fisted her hair, as tears ran down his cheeks too. "Try to relax, it's okay, I'm here."

I'm impressed he could even come up with anything to say at a time like this. That was what good defense attorneys did, found the right words for horrible situations.

When she felt like it was mostly over, she put on something comfortable and went back to bed. When Daniel called the doctor's office, they told him she only needed to go to the hospital if her bleeding became severe.

"I'm going to call everybody and tell them not to come. Or maybe I'll ask my dad to come and get the food and he can do the barbecue at his house." Daniel picked up the phone beside the bed.

"What are you going to tell them?"

He sighed, and just looked at her.

"Call Clark. Tell him what happened. He's a physician. I mean I know he is in internal medicine but ask him to come. Let him or Annette tell the others." Daniel nodded and made the call.

CHAPTER THIRTY-SEVEN

October 17, 1969

Yvonne and Debbie had decided to go to the Capital High's Homecoming football game on a whim. Debbie had heard from Linda the twirlers would be putting on a big show once again and twirling with fire.

They arrived about ten minutes before the time they thought halftime would start. As they were climbing up the bleachers they stopped to chat with the twirlers and other band members. Debbie was seven months pregnant and couldn't button her old Varsity jacket, but they wore them for nostalgia.

When Nancy saw them, she hugged them both. As she

hugged Yvonne, she whispered in her ear, "I need to talk to you, Yvonne. Will you be here after the game?"

Yvonne saw something troubling in Nancy's eyes. She nodded.

Debbie and Yvonne cheered unabashedly during the halftime show. Yvonne was surprised Mr. Humphreys had let the twirlers move through the ranks of the marching band with the fire batons, but it made a beautiful spectacle. One of the younger twirlers had done some solo work with batons and had a segment to herself where she did many fancy tosses. Linda even incorporated cartwheels and jumps in a segment she performed. After the show, they went down and congratulated their former protégées.

"This show was even better than last year!" Debbie gave a little squeal with her fingers splayed on her cheeks.

"You did us proud!" Yvonne said.

Nancy grabbed Yvonne's hand and said, "Meet me down at the far end of the bleachers after. Alone please."

Yvonne glanced at Debbie who was busy hugging the new twirlers. "Okay."

Debbie was ready to leave midway through the third quarter of the game.

"I have to talk to Nancy," Yvonne said. "I don't know what it is about, but she asked me to meet her after the game. I have a feeling she needs my help."

"I should get home and rest. My feet have started swelling." They decided Debbie would drive them back to her house and Yvonne would take her father's car back to the game. Their hands had been stamped at the entrance so they could re-enter.

The game was almost over when Yvonne returned and many of the fans were leaving. The football team was trailing by two touchdowns and that was thinning the crowd. Rather than taking another seat, she stood at the far end of the bleachers where Nancy had designated. The bleachers and football made her think of Dick Dunn. That whole mess had been eighteen months ago now and it seemed like another lifetime.

Nancy approached after the game. She was a cute little thing. Her auburn hair was pulled up in a bun for the fire twirling that night. Nancy had learned to play up those big emerald green eyes with dark eyeliner that extended beyond the outer edge of her eyes and lots of mascara. She was even wearing bright orange lipstick, but the makeup might have only been for the show. Nancy put her arms around Yvonne's waist as soon as she reached her.

"Let's sit down, Nancy. Tell me what's going on." Yvonne said.

"We don't have much time. I have to get my oboe back to the band room." Nancy looked into Yvonne's eyes and shivered. "I'm pregnant. I know. Nothing you haven't heard before. I don't know what to do."

Yvonne was sure her mouth flew open. Not Nancy. She was the most modest and conventional of all the twirlers. Nancy hadn't approved of Debbie dating Robert. She hadn't agreed with Linda when she decided to end her pregnancy. Nancy was . . . she searched for the right word. Catholic. That's right, she'd forgotten, Nancy was Catholic. Yvonne had gone to mass with her once and thought it was beautiful though she didn't understand it all. *Oh, this was bad.* How would Nancy explain this to her parents when "Daddy's from Mississippi?" Yvonne had never been to Mississippi, but she inferred from what Nancy had said it was conservative.

"Let me catch up. First, are you sure you are pregnant? Have you seen a doctor?"

"Yes. I went to my family doctor last week. He wanted to tell my mother, but I swore him to secrecy."

"How far along are you?" Yvonne looked at her tight-fitting

twirler uniform and couldn't tell much difference.

"About three to four months." Nancy hunched her shoulders. "Peter said he'd heard you couldn't get pregnant the first time. But I think I did."

"Peter Thompson is the father?" Yvonne hadn't seen him tonight, but she still pictured him as a gangly kid with braces on his teeth. "What does he have to say about this?"

"I just told him a few days ago. He's still in shock, I think. I don't know how to tell my parents. I'm afraid they will send me away to one of those homes for expectant mothers." Nancy's lips were trembling.

"What do you want to do about this?" Yvonne asked, putting her hand on Nancy's shoulder.

Nancy started to cry. "I want to finish high school with my friends." Yvonne pulled her close and let her cry. When she looked up Peter was standing in front of them.

Where had he come from? He must have been watching from the stands. He wasn't as tall as Yvonne, but he'd filled out a little bit and his braces were long gone. His sandy-brown hair sat on his collar and he had to keep sweeping it out of his eyes.

He is nice-looking. He swings that shaggy hair around like a rock star. Still, his face is so innocent. I can't imagine him with a baby. Heck, I can't believe he knew how to make a baby.

"Nance, can I talk to you?" Peter sat next to Nancy on the bleacher.

Nancy tried to dry her eyes and looked at Yvonne, as though she had something to say about it. Yvonne took out a small notebook and a pen and scribbled down her phone number at the dormitory.

"Why don't you talk to Peter? The two of you need to figure this out. If you want to reach me, Nancy, here is my number at college." Yvonne headed back to the gate. When she looked back at them, Peter had his arm around Nancy. Yvonne just shook her head.

CHAPTER THIRTY-EIGHT

A week later, Yvonne got a phone call from Nancy. Yvonne was in class, but her roommate took the message. When she called her back, she was surprised when Linda answered. It was Linda's teen line and she put Nancy on the phone.

"What's going on Nancy? Did you and Peter decide what to do?"

Nancy sighed. "It's a big mess. I think we're getting married. My parents hit the roof, which was pretty much expected. They want me to go to a Catholic Charities home in Omaha or one in Kansas City. Our parish priest tried to convince me it was the best thing for the baby. I said I wouldn't give up my child, and my parents kicked me out of the house. That's why I am at Linda's. Peter's parents agreed to sign papers permitting him to get married, but mine won't."

"When do you and Peter turn eighteen?"

There was a pause on Nancy's end as she spoke to Linda. "What? Oh, well my eighteenth birthday is November 28, and Peter's is December 16. We were thinking we could get married over Christmas break from school."

Yvonne doodled on her notepad by the phone. "So, you are going to Kansas to get married?"

"Kansas?" Nancy said something to Linda which Yvonne couldn't quite hear. "Do we have to go to Kansas?"

"If your parents won't sign a consent form, you can't get

married in Nebraska until you are nineteen. We discussed this when Debbie was getting married."

Linda took the phone.

"Can they get married in Marysville? That's barely over the border, and I have heard about kids getting married there. I could probably drive them down there, or Tom might drive."

"I suppose if they have a justice of the peace there. You might want to try to find out. Linda, when is your eighteenth birthday? In February sometime?" Yvonne remembered celebrating their birthdays last year, but her memory was foggy on the dates.

"February 10, but I don't have to be eighteen," Linda said.

"Well, as long as she has two witnesses over the age of eighteen, you don't." Yvonne heard Linda repeat this to Nancy who got back on the phone.

"Are you saying the witnesses have to be eighteen too? Holy smokes. Do you think I can find a priest who will marry us there?"

"I guess you can call directory assistance and find out if there is a Catholic Church in Marysville or near there and call to find out."

"Yvonne, would you go with us? I know Debbie's baby is due in December so she's out, but it would mean a lot if you could go. And you are eighteen," Nancy said.

Yvonne could feel the headache starting across her forehead. *How do I get myself roped into these things?*

"Um, maybe. I don't have a car, you know. I'm not sure my dad would let me drive his car that far, especially if he knew your parents weren't on board with this. I definitely couldn't go before December 21, due to finals."

"Okay. I'll call you back when we have more details. I can find you a ride," Nancy said, and they ended the call.

On a sunny afternoon two days before Christmas, Yvonne stood by while Nancy Evans and Peter Thompson said their "I dos" in the home of the justice of the peace in Marysville, Kansas. Yvonne began to wonder if maybe there was something wrong with her. This made four of her friends, all of them twirlers, who had gotten pregnant as teenagers. Why hadn't they shown any restraint? Why hadn't they used birth control? The pill was easily available. She did know that from experience.

And there were condoms too. True, she supposed they were behind the drug store counter and you probably had to ask for one, but boys could do that if they were really motivated.

Hmmm. Maybe they are behind the counter because there is an age limit. They must keep them back there with the cigarettes and nudie magazines. Well, that's dumb. Who needs condoms more than high school boys? Heck, they should put them in vending machines next to the candy bars in the gymnasium hallways. Someone was confusing morality with common sense.

But maybe that is what Yvonne herself had done. Maybe she was holding out trying to sustain some moral high note while everyone else was having fun enjoying their sexual liberation. She supposed the only real chance she'd passed up was with Dick. Oh, she'd had a few drunk fraternity boys try to worm their way into her good graces and her pants, but there had always been a room full of people present, making their advances easy to rebuff. This is why she made it a habit never to have more than two Solo cups of beer. *Huh. So not getting drunk meant not having sex. Maybe I do need to live a little. After all, I am on the pill. Huh.*

After the wedding ceremony, the guests convened at a nearby diner. Peter's twenty-two-year-old brother, Terry, and his girlfriend, Iris, had driven Peter and Nancy from Lincoln. Linda had picked up Yvonne. Nancy had two older sisters in their twenties, but they weren't there, and Yvonne didn't ask if they knew.

"What are you going to do when you get back home, now that you are married?" Yvonne asked the newlyweds.

"I'm hoping my parents will change their minds," Nancy said.

"My mom said that Nancy should live with her husband once they got married, so she can't stay with me anymore," Linda said.

"We didn't think living together was such a good idea right now because we don't want the school to know about this," Peter said. "Nancy is going to try to finish high school. I don't know if they would expel either one of us if they knew we were married. For right now, Nancy is going to stay with Terry and Iris."

"But Nancy, don't you think the teachers will notice you are expecting a baby?" Yvonne asked. Nancy had hidden it pretty well in her bulky coat, but when she took it off at the ceremony, she was visibly pregnant. Yvonne felt sorry for the bride. She was wearing an oversized sweatshirt and baggy pants instead of a wedding dress.

"I should be able to wear big sweaters. I'm going to tell people I am on some medication that made me gain weight. Then when I lose it, they will just think I stopped the medication," Nancy explained.

"I suppose that might work. Right up to the point where you go into labor and your water breaks in the middle of algebra class!" Yvonne didn't intend for it to sound so snarky. Everyone else shifted uncomfortably. Nancy looked at her with tears in her eyes.

"I think we'd better head back. It's a long drive and it gets dark early," Terry said.

Yvonne felt like she'd insulted everyone and hugged Nancy before they departed. "I'm sorry, I didn't mean to make it worse." Nancy just nodded.

As Linda pulled back onto the highway, Yvonne looked out the window at the snow-covered fields.

How much worse could it get for Nancy? Her parents cut her off, Peter's parents declined to attend the wedding. She has to keep lying to try to finish high school. Oh, and pretty soon there will be another mouth to feed. Nope. That moral high note still sounds pretty sweet.

CHAPTER THIRTY-NINE

June 12, 1973

Yvonne brought her old baton out to the patio behind her parents' house at dusk and snaked it languidly from one finger to the other. She'd gone out to dinner for her twenty-second birthday with her parents, Clark, and his fiancé, Annette Anderson. They were getting married in August.

She'd graduated with honors two weeks ago with a bachelor of arts degree in journalism from the University of Nebraska. Next week, she would start her job as a reporter for the *Lincoln Evening Journal*. She felt good about that. But she also had a nagging feeling something was missing.

Why am I feeling sorry for myself? At twenty-two, I graduated from college. Check that off the list. I guess when I started college, I assumed I would be with my future husband by the time I graduated. There were several who auditioned but didn't quite make the grade. And now I am comparing dating to when we conducted twirler tryouts.

She smiled remembering the drama when she'd gotten those first birth control pills. She hadn't needed them right away, not until Michael Conyers came along. Slowly, she started doing the familiar twirling routine from the pregame show.

It's hard to think about Michael without melancholy. There were other boys she liked in college before him. But Michael had come at her like a gale-force wind, and she couldn't help but be blown away. She stopped twirling her baton as the memory came into focus.

"I can't decide which feature on your face is the most perfect," Michael had told her one afternoon when they laid entwined on his bed in the dappled afternoon light. "I think it is the third hair from the left on your right eyebrow."

"Your right or my right?"

"No, never mind. The most perfect is the longest eyelash on your left eye." He bent to kiss her eyelid. "It wins by a hair."

She had laughed. "My eyelash is your favorite thing?"

"It is so hard to choose. Every single part of your body would make a goddess jealous. Your nose is almost insultingly symmetric. Your lips shimmer with ripeness. Your chin is the perfect point of a heart-shaped face. And then there is a little spot right here that is unobtrusive but ever so seductively sensitive."

He had run his mouth over her neck below her ear. Even now it gave her goosebumps. He had an arsenal of moves like that.

I guess I'm feeling sentimental because of my birthday. And seeing Clark and Annette so happy together. Time to focus on the next phase of my life as a working woman. She grabbed her baton and was heading indoors when she heard the familiar sound of his Plymouth Fury.

She crept in the shadows around the side of her house, wondering if Daniel was alone. She hadn't seen him at all since Christmas, and then it was only from her window. Debbie had told her he'd dated a girl who lived near Lawrence, Kansas, for about half of his college time. But Debbie had given her the impression he hadn't gotten serious about anyone.

He emerged from the car with a big laundry bag. He stopped in the driveway and looked at her house, up at her bedroom window. Then his eyes fell on her when she moved into the light, and he broke into a grin.

"There's the birthday girl," he said, dropping the bag next to the car and striding up to her. "I'm surprised you don't have a hot date."

She smiled, "No, no date, hot or otherwise, I'm afraid. All by my lonesome—" The way he grabbed her and kissed her caught her off guard. Every time she saw him, he seemed bigger.

He broke away and stepped back. "Wow. Sorry. I didn't plan to do that. Happy Birthday."

"You too. I mean, uh nice to see you too." She gestured aimlessly with her hands, surprised she still held her baton. She had no idea what she was saying. "You're back. You're home." She took a breath to try to calm her racing pulse and dropped her baton next to the house.

"I'm home," he repeated. "Starting law school here in September." He put his hands on her hips this time pulling her to him gradually and kissed her again. She wrapped her arms around his neck. "It feels good to be back."

"Uh-huh," she agreed. She reluctantly retreated. "I'd better be going inside and you should go in and um . . . see your parents. They have probably gotten used to the quiet now that Debbie, Robert, and the kids have moved away."

He turned to go back to his car, smiling. "I'll talk to you tomorrow. We can do something."

CHAPTER FORTY

She hadn't seen much of Daniel even during the summers while they were in college. Debbie told her he'd gotten a job working in Kansas City the summers after his freshman and sophomore years. Yvonne worked at the swimming pool after her freshman year and she went to summer school after her sophomore year. She'd been a camp counselor in Minnesota after junior year. Daniel had been home for a month or so after his junior year while she was gone. They had run into each other on occasion when he was home visiting, but there were always other relatives present.

Being with Daniel felt different now. For one thing, they'd always had Debbie as a go-between in their relationship. Debbie and Robert had two sons, André, who was four, and Jamal, who was nearly one. Robert had graduated from the University of Nebraska as a mechanical engineer and had taken a job in Columbia, South Carolina. They had left at the end of May.

It seemed awkward being back in their parents' homes after all this time and trying to date. Daniel started looking for an apartment at once. He found one available in July and they spent time trying to furnish it.

They had a lot of catching up to do. One evening at King's Restaurant over dinner, they had a chance to talk about their college romances.

"I tried to pry this information out of my sister, but she was pretty tight-lipped about your boyfriends the past four years. I know you didn't join a convent. Tell me all about your love life," Daniel leaned back in the booth lacing his hands behind his head while they waited for their order.

"Gosh, a convent. I hadn't thought about that option. Somedays I might have preferred it," Yvonne said. "All right. Let's see. I had the party girls on my dorm floor my freshman year. And one of them always knew about a fraternity kegger off campus."

"You weren't old enough to drink. Not even beer."

She shook her head and grinned. "Like you didn't drink before you were old enough?"

He put his finger to his lips like it was a secret.

She pushed her hair back behind her shoulders with both hands and watched his brows rise. "Unfortunately, all the eighteen-year-old frat boys thought it was their God-given right to get blindly drunk. It didn't take long to figure out I'd have to spend those nights fending off passes from obnoxious strangers. No thanks.

"Then I met Steve. He didn't drink, well hardly ever. He was on a full-ride wrestling scholarship and kept himself in shape."

Boy was he in shape. Quite the hunk.

"Another jock? What is it with you and the jocks?" Daniel narrowed his eyes, but a smile toyed with the corner of his mouth.

"Well, it was nice walking around campus with him. He was big and strong and looked intimidating. As a wrestler should, I guess." She watched with amusement how Daniel's jaw tensed up. "Once the wrestling season ended we spent more time together." She leaned forward onto her elbows. "That's when I discovered he was a male chauvinist pig."

"Yeah?"

"Yeah. He made some comment about working women. He thought only single and childless women should be in the workforce. Mothers had to be home with the babies."

Daniel shrugged. "Something wrong with that?"

She scowled at him. "I set him straight. I told him I wouldn't have gone to college if I didn't expect to have a good job. Which didn't mean I wasn't having children. I couldn't go out with a boy who had such outdated thinking."

"Oh, of course not. Heaven forbid." The food arrived then, and they dug into their French fries first.

"That summer I dated Gary again. You remember Gary White? He went to the Lincoln School of Commerce. I guess he must have gotten his accounting certificate by now. He played drums in his cousin's combo. Started driving around a big old VW van to haul equipment. I went to one of their shows. They weren't too bad."

"Did you finally get tired of the Neanderthal?"

"I dunno. We were friends and somehow, we never became more. He tried to kiss me once and I laughed."

"Ouch. That must have hurt his ego."

She shrugged. "He laughed too afterward. But he wasn't for me."

"Good riddance Gary," Daniel said.

Before continuing her tale, Yvonne ate some of her cheese Frenchie. A bit of the gooey yellow contents oozed out of the deep-fried sandwich. "Sophomore year, I dated this guy named James Hedges. He was in the fraternity that was across the street from my sorority house. One day, I was coming back to my house and he called out to me from his second-story sundeck. 'Hey, Gorgeous! What's your name?' Guys were always heckling me. You could either dish it right back out or ignore it. So I said, 'if you want to know, come down here.' And he did. At first, I thought he was going to jump from that sundeck."

Daniel squinted. "You thought the first guy, Steve, was insulting because he thought women should be homemakers, but you weren't insulted when this stranger started catcalling you?"

"Oh, I gave him a bad time too. He asked me my name. I said, 'Puddin' Tame. Ask me again and I'll tell you the same.'"

I can still picture James standing there, toe-to-toe with me.

About six-foot-two with bleached blonde hair and freckles. And he hadn't smelled like he'd been drinking. That had been a plus.

"Sounds like you had some stimulating conversation." Daniel bit into his burger.

"He did know how to flatter a girl. He said after he saw me up close, he was in love. So he really needed to know my name."

"Don't tell me you fell for a line like that."

"We dated for about six months, so I guess I did. He was always fun. He'd hang around the rec room at my sorority house. The housemother even liked him." She sighed and drank a sip of her milkshake.

"And?"

"I guess no one told him he was in college to learn things, to study, to get a degree. He flunked out second semester."

"You gotta watch out for the pretty boys." Daniel smirked as he squeezed more ketchup on his bun.

"I didn't say he was pretty."

"Your expression did."

He was pretty. He could have been a model. Maybe for men's cologne.

"Then there was Michael. I shouldn't have fallen for Michael Conyers. He was trouble." Yvonne bit her lip.

Daniel eyed her cautiously. "What happened?"

She shook her head, eyes cloudy. "I was in summer school before my junior year. I was taking a couple of English courses. We met in the student union, waiting in line for coffee," she said.

Was it his luminous hazel eyes that took me in? He was such a charmer, so romantic. Maybe it was just me. I was ready to fall in love and into bed with a handsome stranger who had an off-campus apartment.

She cleared her throat. "He was pre-law. I guess you must have been pre-law as an undergrad, huh? I thought he was so smart and sweet. He wrote me songs and poetry. He even brought me daisies."

The swell of that wave was blissful, but when it crashed on the rocks it was brutal. I didn't see it coming. Even now I can feel the blow.

"Something went wrong," Daniel said.

"We'd been together a few months when I had a notion to walk to his place and surprise him. I was the one who was surprised. He had another girl in his room. He didn't bother denying anything. 'Free love,' he'd said. I freed myself from him rather abruptly."

"He broke your heart. I can see that." Daniel rubbed her arm.

Yvonne inhaled. "Not for the first time. I suppose it won't be the last either. But yes, that one hurt."

"Then what?" Daniel said.

"Oh," she sighed. "I swore off boys for a while afterward. I was tired of them thinking they could be so irresponsible without consequences. Besides, there were more important things happening on campus. I worked for *The Daily Nebraskan*, the student newspaper. Political unrest was all around me. Sit-ins, strikes, and marches protesting the War in Vietnam and bombings in Cambodia."

"You were a protestor?"

"Well, mostly I had to write about it. I had read Betty Friedan's *The Feminine Mystique*. Very enlightening. So then I joined the Women's Liberation Movement. There were so many great young women sharing ideas, and Cheryl Potter was an organizer. She and I became good friends. I was convinced men were trying to mold me into someone to satisfy their needs."

Daniel rolled his eyes. "Men are always doing that."

Yvonne smiled. "That wasn't meant as an accusation. I went to seminars and rallies where coeds talked about the Bill of Rights for Women and the Equal Rights Amendment. I also joined the student chapter of the National Organization for Women. We had a big party the night the Nebraska Unicameral passed the E.R.A. Nebraska was the second state to ratify it. A year later, those idiots tried to rescind the ratification. It got very political.

"I even bought one of those bumper stickers that read, 'A woman needs a man like a fish needs a bicycle.' I pasted it on my book bag. Then I cut off all my hair."

"What? How much?"

"Oh, you know. Like Joan Baez. It was midway down my back and I just started hacking away," she laughed. "It looked pretty awful, so I had to go to a hair salon to have them fix it. It's grown quite a bit since then though. But after joining N.O.W. I rebelled against the glamour girl image that my sorority maintained. I stopped wearing makeup, and my contacts, and even wore black jeans and ratty sweatshirts all the time. I think my sorority sisters thought I was having a nervous breakdown!"

"You thought feminists couldn't be pretty? Have you ever seen Gloria Steinem? She's hot," Daniel said. "So that was the end of your college flirtations?"

"No. I kept a moratorium on dating, but when the spring formal rolled around I had no one to invite, and I had to rethink my stance. The truth was, I wanted it all. Education, career, romance.

"I remember in May, I'd started dressing stylishly again and I went to buy some platform sandals. They were pretty high, adding two or three inches to my height. They were so comfortable though, and those shoes made my legs look about ten feet long."

Daniel just leered at her.

"I remember the shoe salesman was a young guy, about my age. He asked me, 'how tall is your boyfriend?' when I was strutting around the store. So I said, 'I don't know, how tall are you?' He wanted my phone number, so I figured I was back in the game. I decided I could still be feminine and a feminist."

"Hallelujah."

"But the guy I dated my senior year was a real departure. Neil Hicks. We met at an anti-war rally. He'd been carrying a sign that said, 'Make love, not war.' His hair was longer than mine. Serious student, political science major. Taught me a lot about the war and the propaganda being foisted on the American people."

But that ratty apartment he lived in. It always smelled like grass. His bare mattress was probably twenty years old. I don't think he owned any sheets. I guess it was his idealism I found intoxicating.

"What happened to him?" Daniel asked.

"The last time I saw him was at graduation a few weeks ago. He'd cut his hair and was wearing a button-down shirt and dress pants. He was off to D.C. to work for a congressman."

"Okay, serious question now," he said barely containing a telltale smile. "Which one of those morons made you dip into that package of birth control pills?"

She made him wait for an answer. "What makes you think I started taking the pill?"

"That was a long time ago. If you didn't take those pills, they have probably expired by now."

She laughed, "Oh, I took them, but maybe I didn't need to." She liked the way they could still play with each other, almost like the past four years hadn't come between.

Why should I tell him who had been my first? It's too bad it wasn't him.

"Your turn. Tell me about your long-term girlfriend," Yvonne said.

"Denise?"

"Her name was Denise? It sounds like she could have been triplets with you and Debbie. Then you would have had two sisters."

"One is plenty, believe me. Denise and I went out most of our freshman, sophomore, and junior years. I even went to her house for holidays sometimes. She was sweet. Her family had political connections and a lot of money. Her father hinted I could run for office someday."

"Why did you break up with her?" Yvonne stirred her milkshake, not sure if she was going to like the answer.

"I didn't exactly. She broke up with me. She claimed I was . . . well, never going to marry her." He grimaced.

"Why did she think that? Was it true?" Yvonne asked.

He dipped a French fry into his puddle of ketchup. "I guess it was true. She said I was carrying a torch for someone else." When he raised his eyes, she studied them. "You didn't get engaged to any of the guys you dated either."

"I tried them on. They weren't quite right." She dipped a fry into his ketchup. "I wasn't trying to get an M.R.S. degree. I'm a liberated woman after all."

"Oh, yeah. I forgot about you and Cheryl." He chuckled, but he picked up her hand across the table. "Let's get out of here. Someplace we need to visit."

When he drove out of town onto a country road, she wondered why it was familiar. By then it was starting to get dark. When he pulled onto the grass off a dirt road, she thought she'd figured it out.

"Is this the spot where we went skinny-dipping the night of Debbie's wedding?"

"You remembered."

"Do you want to go skinny-dipping again? Cuz I remember there were snakes."

"There were no snakes. Just fish. But that isn't what I had in mind."

He handed her the flashlight and got a couple of thick blankets and a paper bag out of the trunk. She followed him down the same path they'd taken before.

He stopped about fifteen feet from the water next to a tree stump and pulled three fat candles and matches out of the bag. He lit the candles on the stump and sprayed the grass with insect repellent. Then he spread the blankets out on the grass and sat in the middle of them.

"You said no skinny-dipping. Is this like a picnic?" Yvonne asked.

"Didn't we just eat? We aren't going into the water, but this activity does involve removing clothes."

His eyes never left hers as he pulled his T-shirt over his head. She could see he wasn't the skinny kid she remembered from their days at the local swimming pool. His taut frame was more lean disciplined lines than bulging muscle, illustrating the journey from boy to man. Her heart fluttered to her throat as she stood in the candle glow and slowly unbuttoned the one-piece short jumpsuit she was wearing and slid it off her shoulders. When she let it drop on the ground, he closed the distance between them and pulled her down on top of him, yanking her mouth to his. He'd never kissed her like that. No one had ever kissed her like that, with so much need and urgency it left her head spinning.

He gasped. "Still taking those pills?"

She nodded. She unbuttoned his jeans and tugged at the zipper. "Part of being a liberated woman."

They'd kicked their shoes off beyond the blankets and he'd slid his pants and their underwear off, but she'd lost track of how it happened. The way he was kissing and touching her made sounds escape her throat she'd never heard, and her bones felt like they were melting.

She forgot they were outside, that there was a house nearby, or someone might come down the road and spot his car. She only relished the feel and smell of him. He was warmly familiar, yet at the same time, they were in unchartered territory, sending frantic ripples of excitement over her body everywhere he trailed his hands and mouth. She had no idea he could create such yearning in her system until they collapsed in a gasping heap on top of the crumbled blankets. She'd never felt like this with anyone else.

She was glad then they'd waited. It wouldn't have been as intense and natural at the same time if they'd consummated their relationship when they were teenagers. They'd already let the passion smolder for weeks getting to know each other again. When he said he was renting an apartment, she assumed he'd invite her into his bedroom once he moved in. She wasn't sure she wanted to wait that long, and clearly his resolve had given out.

They lay on the blanket letting their hammering hearts recover. Staring at the stars, and listening to the bullfrogs, Yvonne pulled the second blanket on top of them.

"No, don't do that. We finally got back to naked. I want to look at you." He pushed the blanket away from her shoulders and her breasts.

"I don't want the mosquitoes to find me."

"I'll tell you what. I promise to be on mosquito patrol and make sure they don't have a chance to mar your perfect skin." She shuddered as he ran his fingers and mouth down from her throat to her belly.

"We've waited so long to do this," she sighed, running her fingers through his hair. "Tell me we don't have to wait another four years before the next time."

"We don't have to wait another four minutes before the next time," he laughed. Then he pulled her face back to his. "I still love you, Yvonne. I think I've been in love with you since I was about fourteen, I just didn't know what to do about it."

Her eyes swept from his face to his torso. "I'd say you figured it out." When he grinned, she went on, "I've been in love with you for a long time too. Why did we spend so much time apart?"

"We're grown up now. I'm not going to mess it up this time."

The next day, she called Debbie in South Carolina. Debbie had called her the previous week after she'd heard from Bonnie that Yvonne and Daniel were dating again.

"So how is it going with you and my brother?" Debbie got right to the point.

Yvonne let out an exaggerated sigh. "Never been better."

"Are you saying you finally got it on?"

"Twice."

Debbie squealed.

"It was very romantic. We went to that fishing pond where we went skinny-dipping once."

"You mean you parked at John Mason's fishing hole?"

"No, we didn't park. He brought blankets and candles. Well, you get the idea."

"Outdoors? Wow, I never would have figured Daniel would be so daring."

Yvonne laughed. "Oh, he's a lot more daring than he used to be."

CHAPTER FORTY-ONE

Yvonne and Daniel were practically inseparable that summer. Once she'd helped him move into and decorate his apartment, they spent a lot of time there. At last, she knew what it was like to be head over heels in love with someone she could trust.

In August, they went to Clark and Annette's upscale wedding. They were married at Westminster Presbyterian Church and held the reception at the Country Club of Lincoln, where Annette's parents were long-time members. Yvonne was a bridesmaid again, but this time she was one of four.

They'd a chance to chat with the bride and groom informally during the reception.

"I am supposed to tell you we bought you place settings of your china for a wedding gift," Daniel said, swigging his scotch. "But that was my second choice."

"Daniel, don't tell them that!" Yvonne could feel her ears and cheeks burning.

"Well, now you have to tell us what the first choice was." Clark's inquisitive gaze ping-ponged between Daniel and Yvonne. "Maybe I'll want to trade the dishes in."

"*The Kamasutra.*" Daniel raised his eyebrows.

"Seriously. Don't say anything more. You'll never hear the end of it." Yvonne tightened her grip on his arm.

"*The Kamasutra.* Is that the book with all of the ..."

Annette's lowered her voice to a stage whisper, "illustrations?"

"What?" Clark's eyebrows winged up.

"Yeah, I wanted to give you a copy of *The Kamasutra*, but Yvonne thought you'd prefer Masters' & Johnson's book. You know, the feminists prefer that one cuz it gets into what women like." Daniel grinned putting a hand on Clark's shoulder. "We've made it about halfway through both and couldn't decide which is better. They are both entertaining."

"The place settings seemed like a safer choice." Yvonne took Daniel's drink out of his hand, setting it on a nearby table. "Maybe you have had enough scotch."

"Hmmm. Honey, is that the book your mother's book club was reading?" Clark's wicked grin was aimed at his bride now. "The ancient Hindu work famous for its 245 sexual positions?"

Annette rolled her eyes. "I'm sure my mother knows nothing about it."

"Men!" Yvonne shook her head. "What are we going to do with them?"

Clark drew closer to his sister. "I suggest number eighteen." With that, he steered his wife away to greet other guests. Annette smiled back at them over her shoulder and nodded.

Daniel nearly doubled over in laughter. "God, I love your brother!"

By fall, they were busier than ever. Daniel started law school and Yvonne was getting better assignments at the newspaper once she was past the probationary period at her job. Yvonne decided against moving in with him, as he spent a lot of his time at the law library, and they sometimes went days without seeing each other.

They were both glad when Daniel got a break at Christmas.

They were enjoying time alone together before they'd spend Christmas Eve and Christmas Day with family. Yvonne made a home-cooked meal at his apartment: meatloaf, mashed potatoes, and peas, with pudding parfaits as dessert. Daniel took charge of the chocolate and vanilla parfaits, putting them in fancy champagne flutes and had whipped cream in a can ready to top them.

When the dishes were cleared, Daniel told her to sit down at the table and he'd bring in the dessert. He sat hers down in front of her, focusing his attention on the parfait rather than looking at her.

"When do you want to exchange our Christmas gifts, on Christmas Eve at your parents' house or on Christmas Day at my folks'?" she asked. "Daniel, why are you looking at my dessert? Are you waiting for me to try it?" She scooped a bite of pudding from the side and put the spoon in her mouth.

"No! Don't swallow that." He bounced up and stuck his fingers into the whipped cream on her dish. "Oh, good. It's still here." He sheepishly pulled a diamond solitaire ring out of her whipped cream. "I put it on top, but it must have sunk underneath when I moved it to the table."

She choked on her pudding and looked at him with wide eyes.

He dipped the ring in a glass of water he'd put on the table and got down on one knee. "Yvonne Edison, you are the love of my life, my reason for living, the whipped cream on my parfait." She laughed at the corny tie-in. "Tell me you'll marry me. Then you get dessert." He winked.

She threw her arms around his neck and kissed him. "Of course I'll marry you. As long as you keep giving me dessert."

They broke the news to his parents on Christmas Eve. Bonnie insisted it wasn't fair to Connie and Harold to make them wait until the next day, and she called them to come over so they could all toast Daniel and Yvonne.

"When are you thinking about getting married?" Bonnie asked them.

"Oh, well, we haven't narrowed it down. Sometime when Daniel has a break from school so we can take a honeymoon. May or June," Yvonne answered.

"You're not having a baby then?" Connie asked.

"What? No! I mean we will sometime, but I'm not pregnant."

"For a while there we thought there was something in the water . . . you did have quite a few friends who were pregnant."

Really Mom? You want to remind Bonnie and Bernard?

Yvonne put her arm around Bonnie's waist. "I can't wait to tell Debbie and Robert. I hope they can come back from South Carolina for the wedding."

"Let's call them!" Bernard grabbed their number off the desk.

"Well, aren't you the big spender all of a sudden," Daniel teased him. Calling on Christmas Eve, or any day designated as a holiday by the telephone companies, was more expensive than the usual rate.

Debbie answered the phone in a whisper.

"Debbie, is that you?" Bonnie asked.

"Yeah, Mom. Robert is putting together a bicycle for André and I am wrapping some gifts for Jamal. We had trouble getting them to sleep, they were so excited about Santa Claus. So we have to be quiet."

Bonnie motioned for Daniel to take the phone.

"Merry Christmas, Sis," Daniel said.

"Oh, Daniel, you're over at Mom and Dad's? That makes sense, Christmas Eve and all. You know maybe you all could call back tomorrow evening."

Yvonne stood right next to Daniel and heard both sides of the conversation. He ignored what Debbie said and plowed ahead. "I thought you'd want to know I asked Yvonne to marry me and she said yes."

"What?"

Yvonne took the phone. "Your brother and I are getting married."

Debbie screamed loud enough everyone in the room heard her. And then they heard Robert telling her to be quiet or she'd wake the boys. Everyone laughed.

Now Debbie was prolonging the conversation. "When are you getting married? How did it happen? Did Daniel do something dopey when he proposed?" Yvonne was laughing too hard to answer. Daniel took the phone receiver back.

"I didn't do anything dopey, thank you. Oh, and Dad is telling me we have to hang up now. Holiday rates and all. Summer wedding. Plan your vacation. Bye now." Daniel laughed. "I think I got her back for all of the crazy stuff you girls pulled on me as children."

"We didn't pull anything on you, you were always tormenting us!" Yvonne said, wrapping her arms around his bicep and leaning on his shoulder. Then she held her left hand out again and admired the diamond. "I don't think I'll ever get a Christmas gift I like more than this."

He pulled her into a kiss. "I'm glad, it has to last forever," he said.

CHAPTER FORTY-TWO

May 25, 1974

I can't believe it's my wedding day.

Once they'd decided on a date for the wedding, it seemed like the planning was all a blur. Now she stood in front of the mirror in Eastridge Presbyterian Church's reception room and fussed with her long lace-trimmed veil. She'd chosen this wedding gown because of the fitted bodice, v-neckline, and cap sleeves that exposed more of her neck and arms than most other wedding gowns she had seen. *I don't want to have the issue Debbie had when she wore a heavier gown. I need to be able to breathe today. Nerves make it hard enough to keep my wits about me.*

But now she was second-guessing the big veil. The voluminous lace and tulle skirt and short train certainly made a statement. Was the veil just overkill?

"Is this veil overpowering me?" Yvonne asked anyone who was listening.

"Don't be silly, Honey," her mother assured her. "You only wear a veil on your wedding day, that's why it looks odd to you. If you want to take it off after the ceremony, you can."

"Are you sure it isn't another symbol of oppression?" Yvonne furrowed her brows in the mirror.

"Stop reading too much into it. You look beautiful," Debbie assured her. As Matron of Honor, she was dressed in a bright pink satin short-sleeved gown. The other two bridesmaids, friends of Yvonne's from college, wore the same dress in Kelly green. Debbie looked wonderful, thinner than she'd been in high school and blonder than ever. Chasing two little boys around every day must have kept her in shape.

Daniel had wanted Robert to stand up with him, but Debbie and Robert decided it was more important he wrangle their sons in the pew during the wedding, so he could take them out of the room if they made a fuss. So, Daniel had his childhood friend, Bill Edwards, Yvonne's brother, Clark, and one of his law school friends serve as his groomsmen.

Yvonne had been surprised when she saw Bill for the first time in years. He had been the most socially awkward kid, who taped his black glasses together with white medical tape and was bullied on the playground. Now he was debonair in a black tuxedo and seemed to charm the ladies when he'd a chance. He was studying at the College of Medicine in Omaha.

Before the ceremony started, Linda and Nancy snuck in to see her. She'd asked them to help serve at the reception. Linda had married Tom Case a year ago, and she was attending college part-time, while Tom worked as a landscaper. They had a baby boy who was nine months old. Nancy was back home again, with her four-year-old daughter. Peter was now on his second tour of duty in Vietnam. She'd lived with him on a base in Germany in recent years.

"Oh my! Yvonne, you look amazing!" Linda gushed, as they hugged and gave air kisses.

"Like a fashion model in that gown!" Nancy added. "But then you always did look like you were stepping off a runway, even in your majorette uniform!"

"Thank you." Yvonne couldn't help but picture the outfit Nancy had worn to her wedding. "I am so happy you both could be here and help us celebrate."

"As if we would miss the wedding of two of our favorite people," Linda sighed.

It wasn't long before Yvonne was walking down the aisle on Harold's arm, carrying a bouquet of white roses and pink lilies. Daniel was sporting a white tuxedo and beaming at her. Her heart wanted to burst with joy. To keep her tears at bay, she shifted her gaze to Reverend Huxtable standing next to him in a black robe. He'd been the pastor of her church as long as Yvonne had attended. When she was a child, she thought God must look like him. But that meant God was balding and wore black glasses. She almost laughed but then remembered she was supposed to look serene. She took Daniel's hand as her father gave her away.

After a myriad of post-nuptial photographs, they adjourned to the reception at East Hills Supper Club for a light buffet and dancing. Daniel knew many of the local bands from his stint in the Lincoln Symphony. Several of his high school friends, including Keith Pritchard, played in the combo they'd booked for the reception. And little André stole the show on the dance floor, taking after his father.

"I can't even imagine being happier than this," Yvonne cooed, dancing with her groom.

"Me neither," Daniel said. "Unless it was to have one of those." He tilted his head toward André who was dancing next to Debbie, along with Robert who was balancing Jamal on his hip.

Yvonne laughed. "No, no. Law school first. Babies later. That was the deal!" He grinned and kissed her neck.

CHAPTER FORTY-THREE

June 26, 1980

"Babies later," Yvonne had said, the day they were married. Now it was more than six years later, and they were no closer to having a baby than they'd been two years ago when she went off the pill.

When her friends got pregnant in high school, part of her had disdained them. They had sidetracked their lives; how could anyone want to have a baby at seventeen or eighteen? Life was just beginning at that age; you finally had some freedom. Why would anyone give that up for a baby? Or a husband? But now she had to wonder. Could she have gotten pregnant easily at sixteen or even seventeen when Dick Dunn was trying to seduce her? What about later? Could she have had a baby at twenty or twenty-two? She'd been married by twenty-three, was that too late? Should she have taken advantage of a time when most girls have the best chance of conceiving? Had she lost her only chance? Or had she never even had a chance and hadn't known it?

She sat in Dr. Mayer's office waiting for him to prescribe the Danocrine that was supposed to put her endometriosis in remission. He'd already done an examination after her miscarriage in May.

"Your husband isn't with you today?" Dr. Mayer asked, studying her.

Yvonne shifted in her chair. "No, Daniel has a big trial coming up and he couldn't be here today. He knows I am going to start this drug."

"He seemed upset about it before."

"Well, yes. But we are both anxious to have a child. If you think this has the highest chance of success, we're going to try it," she said with more confidence than she felt.

"All right. But you are going to have to tell your husband all about the side effects I am going to explain. I will give you a handout to take home. Some of the side effects may appear a month or two from now, or not at all. Sometimes, the husband is more aware of changes in his wife than she is. If he has any questions, he can make an appointment to come and see me." He handed her a six-page summary of the drug interactions and side effects.

"First of all, I want to reiterate that you need to use a barrier method of birth control while taking this drug, as it can cause birth defects. This drug is a steroid and can cause the following side effects: acne or other skin problems, oily hair or skin, unexplained muscle pain or tenderness or weakness, pressure inside the skull, severe headaches, ringing in the ears, hair loss, sudden weight gain, swelling in your feet or legs, bruising or spotting on your skin, nausea, dizziness, vomiting, heart problems, liver problems, excessive perspiration, bleeding gums, or blood in the urine.

"Because it is suppressing your female hormones, you could see hair growth on your face, your voice could get deeper, your breasts might get smaller, you could have vaginal dryness, severe mood swings, hot flashes, burning, itching or bleeding, and your menses should cease. These are all symptoms associated with menopause. As I said before, the purpose of this is to convince your body you are in menopause, which will cause the endometriosis to shrink. Then ideally you will be able to get pregnant after you are off the drug and before the endometriosis returns. I want to see you again in three months. I encourage you to bring your husband with you then," Dr. Mayer said.

He handed her the prescription for Danocrine. "You need to take this twice a day for at least six months; eight to nine months would be better. Do you have any questions?"

Yvonne shook her head, blinking slowly, unable to stand at first. Her mind seemed blank she walked out of the doctor's office into the stairwell. She started shaking uncontrollably then and grabbed onto the railing so she wouldn't fall down the stairs.

I won't have to worry about birth control. If I have half of these symptoms, I won't be in good enough shape to have sex. I can't go through this list with Daniel. There is no way he'd agree to me taking this drug if he heard what I just heard. I can't tell him. That's all there is to it. She stuffed the list of side effects in her bag and inhaled deeply. She regained her composure enough to make it to the pharmacy.

She started taking the medication as prescribed. In the first month, she felt no different and used a diaphragm for birth control. Daniel had been busy, and he often didn't come home until late because of the trial work. She'd told him she was taking the drug, but he didn't seem to want to discuss it. He picked up the bottle of pills once when they were both sharing the sink in their bathroom, but the side effects weren't listed on the bottle since the list was much too long. He didn't ask to see the list of side effects, and she didn't offer to tell him. *I'll tell him when I notice something.*

She noticed when her period did not resume, but that was to be expected. She had a few headaches but simply took some aspirin. She noticed a few pimples and her hair did seem oilier, but she just washed it every night. This is manageable. *Not as bad as I feared.*

CHAPTER FORTY-FOUR

Yvonne had been covering news stories mostly at the state capitol and had been to the Nebraska Attorney General's office several times in connection with a story about the Supreme Court lifting a ban on the Hyde Amendment, which limited Medicaid abortions. One of the clerks working the front counter at the Attorney General's office, Noreen, had been particularly friendly and helpful in getting her contacts to follow up with. Yvonne thought Noreen looked and dressed like she was about twenty. This impression was reinforced when Noreen needed to ask several more senior clerks for direction. At the same time, Yvonne liked her eager-to-please disposition.

So she was happy when she found Noreen upfront dealing with visitors when she came back to the Attorney General's office.

"Hi Noreen, how are you today? I need an update on how this office is going to deal with the Hyde Amendment restrictions. I think there's a deadline in September. Who should I talk to?"

Before Noreen could answer, someone else called out to her. An attractive dark-haired man strode out of a side office and walked up behind Noreen. Noreen blushed and giggled when he stood close. Yvonne was shocked to find it was Michael Conyers, her old college flame. She immediately dropped to a squat, on the pretense of tying her shoe, hiding behind the counter. *What in the world is he doing here? He must be an attorney by now.*

"Noreeeeen," Michael said, "Did you eat the last chocolate doughnut? You know they are my favorite."

"I know, so I took a maple one," Noreen cooed.

When Yvonne saw him exit through a gate in the long counter, she rose back up to meet Noreen's inquisitive stare. It appeared Michael hadn't spotted her.

"I had to tie my sneaker. I always change to sneakers when I walk over here. More comfortable on these marble floors." Yvonne pulled out her notebook from her bag, hoping to regain some professionalism. "Who was that man? He sort of looked familiar, like maybe I have seen him on the news."

Noreen smiled broadly and placed her hand over her heart. "Oh, that's Michael Conyers. He's a staff attorney and the official dreamboat. Recently divorced. Gorgeous, isn't he? And he couldn't be more charming."

Watch out, Noreen. You don't want to get involved with him.

But I know what she means. He looked good, too good. First time I've seen him in a suit, and he wore it well. There may have been a hint of gray at his temples. He didn't look like that nine years ago. How do men get better looking? Even his voice seemed familiar, smooth, and seductive.

Why am I even thinking about this? My hormones must be going wacky.

"The Hyde amendment recommendation. Who can I speak with about that? Oh, and I also need an update on the lawsuit on the Local Government Revenue Fund." Yvonne wrote down the names and phone numbers for the attorneys Noreen gave her.

She couldn't get Michael off her mind as she walked back to the office. *I'm at the capitol building nearly every day covering stories, I am almost certain to see him again. Should I pretend I don't know him? What if I acknowledge we had a thing and he doesn't remember me? It was nine years ago. Lord knows how many women he has charmed since then. Probably best to pretend we don't have a history and see if he brings it up.*

CHAPTER FORTY-FIVE

About six weeks after she started on the Danocrine, she woke up in the middle of the night.

Why am I so cold? It's August. Maybe I turned the thermostat on the air-conditioning down too low.

Then she sat bolt upright. *What happened? I'm wet! My hair is wet, my whole body feels wet and clammy.* She turned on the bedside lamp. Even the pillow and fitted sheet were soaked. *What is this?* She shivered.

Daniel rubbed his eyes and looked at her. "What's going on?" He put his hand out to reach for her and touched her wet nightgown. He sat up and looked at her. "Yvonne! You're all wet. You look like someone just doused you with a glass of water."

A torrent of heat raced up to her face, even to her scalp, then flooded her chest and neck. She was cold and hot at the same time.

She was sweating and shivering. And scared. *Night sweats? Could they be this intense?*

She went into the bathroom and took a shower, throwing her nightgown in the hamper. She came back to the bedroom with a towel wrapped around her and another twisted around her hair. Daniel was putting clean sheets on the bed.

"Yvonne, what's going on?" He took her hand when she began trembling.

"I don't know. I think it is a side effect of the medication. Women get night sweats and hot flashes in menopause. I'll ask my mother about it tomorrow. She may have had them before; she's never mentioned it." She sat on the edge of the bed. "Now I don't even know what to put on. I don't know if it will happen again."

He studied her and put his hand on her shoulder. "You still seem warm, but maybe it is from the shower. Where did you get these brown spots?"

She hadn't noticed any brown spots, but she started examining her arms. She had more freckles than usual, and they seemed to be larger. "I must have been out in the sun."

"What other side effects have you had?"

Mustn't panic. Have to downplay the side effects. I can handle this.

She took a deep breath. "I've had some headaches behind my eyes. I haven't had that kind of headache before. A little nausea, nothing compared to this." She went to the closet and donned her terrycloth bathrobe, returning the towels to the bathroom.

Daniel tilted his head, narrowing his eyes as he watched her flitting about.

"Go back to sleep, Babe. I think I'll sit up for a little while in case it comes back. I don't think I can sleep anyway right now." She put a sheet over the sofa and sat there. The dog stirred from his spot on the overstuffed chair. Soon she was chilly, so she draped a quilt over herself and fell asleep.

My God, I'm burning up! Is the house on fire?

Prosecutor barked in alarm when she cast off the quilt, jumping to her feet.

It's happening again! Sweating from my scalp, face, chest, back, every pore in my body. Like my blood is boiling over! Or a hot water pipe burst inside me! I've got to get this robe off!

Daniel stood in the living room doorway wearing pajama pants. "I suppose if you're going to start running around the house naked in the middle of the night, I shouldn't complain, but—you're red as a beet! You'd better sit down."

"I can't sit down, I need air. Why is it so freaking hot in here?" She crossed to the back-patio door and slid it open, but quickly shut it again. "It's even hotter out there."

He pulled her away from the door. "I don't think you want to flash the neighbors in the back. Old Mr. Hancock has a heart condition, you know." He pulled her to his bare chest. "You do seem very warm."

"Cold water. I need a cold washcloth."

She broke away racing to the bathroom. *Ooooh. That helped. I need to keep this on my face, and one on my chest or back. Just until I cool off. I can't have a washcloth in bed though, the sheet will get wet again. I need a bowl.*

She put the wet washcloth in a big bowl and put it next to the bed. She climbed back into bed and hoped she would wake up in time to use the washcloth to cool herself down if it happened again. She was able to sleep this time. When the alarm sounded, she felt sticky and took another shower.

She had the night sweats frequently and started sleeping in the spare bedroom, so at least she wouldn't keep disturbing Daniel.

He was asking too many questions.

CHAPTER FORTY-SIX

September 2, 1980

Yvonne put her head in her hands on her old oak desk in her newsroom office. The intermittently-blinking overhead florescent light was tormenting her. When the headaches made wearing contact lenses uncomfortable, she'd started wearing her old glasses that were anything but stylish. She opened the desk drawer and retrieved the bottle of aspirin and stared at the three remaining tablets.

How many of these have I taken today? How many this week? I think I just bought this bottle on Friday. It says on the label to take no more than eight a day, but that doesn't begin to treat my headaches. Every freaking hour my head pounds like a jackhammer. I never used to get sick at all. And my poor ankles, they disappear at the end of the day. Where did my ankles bones go?

She stood and started pitching as soon as she was on her feet. *And I get dizzy a lot now.*

When she took a deep breath, the dizziness receded. She picked up her mail and read the latest state government press release. She'd been on the capitol beat, but her editor had reassigned her since she'd missed so much work.

This wouldn't be so bad if one symptom replaced another. But no, they are piling on top of each other. I still have the night sweats, but now I get them in the daytime too. Poor Daniel. He's not happy I am sleeping in the guest room, but I am trying to make this easier on him. I don't need him worrying. At least I haven't had to mess with the diaphragm lately.

She was now working on feature articles, human interest stories that could run whenever they had space to fill in the newspaper.

"What ideas do you have for your next feature, Yvonne?" her boss, Justin Haden, asked as he stopped by her desk.

She flipped her notebook open to her list of ideas. "I was thinking about doing something on infertility. It's kind of a hot topic right now among career women. I could even do a series of articles about different women," she began. She had found several other young women who had problems like hers, and they were thinking about starting a support group.

"Yuck, that sounds depressing. No one wants to read about that. What else you got?" She swallowed and pinched her lips together. Justin was a year or two older than she was, but his uncle was one of the editors, and he seemed to think his opinion should carry the day.

"Well, I got a call about a couple who is celebrating their seventieth wedding anniversary. He is ninety and she is eighty-eight. I thought it would be fun to interview them."

"No one who isn't on social security would care about that. We need to get some fun youth-based stories. What about the new skateboard park? You could even get some pictures of kids doing tricks."

She was picturing him on a skateboard ramp about then, and she was going to run over him with a skateboard the size of her car. Oh, maybe it was her car. "Sure, Justin, I could probably do that, where is it?"

He shrugged, "I don't remember. Call Parks and Recreation. They'll set you straight. Keep working on your list though."

Two days later, when she had most of the skateboard park article done, her headache was so bad she was vomiting, and she had to stay home in bed. When she returned the next day, she found someone else had been assigned her article and Justin had left a letter on her desk reprimanding her for excessive absenteeism. The letter stated if she had any more absences within three months her employment would be terminated.

I'm not going to cry. No crying at work, no matter how crazy my hormones get. There must be something I can do to improve the situation. He doesn't understand what I am dealing with. How could he? If he knew how difficult this has been to hang in there, maybe he'd be more understanding. I guess I could try to tell him. What do I have to lose?

She found him working alone in his office and dropped into a visitor's chair.

"Justin, I read the letter you left for me. I know I have been gone more than normal. I wanted to share with you what was going on," she began and took a deep breath when he appeared to be listening. "I have something called endometriosis, and I am taking medication for it. The medication causes many side effects, such as the blinding headache I had yesterday, nausea, dizziness. It's like you are going through menopause."

"Jesus, Yvonne. How old are you?"

She shifted in her chair and crossed her legs, but she couldn't hold her leg still. She felt like she was getting one of those hot flashes and a bead of sweat ran down her forehead. "I'm only twenty-nine. I'm taking this because if I can't get rid of the endometriosis, I can't have a baby."

"You're trying to have a baby? That is bound to put you over the limit on sick time. Bad idea. Upper management is looking at these things closely. They now allow pregnancy to count as a sickness, and you could be paid for maternity leave. But there's nothing that provides for extra sick time for trying to have a kid." He paused and gawked at her. "What the hell is wrong with you now? I've never seen anyone sweat so much while just sitting there. It's not even warm in here."

Her leg was twitching noticeably now. *I have to escape. I'm getting drenched in sweat again. Dammit, I'm about to start crying. I hate this. It's pathetic.*

She flew out of his office and into the restroom across the hall. She doused paper towels with water and cooled off in one of the stalls. When she came out about twenty minutes later, Justin wasn't in his office, and she went back to her desk and tried to work.

Every ten minutes, she checked her watch. *Will this day ever end? Am I crazy to think I can handle this drug? He's gonna fire me, it's just a matter of time. And he may be a colossal jerk, but he's not wrong. I am not doing my job well enough. I can't.*

She pulled the car into their garage, and broke down, and cried her eyes out.

I've only made it through two months, I can't stop now. I must be stronger. I should stop thinking about myself. What can I do for Daniel? He's been working so hard to prepare for that trial. Dinner. I should make a nice meal and we can talk and reconnect tonight.

She put on his favorite halter top which exposed her whole back, and a pair of shorts. It was cool clothing if she got a hot flash. She roasted a chicken, made some pasta as a side dish, and a fresh fruit salad. And waited for him to come home.

Where is he? It's already forty-five minutes later than he usually gets home. I guess I'll put the fruit in the fridge again. The chicken is a little overcooked already, and the pasta is getting mushy. I'd better take it off the stove. She checked the clock again and started wringing her hands.

Why hadn't he called? Is he avoiding coming home? Have I been that disagreeable? Dr. Mayer asked me if I'd been losing my temper, but I told him it was the least of my worries. But have I been taking it out on Daniel? Some wives might worry about another woman if their husband didn't come home on time. But he's never given me any reason to suspect that.

Three hours later, he came in, and it smelled like he'd been drinking. The dinner was ruined by then. She'd eaten her plate of food, although by the time she did, it was cold, and she'd been too stubborn to reheat it.

Daniel walked into the dining room, looked at the dinner on the table, and groaned. "I'm sorry, Baby. I should have called. We were in a big pow-wow, and then it was getting late, so we went over to the University Club to get a bite, and I guess I lost track of time."

"Yes, you should have called," Yvonne said. "I made you a plate. Have it now." She stood and heaved the plate across the table at him. He was quick enough to duck but food splattered on his face, shirt, tie, and jacket and the plate went sailing past him, smashing to pieces when it hit the kitchen floor.

He stared at her with wild eyes, wiping food off his face. "What the hell? I said I was sorry. Are you crazy?" She stalked into the bedroom and left him to clean up the mess, with the dog jumping in to lick the broken plate.

Fifteen minutes later, Daniel was pounding the bedroom door. "Yvonne, open the damn door! I don't know what's gotten into you, but something is very wrong."

She opened the door a crack and he pushed his way in. When he saw her red eyes and tears, he wrapped her in his arms despite his anger. He sat on the edge of the bed and pulled her into his lap.

"Tell me why you did that. If that plate had hit me in the head, I might be on my way to the hospital. Or the morgue."

She started crying again. "I had a terrible day. My head hurt and Justin gave me a letter threatening to fire me. I went in to talk to him. I thought if I told him about the endometriosis, he might understand why I have been sick so much. He told me it was a bad idea for me to have a baby if I wanted to keep my job. Then I got a hot flash and started sweating like a pig. It was horrible, really horrible."

Daniel chuckled. "It sounds like he was the one you should have thrown something at. He's a snot-nosed little weasel anyway. But you know, if you kill off your husband it might be hard to have a baby."

"I know. I'm sorry. I was trying to make a nice dinner for you, I thought it would make me feel better and we haven't been spending enough time together. Then you didn't show up. I feel like I am going through this ordeal alone. I don't think I can do it without your help."

"Maybe I could be more supportive. But it's been hard to talk to you lately. I never know when you are going to yell at me, but I wasn't expecting violence."

"I wasn't expecting to do that either. Have I been moody?"

"Uh, yeah. It's like you wake up on the wrong side of the bed every day."

"Maybe cuz I'm not sleeping in my own bed. I don't want to keep you up at night with the night sweats or the head pounding. You need your sleep." She kissed his cheek.

He ran his fingers down the length of her bare back. "I also need my sexy wife next to me in bed. I need to have sex with my sexy wife in my bed."

Yvonne laughed, "You want to have sex with a wife who sweats and screams and cries and throws things at you?"

"You're the only wife I have." He started planting kisses across her shoulders. "So that's a yes."

She smiled through her tears. "You're on. I'll be right back.

Get those dirty clothes off."

CHAPTER FORTY-SEVEN

April 14, 1970

Debbie and Yvonne arrived at Linda Bridges' house about an hour before the baby shower for Nancy Evans was supposed to begin. They had offered to help Linda throw the party. Nancy had given birth to a baby girl on March 24, 1970, during her spring break, and had returned to school without any of her teachers asking about her pregnancy. But her classmates started questioning her. Several knew she and Peter were married, although she kept using her maiden name.

So Nancy opted to include a few high school friends. Nancy's mother and sisters would normally be invited, but Nancy's parents still hadn't welcomed her back. They had visited her in the hospital, so they had seen their granddaughter. Linda's mother invited some of her friends to try to fill the room, and at least they brought nice gifts, even though they didn't know Nancy. Bonnie and Connie had agreed to come to help Nancy out too.

Debbie and Yvonne had decorated the recreation room with streamers and balloons and had set out the cake and tea. They had a minute to sit and catch up with Linda.

"Do you ever think about how old your baby would be now or what he or she would look like?" Debbie asked Linda.

Linda jerked her head toward Debbie. "Of course not. I don't think of it as a baby. I think of it as an accident." She got up and paced the room. "I can't believe you would even say that. It's like saying, 'Debbie, do you ever wish you hadn't had your baby?' You should respect my choice as much as I respect yours. And Nancy's for that matter."

"It isn't the same thing at all," Debbie slammed a notepad on a nearby table so someone could record the gift list.

"Whoa. Let's remember we're here to help Nancy and her new baby," Yvonne said. Her words were drowned out by the sound of the doors opening and guests arriving. Peter brought Nancy in with the new baby. Much to the surprise of the hostesses, Nancy's mother and two older sisters also came in with them. Peter returned to their cars to retrieve the shower gifts while the girls admired the infant.

"Oh, she is so little. What's her name?" Debbie asked.

"Jennifer. We'll call her Jenny." Jennifer had wisps of light hair like her father and big blue eyes. They passed the swaddled baby around among the group. Yvonne had never held a baby this young and wasn't sure how to handle her. "You have to support her head, Yvonne. One hand under her head and one under her back."

Yvonne smiled at the infant. "How do you even know what to do with her?" *I wouldn't have had a clue.*

Nancy said, "They gave us some tips at the hospital, thank goodness. And we just decided this weekend I am going to go back and stay with my parents in June when Peter goes to basic training."

This was a turnaround. Yvonne handed Jennifer back to Nancy. "What do you mean, basic training?"

Peter had returned and spoke up. "I joined the army. I am going to go to Fort Sill in Lawton, Oklahoma, two days after graduation." Then to Nancy, he said, "I'll be back to pick you up at four-thirty."

Wow. I would never have pegged Peter as the military type.

"There are a lot of opportunities for education, for jobs, for families. Once he talked to the recruiter, he was sold," Nancy explained when she saw Yvonne's questioning gaze follow Peter to the stairs.

The shower was more successful than the hostesses expected, partly because they hadn't anticipated Nancy's relatives attending. Peter's mother and his brother's girlfriend came too. And there were five of Nancy's friends other than the hostesses. After a couple of hours, everyone else left except for Nancy, baby Jennifer, Yvonne, and Debbie. Linda's mother had gone upstairs to say goodbye to her friends.

"It must be weird to be married," Linda said. "Married with a baby and a husband going into the army. Aren't you worried?"

"You mean about him going to Vietnam? Well, sure. But we're not thinking beyond basic training now." Nancy carefully placed Jennifer in the infant carrier trying not to awaken her.

"Naturally," Yvonne scoffed. "That would mean planning. Having goals instead of babies."

"What are you talking about, Yvonne?" Debbie squinted.

"I don't know. It struck me somewhere in the middle of playing the stupid word scramble game that all of this was avoidable. Sure, little Jennifer is a doll, but her mother, Nancy, is still a child herself. Nancy should be planning her future after high school, going to college, or she should be allowed to have a career in the military if she wanted that. She shouldn't be tied to some guy for life because they had a quickie in the backseat of a ten-year-old car."

Nancy's mouth flew open, "Excuse me?"

"That's a little harsh," Debbie scolded.

"No, I am just getting real. I'm trying to get you all to take off the rose-colored glasses. You slept with your high school boyfriends. As far as I can tell, no one forced you to do that. I could have done that too. But even before I realized what a liar Dick Dunn was, I knew I was too young to get sucked into a no-win situation. One that could potentially destroy the rest of my life. Is saying 'no' really that hard?"

"Yvonne, you think they ruined their lives by having babies?" Linda said.

"Oh, you're not off scot-free either, Linda. Don't think your choice isn't going to follow you around forever. The right thing to do . . . well, my point is by the time you were pregnant, you'd already missed your chance to do the right thing. The right thing was to show some self-control, or failing that, use birth control."

"Why are you on a high horse all of a sudden?" Debbie's nostrils flared. "We all tried to make the best of bad situations."

"You shouldn't have gotten yourselves into a bad situation. I thought I could help put a pretty spin on this with a baby shower, but I realized I can't. It was wrong. What you all did was wrong, and nothing you do afterward makes it right. Women owe it to themselves to become more than support systems for men."

"You think because we got married we are demeaning ourselves?" Nancy fisted her hands on her hips.

"I think because you got married before you even knew what the world was all about, because of one bad decision, you have locked yourself into a second-class role in life. I mean look at how this is shaping up. Debbie is working part-time for minimum wage so her husband can earn a college degree. That way he'll have a degree in four years, and she'll have what? Another baby? And Nancy, you're going to be an army wife and probably follow Peter around wherever he is sent to serve. You know what army wives do, don't you? Play bridge and hostess and have more babies. Linda, you might at least have a shot at breaking out of this mold—"

Debbie crossed her arms. "You're being bitchy, Yvonne.

Where is this coming from?"

"*The Feminine Mystique.* It's a book by Betty Friedan. She says the Feminine Mystique is an assumption women can find fulfillment by doing housework, raising children, being sexually passive, just passive in general when it comes to marriage. She's saying the assumption is a load of crap. Women want more, they deserve more, exactly like men do. You should read it. But maybe it is too late." She looked around at her friends who had matching sets of furrowed brows. "I'm cutting out. I suppose I already said more than you wanted to hear."

Yvonne made a beeline for the door, and nearly upended Peter who was coming down the stairs. She merely snorted at him, as he got out of her way.

CHAPTER FORTY-EIGHT

October 31, 1980

Yvonne had been looking forward to the Halloween party Daniel's boss was having. Reginald Tisdale and his wife, Marsha, lived in the Country Club of Lincoln neighborhood and had restored a lot of the Art Deco style of their home that had been part of the original design in the 1920s. Yvonne had picked out the perfect costume for the party, a sexy witch. She had a long black wig, a good six inches longer than her actual hair, a voluminous velvet cape, a skimpy black dress she once had bought for a brief stint as a cocktail waitress, black fishnet stockings, and black leather boots. She had everything on but the cape.

She looked in the bathroom mirror and painted bright red shiny lipstick on her mouth. Her makeup was exaggerated from the bright blue eyeshadow to her bronze cheeks and fake eyelashes.

She tugged at her black pushup bra. It was going to be hard to keep it from showing, the neckline of the dress plunged so low. But it matched well enough with the dress it was hard to tell where the dress ended. She usually liked the way this bra gave her cleavage, but that had almost deserted her. Another side effect of the Danocrine. At least the pushup bra kept her ribs from showing.

Surely Daniel would see the humor in her choice to dress up as a witch. But it was hard to find humor at all between them lately. It was her fault. Frequently she was in so much pain or so exhausted, she would snap at him over nothing. He'd taken to walking out of the room when she started a tirade. Just that morning she'd had a fit about coffee of all things.

"Daniel, you went to the store last night. Where is my Folgers decaffeinated coffee?"

"Oh. I guess I got regular, not decaf. You didn't write that part on the list."

"Do you think I need more caffeine?" She'd slammed her coffee cup down on the counter and had been surprised it didn't break. "That makes my headaches worse. I really want my coffee. I asked you to do one little thing for me. Why can't you get it right?"

He'd shaken his head as he tried to get his coat and briefcase ready to head out the door. "I guess I am just an inconsiderate imbecile."

"Is that supposed to be a joke?" Her voice had been nasty, and she had regretted it almost at once.

"God, no. I know better than to joke with you. Especially about something as serious as coffee." He'd been nearly out the door when she tugged at his arm.

She'd held him with a scathing look. "You are mocking me!"

"Yvonne," he'd sighed. "I have to head for work. You'll have time to chastise me at length tonight." There had been a hint of sarcasm in his eyes. He hadn't kissed her. He'd seemed to want to escape as quickly as he could.

I hope he isn't still upset. Tonight needs to go perfectly. I've met some of his work colleagues, but I don't know any of them well. I think I can pull it off tonight. I don't look sickly, with all the makeup.

He came in a few minutes later and gave her the once over.

"Wow. That is quite an outfit. What are you supposed to be?"

She detected desire in his eyes, if not approval. "A witch. A sexy witch. Not your garden variety *Wizard of Oz* type."

His eyes flickered to her dress as he moved toward her. He slid the wide "V" of her neckline off her shoulders as they stood inches apart. "Well, it's sexy all right," he tilted her chin up to kiss her throat, avoiding her dripping-with-color lips. "Too sexy to wear to a work function."

"No," she purred, "It can't be." He was running his fingers lightly across her shoulders.

"I don't know where you dug up that dress, but you shouldn't wear it out of the house. You can certainly wear it just for me though."

She pushed him back, trying to clear her head of the sensation he'd stirred with that brief touch. "Are you serious? You don't want me to wear this dress?"

He combed his fingers through his hair. "I'm sorry. It is just too short and too low cut. Don't you have another black dress you can wear with the rest of the getup? How about the dress you wore to Uncle Jim's funeral last summer?"

She crossed her arms. "What is it you are worried about? Other men in your firm might think your wife is attractive?"

He sighed. "I am more worried about the other women, the wives, the associates, and paralegals. Law firms can be very conservative. I'm not looking to upset the apple cart."

She stalked into her closet searching for another black dress, then not finding what she wanted, stomped to the closet in the second bedroom. She found a straight black leather skirt she rarely wore because it had a high slit in the back. That wouldn't show with the cape. She came back into their bedroom wearing the bra and skirt and went to his side of the closet and snatched his black T-shirt off a hanger. It was baggy on her, and she pulled out a wide leather belt and cinched it around her waist. Then she put the cape on.

"Is this better? No one will even know I am female now."

"They'll know you're a witch though. Especially if you make that face."

Why can't he understand his little jokes are hurtful now? Trying hard to keep her lips from trembling, she went to the hallway to reassess the outfit in the full-length mirror while she waited for him to put on his Hercule Poirot costume complete with a bowler hat and an exaggerated mustache.

Maybe if I move the slit in this leather skirt around to the front, you can see the fishnet stockings. No, not like that. There, centered over one leg. That works. A little bit sexy at least. I'll have to be careful if I sit down it doesn't show too much.

She tried hard to get over her pout once they got to the party and Daniel introduced her to his staff and peers.

"Tell me, Doll," one of Daniel's associates said. He was ogling her and standing closer than she wanted him to. "What are you drinking?"

"How about a Fuzzy Navel?" another of her husband's colleagues offered, tilting his head toward her. "You'd like it, sweet but with a little kick. I'll bet that describes you, doesn't it?"

He plucked a drink off the tray being circulated by a server and handed it to her.

I'm starting to see why Daniel didn't want me to wear that sexy dress. These guys are at least ten years older than I am, half-drunk and leaning toward lecherous. I guess I'm safe enough here. If anyone tries anything, I'm surrounded by lawyers. I could sue. If I learned anything as a reporter, it was that people just want attention. Maybe this is a chance for middle-aged men to flirt with younger women. All I have to do is listen. Or pretend to listen.

After a while she looked over and spotted Daniel across the living room, talking to a younger woman she hadn't met. She appeared to be dressed as a flower child from the 1960s, with a leather headband around her long straight blonde hair. And she was wearing a very short dress.

He can feel me looking at him. Yes, Dear, I see you. And I see Miss Miniskirt too. I hope you told her that outfit is too scandalous for a work function. To add insult to injury, her legs aren't even great.

She forced herself to feign interest in the story the managing partner was telling next to her about his argument with a famous union leader in Washington.

Daniel's hand was on her elbow a few minutes later, as he ushered her into the solarium. The home was on a hill, and there was a view of the surrounding neighborhood and a kaleidoscope of lights.

"How much have you had to drink?" He pulled her face to his looking at her eyes.

"Not much, but someone keeps bringing me Fuzzy Navels. My head is a little fuzzy now that you mention it." He had his hands on either side of her face and suddenly she had trouble breathing. Her heart started pounding as her fear mounted.

"C'mon outside, let's get some air." He opened a door to a

patio overlooking the vista. When she shivered, he took off his suit jacket and put it over her cape.

She put her hand on her mouth. "I think I might be sick." She made it as far as the hedge of rose bushes before she threw up and started to cry and gasp for breath.

"I don't think you should drink while you are taking Danocrine. Let's get you home."

She took the handkerchief he offered to wipe off her mouth.

That was a very Hercule Poirot move.

She kept the hanky pressed to her lips while he made excuses to the Tisdales about her not feeling well and ushered her out to the car. She leaned back in the seat and pondered how to get a bright red lipstick stain out of a white cotton handkerchief.

CHAPTER FORTY-NINE

April 15, 1970

"Dear Debbie,

I'm so sorry. I can't believe I said all those awful things to you at the baby shower. I know you are a wonderful mother, even if you are too young to be one. I can't explain it, something snapped at that shower. I was watching Nancy's mother and sisters act like they were thrilled with her baby. They seemed very hypocritical to me. Weren't they the ones treating her like a slut before the baby was born? And then there was Peter. He's decided he should run off to army camp before the ink is dry on his high school diploma? And leave Nancy high and dry with a newborn? Like it is her problem

216

now. Maybe that was what set me off. What if Nancy was the one who left town to pursue some career opportunities? People would have said she abandoned her husband and child. Yet somehow it is noble if he does the same thing. Of course, serving his country is patriotic, ~~but is that the best thing for a new father? It's dangerous!~~

Maybe this has nothing to do with Nancy and Peter, or any of you. I have been taking two courses this semester that seem to contradict each other. One is Marriage and Family. My sorority sisters told me it was an easy 'A.' But the graduate assistant that is teaching it seems to have walked off the set of *Ozzie and Harriet* where the wives stay home and raise children and the husbands go do something interesting with their lives. There are two or three of us who keep challenging the basic premise of the material she is trying to foist on us. Not sure I am getting that easy 'A,' Ladies.

Then the other course is about the Women's Role in the Workplace. It talks about how the Supreme Court and federal court decisions have affected women's livelihood; what political action needs to happen to create a truly level playing field for women at work. Not just for today, as change happens slowly sometimes, but for the next generation. I love this course. And the grad student who teaches this one is a man, believe it or not. ~~A very attractive man. But I think he knows he has all of the coeds eating out of his hand.~~

It has me thinking. Women are changing the world. I know living on a college campus has given me an enlightened point of view that none of you have had a chance to experience. I've seen women marching in protest and burning bras and textbooks. But sometimes it seems like it is not the men who are trying to keep women behind, it is the women who embrace traditional ideas such as marriage. No woman should ever vow to 'love honor and obey.' Not unless her groom says the same words."

Yvonne sighed and crumpled up the draft of the letter she had written. She had meant to copy the content for all three friends. *This is the coward's way out. I am going to have to go see Debbie, at least, in person.* Maybe she'd write to the others.

She caught a ride with Clark from campus back to her house and figured she had time to eat some crow next door before the Edison family dinner.

When Debbie opened the door of her parents' house, she looked at Yvonne blankly.

Yvonne took a deep breath and smelled baby powder. "Debbie, I came to apologize. May I come in?" Debbie opened the door to admit her and Yvonne found Robert sitting on the couch in the living room with baby André lying on a quilt on the floor batting at a baby mobile with his hands and feet. He was making a cooing noise as the plastic pieces rattled together. Robert was studying her like something he'd scraped off his shoe.

"Oh gosh, look how André has grown since I saw him! What a little doll!" Yvonne saw the skepticism on Debbie's face. "Can we talk somewhere by ourselves?"

Debbie stiffened. "I think whatever you want to say you can say in front of my husband. After all, you think he controls me, or we are joined at the hip or some such nonsense."

Yvonne pursed her lips as the color rose to her face. Debbie wasn't going to make this easy. "Okay. Look, I know I was out of line yesterday. I said some things that were a little extreme, and I may have hurt your feelings. I never want to do that. I'm sorry."

Debbie tilted her head. "You didn't mean to hurt me, but you did. You honestly think women are less important in society if they get married, or have children?"

"No. That's not what I meant. I think women should support each other. Everyone has different choices. That doesn't mean they can't find their power."

"But you think when a teenage girl gets pregnant, she's already given away her options right along with her virginity. She's doomed to a second-class life. Isn't that what you said yesterday?"

Yvonne looked down at her feet. She could feel Robert's stare trying to bore through her. "I don't think I was quite that nasty, but I shouldn't have said it. Whatever I said, it was wrong of me."

Debbie stood right in front of Yvonne. "I'm not talking about what you said. I want to know what you think. Do you think I am less than you are because I got married and had a baby and you went to college?"

For a minute, Yvonne was afraid Debbie was about to hit her and Robert wouldn't have stopped her. She stood up straighter, grateful for the four-inch advantage. "No," she said. "I believe what you are doing is remarkable. I don't think I could do it. Not at our age. I admire the way you are making things work, living with your parents, and keeping your husband happy, holding down a job, and taking care of a baby."

Debbie stepped back and her eyes softened slightly.

"It's different being on campus, everything seems so political," Yvonne's gaze flicked to the couch. "You must have felt that too, Robert." She needed an ally.

He raised one eyebrow. "Don' look at me, Sugar. She pissed at you. Can't say I blame her."

Yvonne crossed her arms. "Well, it is political, and it can be confusing. Women are protesting and burning bras, demanding equal rights. Then there are other professors trying to tell you women can still excel as the heart of the family. They would like you to believe we can have it all, but it just sounds exhausting." She paused and looked back at the baby. "We may have things we don't agree on now. Look at you, you're a lot more grown-up than

I am. I am still figuring out who I am. College gives you that opportunity. I didn't intend to be cruel. I hope you can accept my apology."

"It's too bad you aren't grown up, Yvonne. I might have offered you some wine." Debbie gave her a sidelong look and started walking to the kitchen. The teasing smile was slowly spreading across her mouth.

She does that just like Daniel. She followed Debbie to sit on a barstool at the kitchen counter.

"Wine sounds nice." Debbie got down two glasses and poured chardonnay from her mother's decanter.

"Now tell me all about this wrestler you've been seeing," Debbie said raising her brows and her glass.

CHAPTER FIFTY

December 27, 1980

Daniel spent the morning at the office, trying to get some work done on a Saturday. He was on his third cup of coffee, but having trouble concentrating. If his calculations were right, Yvonne had been on the Danocrine for five months, five-and-a-half, he supposed. The doctor had said six months minimum, eight, or nine months was optimal. It seemed like every day there was another complication. He wasn't used to her feeling sick, and he certainly wasn't used to her being cranky. Cranky didn't cover it. She was hell on wheels most of the time. He knew the temper was partly about the headaches she had been getting, the hot flashes, and the hormones. But she said mood swings were another symptom. He couldn't imagine women went through all of this during menopause. No marriage could survive it.

He should have tried to go with her to the doctor. She may have been downplaying her symptoms with Dr. Mayer. Yeah, that was typical of Yvonne. She'd look on the bright side of things normally; she'd be cheerful and optimistic. But she needed to be honest about what was going on with her health. He was starting to believe having a baby wasn't worth the torture she was inflicting on both of them. He wasn't the one suffering the side effects, but it tore his heart out to see what it was doing to her. And she was too stubborn to admit defeat. He was going to have to do it for her, and she was going to hate him for it.

He'd planned to suggest she make a doctor appointment that worked with his schedule so he could go along. Then she came home a week before Christmas saying she'd been fired because she had missed too much work. It was a blessing because she no longer had to worry about going to work when she felt sick, but now she seemed to be even more depressed. He'd been walking on eggshells ever since. Maybe they could hang in there with this one more month.

He gave up trying to work in his office by noon. When he got home, Yvonne was laying on the sofa in a bathrobe with a wet towel on her forehead. The sunlight was streaming in from the patio door dancing on her hair. He sat down next to her on the edge of the sofa.

"Headache?" he asked. She nodded. "Hmmm. What did you eat? It looks like you have chocolate on your upper lip." He took the wet cloth and wiped the skin between her mouth and her nose. "It's not coming off." He bent over her and looked closer. "It isn't chocolate. It looks like hair. Like a mustache sort of."

Yvonne bolted upright glaring at him. She threw the towel in his direction and ran into the bathroom. He assumed she was looking in the mirror when he heard screaming. Then he remembered Yvonne's great aunt had favored their Greek ancestors, and she had olive skin and a mustache. In her case, she was at least seventy-five years old when he met her at their wedding.

Daniel had no idea what he could say to comfort Yvonne. He raked a hand over his face. This was a very strange side effect if that was what it was. And certainly not an appealing one. He walked into the bathroom where she was scrubbing her face with soap and water at the sink.

"I can't believe it," she said. "I thought I had at least avoided this side effect. I swear I have had every one on the damn list."

"Do you have a list? A list of side effects?" Daniel met her eyes in the mirror before she evaded his gaze.

"The doctor gave me one last summer. I may have thrown it away or something."

"No, that isn't like you. You wouldn't throw away something like that," Daniel said. He tried to put himself in her head, thinking where she would have kept something the doctor gave her. He walked to the closet and looked in her oversized bag where she kept reference material and her notes regarding treatments. She followed him and stopped short. He had found the six-page list stapled together.

"Don't look in my private bag."

"Side effects of Danazol, brand name Danocrine. Is this what you threw away?" He narrowed his eyes at her, and she turned and walked out of the bedroom. He sat on the bed and started reading. *Well, she's right about one thing. She has hit almost all of these.*

Except for the weight gain. If anything, she hasn't eaten enough. She'd told him she couldn't eat when her head was pounding. But as he read the list, his stomach began to churn. It wasn't just the side effects, but the detailed descriptions of them that read like the nightmare they had been living.

He found her sitting on the sofa in the living room, head in her hands, elbows on her knees.

"Why didn't you show me this list? Did Dr. Mayer give this to you when you started the drug?" She nodded but didn't look up.

"You knew what I would say if I read it, didn't you? That no one in their right mind would take a drug that did these things to them?"

She nodded again and started crying.

"Save your tears, Yvonne. You should have been honest with me. We could have stopped it before it got this bad. You didn't give me a chance to be a part of that decision. How the hell do you think we could be parents if you're going to make decisions without even telling me?"

The look she gave him almost singed his eyes, as tears coursed down her cheeks. "You would have said no. You wouldn't have let me even start the drug if I'd let you read that list. You would have taken that choice away from me. The only choice I had left to have a child."

"That would have been the sane thing to do. You've been sacrificing yourself, your own health, for a hypothetical child. You might go through all of this and still not get pregnant."

Her words came out in ragged breaths. "Don't you think I know that?" She pressed the wet towel back to her forehead. "I still had to try."

"Not anymore." Daniel threw the list down and strode back to the bathroom. He opened the bottle of Danocrine and dumped the contents into the toilet. She was a few steps behind him. She tried to grab his hand and a few of the pills scattered on the linoleum floor. She sank to the floor and retrieved the ones she could find.

"Dammit, I have to take two of these a day. Now I will have to have the doctor write a new prescription. And they weren't cheap either. That's about fifty dollars' worth of pills you threw away."

"No! You're done. Don't take any more of these. They're too

expensive, not in terms of money but look at what they've done to you. They turned my beautiful wife into a menopausal monster. You're in so much pain, you can't even think straight anymore. You need to stop and hope to God the side effects will go away."

She looked up at him from the bathroom floor with fury in her eyes. "You need to go away. Just leave me alone. I knew you would ruin everything."

He met her eyes then flushed the toilet as she started crying again. He grabbed his toothbrush and Dopp kit, then marched into the bedroom and threw some clothes in a suitcase. He could still hear her crying in the bathroom when he put on his coat and walked out.

CHAPTER FIFTY-ONE

January 11, 1981

"Mother, what are you doing here?" Yvonne asked, pushing Prosecutor back with her leg, while she opened the front door. She wasn't expecting company. There were dirty dishes on the table and next to the sofa, and she looked like she hadn't slept or taken a shower in days. She ran a hand through her hair, which was partially slipping out of her ponytail.

Connie took a step in, petting the dog, and taking off her winter coat and snow boots. "You aren't answering your phone, so I had to come and see how you were for myself. If you didn't let me in, I would have been forced to confront your husband, whom I can clearly see is living at Bonnie and Bernard's house."

Well, that was news to her. He might have been staying in a motel or at one of his friend's houses. He should have figured out her parents would see him. Yvonne sat back on the sofa. She was wearing a pajama shirt of Daniel's, baggy sweatpants, and mismatched socks. "I haven't been feeling well enough to talk on the phone. I just let it ring."

"You might miss an important call. Exactly what is going on, Vonnie?" Connie plopped down on the hassock.

Yvonne sighed and covered her mouth with her hand. "Daniel and I had a big fight. He thinks I should quit taking the Danocrine pills because they are making me feel terrible. But I have to keep going at least until February to make sure all this hasn't been a waste. Anyway, he threw the pills away, and I told him to get out. It might be better he isn't here. He doesn't have to put up with my symptoms and I don't have to try to hide them from him."

Connie gave her the mother look, full of judgment and concern. "You do see the irony in this, surely?"

"Of course, Mom. Daniel and I love each other. This is just temporary. He'll come back as soon as I stop taking the medication." Yvonne struggled to keep her tears at bay.

"I wouldn't be so sure if I were you."

Yvonne flinched. "Why do you say that?"

"It is never good to be separated from your spouse. Sometimes you can't avoid it, because of a job. But in my experience, a temporary separation is almost always the beginning of the end."

Yvonne pulled the ponytail elastic out of her hair, then smoothed her hair back again and replaced the holder. She looked at her hand that held a clump of her hair. "Shit," she said. "Now my hair is coming out."

Connie moved next to Yvonne on the couch. "Let me see that." She took the ponytail holder out again and combed through Yvonne's hair with her fingers, looking at her scalp like she did when she was a child. "You have some sparse spots all right. You shouldn't put any tension on your hair, don't pull it back," Connie continued. "Debbie hasn't called you?"

"No, Mom. Well, I dunno. I haven't answered the phone. I should call her I guess."

"She might come over here to talk to you. Do you want me to help you clean up since you don't feel well?"

"How could she . . . are you saying Debbie's here for a visit? She said she wasn't coming home until summer."

"I'm sure that was before Bernard had a heart attack."

Yvonne's jaw dropped. "What? Oh my God. When? How is he?"

"Last Monday, almost a week now. He got to the hospital in time. But he is having open heart surgery tomorrow."

"Geez Louise. I had no idea. Poor Bernard. And Bonnie. Daniel must be worried sick. He didn't call me. Or maybe he did." The tears started in earnest then. "I can't believe how I messed this up." Connie pulled her into her arms and let her cry.

"I'll tell you what, Baby. Why don't you go take a shower? Prosecutor and I will do a little cleaning up and then, if you are feeling up to it, I'll take you to the hospital to see Bernard."

"Thanks, Mom," Yvonne said, wiping her eyes, and heading to the bathroom.

Twenty minutes later, she was dressed and trying to put makeup on and style her hair. Every time she ran a brush through her hair, she saw more hair caught in its bristles. But looking at her face scared her more. People had always told her she was beautiful. She thought she looked fine most of the time. She did make an effort to enhance her features with makeup if she was leaving the house. But now she looked sallow. The whites of her eyes looked a bit yellow. She knew that could be a liver problem, another side effect. In addition to her hair being thinner, there were dark circles under her eyes and a few brown spots on her forehead. Even her neck was red and dry like she had a skin rash. She'd used a hair bleach on her upper lip and plucked out as many of those new hairs as she could find, but she still saw a mustache.

I look like death warmed over. No wonder my husband left me. She automatically popped a couple of aspirin before she left. The headache was mild right then, but she wanted to keep it from getting worse.

As they walked into Bryan Memorial Hospital, Yvonne's hands started shaking. When she pushed the elevator button, she couldn't hide the trembling. She'd have to face Daniel and his whole family. What had he told them? If he'd moved back into his old room, he had to have told them something.

Connie felt Yvonne's tension. "Darling, everyone in their family loves you. Just relax. No one is upset with you."

Yvonne gave her mother a sidelong glance. "I'm sure Daniel is still upset."

"Well, maybe that is different. But we all need to think about helping Bernard get better right now."

She let out her breath when they got to Bernard's room and found Bonnie and Debbie, but not Daniel. She embraced Bonnie first. "How are you holding up, Bonnie?"

"I'll feel better once I know the operation is a success. Thanks for coming, Sweetie. I know you are dealing with a lot yourself."

She'd just spent Christmas Day with Daniel's family. She and her husband had tried to put on happy faces for the holiday.

Debbie wrapped her arms around Yvonne, then held her at arm's length to look into her eyes.

"I know I look terrible, Debbie. You don't have to tell me." Yvonne tried to make a joke.

"You don't look like yourself. How are you feeling?" Debbie said.

Yvonne sighed, "Oh, some days worse than others. Not bad today." She walked over to put her hand on Bernard's on the hospital bed. "How's this big fella? Are you driving the nurses crazy yet?"

Before Bernard could answer, Daniel walked in with three cups of coffee in a cardboard carrier and Yvonne felt the color draining out of her face, and she staggered back. Daniel set the coffee carrier down on Bernard's table and put his hands on her waist to steady her.

"Are you okay, Yvonne? Here, hold onto my arm," he said. There was a waiting area a few steps from Bernard's room, and he steered her out there and set her in a chair.

"Thank you. I just suddenly got dizzy. I guess you have always had that effect on me."

He sighed and met her eyes. "I miss you."

"Then come home," she said, as tears welled, then looked away. She hated that everything seemed to make her overly emotional.

"Are you still taking that drug?"

"Yes," she said. "I've got another month or so."

"Then no. I'm not coming back if you are taking it. Can you stand up now? I'm sure Dad wants to see you. I'll bring you a chair."

He sounded so matter of fact. That was his attorney's voice. She'd seen him in court a few times and he was truly professional and formal, not at all like he usually was with her. She loved how he used to tease her and grab her when she wasn't expecting it and kiss her like she was his favorite thing in the whole world. She missed that. Would she ever get that again?

She spent some time sitting and talking with Bernard. Connie took Bonnie out to the waiting room to talk, and Debbie and Daniel disappeared together somewhere.

"You know the only good thing about having to be rushed to the hospital, don't you?" Bernard asked Yvonne, holding her hand.

"There's a good thing?"

"It just reminds you of the most important things in life. The people you love who love you too. Bonnie and I have been married thirty-four years, been together thirty-seven. I've never seen her so scared. I guess I was scared too," Bernard said. "My point is that we take our loved ones for granted. It's easy to do when we're busy living our lives. But that's a mistake. Don't take love for granted, Yvonne."

This is the most personal thing he's ever said to me. How can I take love for granted when it is constantly making me weep? She just nodded through her tears.

As she and Connie were leaving the hospital, Debbie told Yvonne she was going to visit her that evening. Yvonne ate an early dinner and got out a bottle of wine and two goblets. When the doorbell rang, she was surprised to see not only Debbie but Linda and Nancy on her doorstep.

"Oh, wow. Not expecting a crowd. How are you all doing? What's it been, years?" Yvonne felt their stares as they all studied her face and body. Does it make them feel more secure now that she was looking wan and sickly? Do women always compare themselves to others or is that just something she'd done? *I need to stop doing that. Especially now, too depressing.*

"We decided this was a good excuse to get together," Linda said. "Debbie called us today and we were both available."

"Gosh, I feel like I should get my baton out to take it for a spin," Yvonne backed up until she hit the kitchen counter. *Why are they here?*

"Let's sit down," Debbie said, then saw the open bottle of wine. "Is this wine for us? Linda, Nancy, do you want some Rosé?" They both nodded.

"This isn't exactly a social call," Nancy began. "We're worried about you. Debbie told us about that drug you had to take and all of the side effects."

"Yeah, I have been a menopausal monster. At least that's what my husband called me. Which is why he isn't here."

"We don't think you should take it anymore," Linda said. "It's not safe."

"Daniel sent you over here to try to convince me, didn't he?"

"No. He doesn't know about this," Debbie answered. "Yvonne, do you remember when you said the doctor told you about artificial insemination, that you could use a surrogate? I offered to carry your baby, but I couldn't because you were married to my brother."

"Sure, I remember. But I don't have to have a surrogate if this treatment works. I may be able to get pregnant if the endometriosis recedes. Besides, you weren't suitable as a surrogate."

"But I am," Linda said.

"And so am I," Nancy added. "And we're even younger than you are."

Yvonne stared at all of them, speechless. When the meaning finally sunk in her eyes overflowed. "You can't be serious . . ."

Debbie offered Yvonne a glass of wine and topped off the others. "We've done some research. Linda and Nancy would have to undergo some testing probably, but they have both had successful pregnancies. Your son Matthew is what, seven now, Linda? And Nancy has two daughters, Jennifer is ten and Allison is five. Neither Linda nor Nancy is married now, so no husbands to consider."

"But I can't believe you'd consider doing that for me. How would you even explain it? To your children, to anyone else?"

"We'd have to be honest with our children. We are helping a friend who can't have a baby. Everyone else would have to get used to the idea. It is still a pretty new concept; we might have to educate people. If they don't like it, screw 'em," Linda made a flicking motion with her hand.

Yvonne sipped her wine. "I guess I shouldn't drink any alcohol. My liver is probably already shot by the looks of my eyes."

"That's exactly why you need to take our offer seriously. You are ruining your health. If you let us help you, you can stop the drug. You're going to need to be healthy to take care of a kid, believe me," Nancy added.

"You must have considered adoption. But I know that may involve a long wait," Linda said. "This way, at least the baby will be Daniel's. And gee, I know you'd prefer the baby look like you or maybe your handsome brother Clark, but how could you lose when you'd have Nancy's or my genes in the mix? And we'd be able to see the child ourselves sometimes. I think it's a perfect solution."

"I'm overwhelmed by your generosity. I never expected something like this," Yvonne said. "I remember how I ragged on you that day at Nancy's baby shower. It's a wonder you all ever spoke to me again."

The others just smiled. "Friends forgive. We haven't forgotten you were also there for us when we needed support. That's all we are trying to do now," Debbie said. "I won't deny I have an ulterior motive. I want a niece or nephew."

Yvonne agreed to consider their offer and discuss it with Daniel. She hugged each of them tightly when they left. She felt something amazing afterward, almost like her heart was glowing. She felt loved. And she felt hope for the first time in nearly nine months.

CHAPTER FIFTY-TWO

July 25, 1961

Daniel found his father sitting out on the patio in a wicker chair, his customary spot on a hot summer night. It was nearly dark, but he saw the lit end of Bernard's cigarette glowing. He knew his father liked smoking out here because he wouldn't have to bother with an ashtray. Even though his father was a contractor and a skilled carpenter, they had an old telephone cable reel that they used for a table on the patio. Daniel climbed on top of it and sat cross-legged.

"Dad, why are girls so dumb?"

"This, my son, is an age-old question. What has your twin sister done now to get your goat?"

"It's not just Debbie. It's all girls. Today, Debbie and Vonnie were playing with their Barbie dolls. They wanted me to bring in my G.I. Joe. G.I. Joe would never hang out with Barbie. He spends his time on the battlefield shooting the enemy. Vonnie had this cute little Austin-Healey convertible for her Barbie though. I allowed Joe might drive that, in a drag race or something. When they weren't paying attention, I took the car out to the garden and had Joe racing around the flowers. When they found out, they were hopping mad. And they were the ones that wanted me to get G.I.

Joe in the first place. Mom wasn't very happy I was playing in the garden, but where else can you do drag racing? Vonnie was mad her precious car got a little dirt on it. Real cars get dirty; you just wash them. No big deal."

"I suppose they figured if they were playing with Barbie dolls and you had a boy doll, you would like to play with them." Bernard took a drag on his cigarette.

"G.I. Joe isn't a doll! He is an action figure! Ken is a doll. Debbie has a Ken doll, but she rubbed all of his flocked hair off and now she thinks he looks bald." Daniel took out his little pocketknife and started poking it into the wooden reel he was sitting on.

"Girls like different things to play with than boys. I don't think that is anything new. You have a unique problem because you have a sister who is your age. Right now that is probably more annoying than it is fun, but when you were both little, you played together all of the time. When you get older, you should watch out for her. That's what men do, they protect the women in their families and once they marry, that includes their wives."

"Yuck. I don't ever want to get married." Daniel shook his head. "Especially to a girl."

"Your mother is a girl. Don't you like her?"

"Yeah, that's different. She takes care of me and makes pancakes and hamburgers and Kool-Aid. Oh, and lemon meringue pie. She's like a necessity."

"She takes care of me too. We take care of each other." His father patted his knee.

"So, you're saying it gets better once you get older?"

"It definitely does, yes," Bernard laughed. "You'll see."

The next day, Daniel, Debbie, and Yvonne rode their bicycles to the Eastridge neighborhood swimming pool where both families were members.

"Let's see your tag, Young Man," the new teenage lifeguard said as they were trying to barge through the gate when the pool opened.

Daniel took the safety pin off his trunks with his family's membership number on it, 147. "See, I am 147-3, cuz I am the third oldest in my family. That one is my little sister."

Debbie poked him with her elbow and showed the lifeguard her pin with 147-4 printed on it. "He thinks he is so cool just because he is four minutes older," she complained.

"Oh, you're twins?" the lifeguard looked from Debbie back to Daniel. "I guess you do look alike."

"Puh-leeease!" Daniel said, "Don't insult me. No one wants to look like her."

"Holding up the line, Daniel!" Yvonne showed her swimming tag to the lifeguard. "Don't mind him. What's your name?" Yvonne asked the pretty lifeguard who had long dark hair like hers.

"Ann. First week on the job. Are the kids here okay?"

"At least the girls are. The boys are impossible!" Yvonne sighed.

"Eddie!" Daniel spotted his buddy mid-pool. "Coming in!" He hurled himself in the air, flying for an instant before the cold water blasted against his sun-seared skin.

"Marco!" Eddie Perkins called.

"Polo!" Daniel emerged closing his eyes.

Debbie and Vonnie spread their beach towels on the sizzling cement and spent more time laying on them than they did swimming. Pretty soon, a couple of other girls put their towels down next to Debbie, and they were all slathering on baby oil and looking at the boys in the pool as though they wouldn't notice.

When the lifeguards whistled a ten-minute break, Daniel walked up to his sister.

"Do you have any zinc oxide in your bag?" he asked her. "Mom told me my nose is peeling too much, and I have to put the white stuff on it."

Debbie pulled a tube out of her bag and handed it to him. "Then you should have brought it yourself."

"You have a bag. Boys don't carry bags." He coated his nose with the thick white cream.

"Hello Daniel," one of the other girls, Janine Meeks, said pleasantly.

He glared at her and walked over to join Eddie, who was sitting on the edge of the pool, dangling his feet in the water. They were only about ten feet away from the girls.

"Here's the plan," Daniel said. "Before they blow the whistle, we'll go behind the girls and get a running start and then do it right by the edge. They'll get soaked."

"And they won't be able to get us without getting their precious hair wet. It's great!" Eddie said.

A minute before the hour and the end of the safety break, the boys got up and leaned on the chain-link fence behind the four girls.

"What are you doing? Don't try to listen to our conversation." Debbie squinted at her brother.

The moment the whistle shrilled, like a champion sprinter Daniel launched his body forward in perfect synchronicity with Eddie's, tromping on his sister's towel, pounding the pavement hard at the lip of the pool as he leaped as high as he could, grabbing his legs, and tilting slightly backward in the execution of a splash-inducing cannonball.

The cool water slapped his back and bottom, forcing his swimming trunks to ride up, and creating what he knew scientifically was a Worthington jet, a hole in the water that creates a giant explosion as it refills.

All four girls were still screaming when Daniel's head burst to the surface and Eddie gave him a triumphant grin. Daniel and Eddie laughed so hard they got water up their noses. The closest lifeguard, a sixteen-year-old neighbor boy, laughed but blew his whistle and shook a finger at the boys.

"Hey, Danny. Who are those boys over by your sister and Yvonne?" Eddie coughed trying to clear his lungs.

A couple of sixth-grade boys were talking to the girls. One of the boys Daniel didn't know, handed Yvonne a towel and she was smiling at him.

"Let's jump off the diving board," Daniel said whipping his head back to Eddie. "Stupid girls. Stupid screaming girls."

At four o'clock, Daniel and Debbie were due home, so they left the pool about three forty-five. Yvonne tagged along, as she was expected home at the same time.

Daniel said, "I want to go look at the creek before we leave. Eddie said he caught a tadpole there yesterday." The creek was right next to the parking lot of the swimming pool. When they reached the creek, Daniel peered in, then he put his feet in the creek and waded around. It was only about a foot deep and murky.

"Mom isn't going to like you getting your tennis shoes muddy," Debbie said.

He ignored her. "I see some. Look, there are a bunch of tadpoles right there."

Debbie wrinkled her nose. Yvonne looked where he was pointing then laid down on her stomach on the side of the creek for a better view.

"I see them," she said. "We should catch some."

Daniel brightened. He didn't expect that. Not from a girl.

"I know. I'll go back to my house and get a Mason jar. My mom has some for when she makes jam," Daniel said.

"Let's go!" Yvonne cried.

Debbie gave her friend a dirty look. They all got on their bikes and rode home. Daniel and Yvonne changed into shorts, got a couple of jars, and went back to the creek, after explaining what they wanted to do to their mothers. They both waded into the creek and filled their jars with water and a couple of tadpoles each.

"Do you think we can watch them turn into frogs?" Yvonne asked. "I helped Clark catch tadpoles last summer and we thought we'd see frogs the next day, but they died."

"I don't know. I'll ask my dad about that." Daniel held his jar up to the sunlight and admired the little amphibians.

Just then, they heard the familiar bell of the ice cream truck.

"It's the ice cream man!" Daniel almost dropped his prized tadpoles. "I want ice cream." Then his joy turned to dismay. "Oh, I don't have any money with me."

Yvonne fished into her pocket and came up with a quarter. "I put this in my pocket the other day when we heard the ice cream truck bell. But then he ran out of popsicles so I didn't get one." She held the coin out to Daniel. He handed his tadpole jar to her and ran over to the ice cream truck.

"What will you have, Son?" The proprietor asked him.

"I'll have an ice cream bar," Daniel said. He looked back at Yvonne holding the two tadpole jars. "No, wait. How much are the twin popsicles? You know the ones you can break in two?"

"Same as an ice cream bar, twenty-five cents."

He sighed. He really wanted that chocolate shell on the vanilla ice cream bar. "Give me a grape twin pop."

When he got back to Yvonne, they split the Popsicle in two and sat down on the curb licking their popsicles and watching their tadpoles.

"You have a grape tongue," Yvonne laughed.

"So do you!" He pointed at her.

When they were done, they put the glass jars in Yvonne's bicycle basket and rode home.

Girls aren't so bad all the time, as long as they don't act stupid.

CHAPTER FIFTY-THREE

February 14, 1981

Yvonne came home after a Jazzercise workout at eleven o'clock in the morning. A long shiny white box rested on her doorstep. *That's odd. Oh, it's Valentine's Day.*

Daniel had been sending her a dozen red roses on Valentine's Day ever since their engagement. She carted the box inside and opened it, revealing eleven long-stemmed white roses, and one red one. The card the florist had enclosed explained the meaning of the color of roses. It said "white roses represented innocence, purity, and charm, and were used in weddings because they represented new beginnings. Eleven roses assure the recipient they are truly and deeply loved. Red roses signify love and romance, and a single rose indicates devotion." In previous years, the enclosure card had been neatly printed by someone at the florist's and it always said, "Love you forever." This time, she recognized her husband's handwriting on the enclosure card. It said, "Our love is just beginning—Daniel."

I don't know what he means, but at least he sent flowers. He's still thinking about me, about us. Turning on the radio, she arranged the roses in a vase and danced around the kitchen in her leotard and leg warmers.

A month ago, after the visit from her twirler friends, she'd taken control of her health. She stopped taking the Danocrine and started taking multi-vitamins. Before she could get serious about working again, she needed to feel better. She got some books at the library on nutrition. *Even though I am eating alone, I can still eat nutritious meals. Thank God my head no longer hurts, and I feel like cooking and eating again.*

They had a family membership at the YMCA, where Daniel worked out or played racquetball, but she hadn't used it as much. She joined a couple of classes and enjoyed interacting with the other ladies.

After three weeks of this, she already felt much better. She hadn't had any more hot flashes, her hair had stopped falling out, and she'd gained a little weight. The most noticeable thing was she didn't feel depressed or angry anymore. If she was feeling down in the evening, she just turned on some music and danced it out. But she hadn't told Daniel about her changes.

She'd spoken to him a few times, checking on Bernard. Daniel had been a big help to both of his parents. Bernard was weak after his heart attack and surgery, so Daniel helped him walk around the house and later took him to physical therapy. Daniel said Bernard was progressing well, and now Bonnie was able to help him get to physical therapy.

I need to call Daniel and thank him for the flowers as soon as I finish my shower. What am I going to tell him? He needs to know about the changes I've made, but am I ready? She called him around lunchtime. She knew he often ate a sandwich at his desk.

"Daniel, I just wanted to thank you for the roses," she said, trying to keep the tremor out of her voice. Why was she nervous? She'd called him plenty of times.

"Yvonne. Funny I was just thinking about you," he said. "I'm glad you liked them. I thought I'd do something a little different this year."

"Uh, I guess everything is a little different this year, isn't it? Which is why it meant so much . . ." her voice broke. She still lost control of her emotions.

"Yeah. I miss you too, Baby. Are you feeling any better?"

She took a deep breath. "Actually, yes, much better. I haven't been taking the Danocrine."

It was a moment before he spoke. "When did you stop taking it?"

"Oh, about a month ago. Right after I saw you at the hospital."

"And you didn't tell me? Never mind. I'm coming over." He hung up.

Oh no. He sounds irritated. That wasn't what she wanted to do. She bit her lip. And how could he leave in the middle of the day? Was he worried about her? She was doing better than she had in a long long time. Maybe he wants to come home. Well, that would be okay. She and Prosecutor had gotten used to it just being them. But he belonged there, after all.

She had changed into a soft silky blouse and palazzo pants and finished putting some makeup on when the sound of the garage door opening signaled his arrival. Her stomach clenched and her feet felt like they were stuck to the bathroom floor.

"Yvonne?" When she met him in the living room, he took her hands and looked her up and down. "My God, you look like yourself again, beautiful and sexy and—" He couldn't finish because he pulled her into a kiss, and then picked her up and whirled her around.

"Happy Valentine's Day to you too, Mister."

"Are you sure you're okay? I mean you look like you did before you started that demon drug, but have you had a check-up?"

"No, but I made an appointment for next week. I've been trying to eat right, and I even started exercising. Can you believe that?"

"I can't believe any of this. But I think I am going to need to do my own examination and check all of your vital signs," he said.

"You're a lawyer, not a doctor." Her laugh became a gasp when he caught her from behind and put his lips and tongue behind her ear, trailing his fingers through her hair.

"*Hmmm.* Your temperature seems normal, maybe rising." He slid his mouth to the vein on the side of her throat. "Nice strong, pulse. That's a good sign, especially for what we're about to do."

She let her head drop to his shoulder. He wrenched her blouse free as his hands found her skin around her waist and back. He deftly slid fingers under her bra over her heart. "Yes, I think you have a good heartbeat. Although it is beginning to race. Does that happen to you a lot?"

She turned to face him, eyes shining and shoved his jacket off his shoulders. "It happens every time you touch me. Sometimes even before you touch me. In anticipation—" The rest of her words were lost in the crush of a kiss. She yanked at his jacket sleeves and he shook it off, tossing it on an armchair, where the dog sat watching. This started a game of whipping off and tossing clothes on the chair trying to cover the dog, but Prosecutor always squirmed free. When they ran out of clothing, he pulled her onto the couch, wrapping her legs around him.

"Don't you have to get back to work?"

"No," he grinned, "I think I've got my hands full right here." He covered her mouth with his again, attempting to rotate her under him until Prosecutor jumped up on the couch and started licking their legs.

"I'd like to request a change in venue, counselor," Yvonne said trying not to giggle.

"Bedroom," he chuckled. "Prosecutor, you stay out here, and stay off the table."

He didn't make it back to work. He picked up his clothes from his parents' house and moved back home.

Later that night, they were holding each other in bed.

"Why didn't you tell me sooner you stopped taking the Danocrine?"

She sat up, crossing her arms on her knees. "I should have, I know. I guess I was scared, depressed. I hoped I would get better quickly and then I would call you. But my hair started falling out. Did I tell you that one?" He sat up to look at her and shook his head. "My hair was thinning, my ribs were sticking out where my breasts were supposed to be, I had to put bleach on my mustache, my eyes were turning yellow, and my skin looked terrible. I was a mess." She turned to look at him. "I felt ugly. I wanted to wait until I felt a little bit pretty again before I saw you."

He pulled her closer and kissed her shoulder. "None of that would have mattered to me. All of your hair could have fallen out, you could have had a Hercule Poirot mustache, your eyes or skin could have been the color of lemons and I would have still loved you. Don't you know that?"

"I don't deserve that. I treated you terribly. I'm really sorry. I'll never be able to make it up to you. I started to think you wouldn't come back. Even my mother and your father warned me . . ." Yvonne put her hand over her eyes trying to stanch the tears.

He put his hands on either side of her face pulling her to him. "What are you talking about? What did my father and your mother say?"

She sniffed. "Oh, your dad said something about not taking you for granted. No, he said don't take love for granted. My mom said something similar."

"Well, I should be annoyed they tried to interfere, but considering where we are right now, maybe that helped." He brushed her tears away and pulled her back to lie on top of him. "We just need to put this whole chapter behind us. Tomorrow I plan to start fattening you up again. More ice cream!" She just smiled and kissed him.

She'd missed him, the way he kissed, the warmth of him sleeping in their bed. And oh-my-gosh the way he'd made her whole body tingle when they'd made love. Something felt different. It wasn't just they hadn't been together in over a month; it was something inside her. Longing. Hormones maybe. She was starting to feel like a woman, like she was supposed to, like she used to. It felt wonderful. She was never taking that for granted again either.

The next evening, they had more time to talk over lasagna. Daniel cleared his throat, "Debbie said something cryptic about your friends offered to help us and I should ask you about it. I didn't know what she was talking about and she wouldn't tell me more. But I could tell there was more."

"Their proposal touched me. I don't know whether I would go along with it but it was amazing they would offer."

"Offer what exactly?"

"You remember Linda Bridges and Nancy Evans . . . oh well, I guess it is Nancy Thompson now. Debbie was the first one who offered, but I told her she couldn't be a surrogate." He had a blank look on his face. "A surrogate has a baby for another couple who can't conceive, or the woman in the couple can't carry the baby to term. The man um . . . donates his sperm and then the surrogate is artificially inseminated when she appears to be ovulating in the hopes that she becomes pregnant. When the baby is born, it is given to the couple who wanted the baby."

"Whoa. That sounds like a legal nightmare if it even is legal," Daniel said. "You're saying the baby would be biologically the surrogate's child and the donor husband's child, but not biologically the wife's child? What's to keep the surrogate mother from keeping the kid? She'd have as much right as the father, maybe more since young children are typically awarded to the mother in a divorce situation."

"Well that's why you'd need a good lawyer, I guess. There would have to be some contract saying the surrogate relinquishes all rights. I don't know if the wife would have to adopt the child to have legal rights."

"I can probably find out more," Daniel said. "I'll talk to Bill over in family law. He's probably familiar with it if this is an option in Nebraska. But how do you feel about doing that? After everything we've been through in the past year, I'd rather not even think about having a child."

She studied him and stopped eating. "Maybe that's our problem. We've been thinking about it too much." She sighed. "You know if you'd said that a month ago, I would have been very upset. But since I stopped taking that drug and started feeling normal again, I have kind of come to the same conclusion. Maybe it will happen and maybe it won't. We can still be happy. We could get on a waiting list for adoption. Maybe we would get a foster child. Maybe we'll get more dogs. I dunno. What did people do about this fifty years ago? I think I have been stressing out about something I shouldn't be. Maybe we should just hang out with Debbie's kids or Clark's son more. I just want to put it aside for now."

"You mean it? A month ago you were willing to sacrifice your health and maybe our marriage for a chance, just a chance, to have a baby. And now you don't care?"

"I wouldn't say I don't care. I just think I needed an attitude adjustment. I'm going to be okay if I don't have a baby. We're going to be okay without a baby. And I wasn't ever trying to sacrifice our marriage. We just had different opinions at the time, and probably needed some time apart." Yvonne's voice trailed off. "I couldn't see it then. It turns out you were right."

He cupped a hand to his ear. "What was that? I don't think I heard you. Say again."

She laughed. She'd missed the way he made her laugh too. "You were right about the Danocrine. All right, you happy now?"

He took her hand and kissed her fingers. "I am deliriously happy," he said. "So now we are rid of the drugs, the stupid schedule, the birth control, the doctor visits. We can just go back to normal life, right? We can just enjoy our marriage."

Her eyes sparkled as he jumped up and took the monthly calendar off the wall in the kitchen.

"You remember last year, we had all the color coding on the calendar, which days we were not allowed to have sex, which days were optimal for fertility?" he said. "That turned out to be a crock. I think we should just make our own schedule this year."

He grabbed a couple of red and green pens they kept in a mug on the kitchen counter and sat back across from her. "Okay, yesterday was Valentine's Day. I am marking that one with a red 'x' because we had sex."

She shook her head, "No, Silly. The red pen meant stop; the green was for the days we were supposed to do it. Don't you remember the system?"

His tongue ran between his teeth. "I'm making my own damn system. I'm going to put a red 'x' on the days I want to have sex. You can use the green pen."

She couldn't stop laughing as he started putting a small red 'x' on every other day. She recognized what this was. He was toying with her. It was like when he brought home the *Kamasutra*. He hadn't meant to try all of those positions, he was just teasing and trying to see if she would accept the challenge. It was a game, and she knew she had to pick up the gauntlet he'd thrown down.

He got through April before she snatched up the green pen and pulled the calendar away from him. She stole glances at him as she flipped back to February fifteenth and put a green 'x' on every date he had left blank.

"Wow, it looks like we are going to be booked for the next few months." He nodded, trying to contain his smile. "I hope no one else will look at our calendar, you know, like our mothers, and break the code."

She studied him in mock concern. Then she picked up the pens again and started writing 'se' before each 'x' in February. She turned the calendar around for his perusal. "Just in case someone can't break the code. We do have a lot of time to make up for. And according to the calendar, today is my turn."

You've been amazingly patient with me for the past six months. You deserve to have some fun. You also deserve to be beaten at your own game.

She stood next to his chair and kissed him tenderly. With a smirk and a jerk on his necktie, she pulled him into their bedroom.

CHAPTER FIFTY-FOUR

Yvonne woke up wanting to stay in bed. A familiar dull ache coursed through her lower back and pelvis. When she sat up, she felt light-headed and weary. Not like she'd just had a good eight hours of shut-eye. She hadn't felt this way in maybe a year. By the time she finished her morning routine in the bathroom, she could cope with the discomfort. She called Daniel at work.

"I can't believe it. I got my period. Isn't that amazing?"

"Uh, I don't know. Am I missing something? Isn't that considered normal?"

"Exactly. That's what is so wonderful. Dr. Mayer said it usually takes at least two months, or longer before you start ovulating again after taking the demon drug. Your body has to start producing estrogen and progesterone or whatever it is you need to be fertile again. I am already ahead of schedule. No longer in menopause!"

"You sure get excited about weird things sometimes, but if you're happy, I am happy for you, Baby," he said. "Where do I sign?" he spoke away from the phone to someone in his office.

"You're busy. I'll let you go. I just wanted you to know that I buried the menopausal monster."

She hung up and started humming to herself, even as the cramps got stronger. She typed up resumes and checked the want ads for job opportunities.

Six weeks later, she started her new job at Lincoln Telephone Company. She was training as a long-distance operator. They were just implementing a new computerized system. She had been told that there were many other jobs available in the company, particularly for someone with her education and background. She was hoping to get a position in the public relations department eventually.

"What's wrong, Yvonne? Is there something bothering you at work?" her husband asked when he found her staring out the window when he came home. He sat on the arm of her chair.

"No. Do you remember how excited I was last month when I

started menstruating again? I thought I was back to normal. But it hasn't happened again. Now I think it was just a fluke. Maybe it will just be off schedule. I need to just chill out, I know. I might make an appointment to see Dr. Mayer. But I'm afraid just doing that will start me back on the mindset that I'm thinking about having a baby all of the time."

"Maybe you should wait awhile then. Let the new job settle in first." He brushed her hair back from her face and tucked it behind her ear.

"You're probably right. I'll wait for another week or two," she said.

By the time she got in to see Dr. Mayer, it was mid-May. She had the usual testing a few days before her appointment. After the exam, she went into his office. She smoothed down her skirt over her shaking knees. *He's going to tell me the endometriosis is back or that something else had gone haywire.*

"There is a perfectly normal explanation for why you only had one period, Yvonne. The next month, you became pregnant. Judging by my physical examination, you are about two months along."

Yvonne squeezed her eyes shut then opened them wide. "I didn't think that was even a possibility, not this soon. Is that a problem, I mean the birth defects from the Danocrine?"

Dr. Mayer patted her hand. "The drug was out of your system by then, almost two months after you stopped taking it. You should be fine. And you didn't even need fertility pills, that's the part that surprises me with your history. But stop at the front desk, they will give you some materials to read about pregnancy. Oh, and here, take this prescription for prenatal iron supplements."

Yvonne put her hand to her heart. She was two months pregnant. She'd had no idea. That was even more pregnant than she had been when she had the miscarriage last year. But now she had a new job. Was that going to be a problem? She hadn't been having morning sickness, but she avoided eating much before ten o'clock anyway. Maybe she should be eating more, she was eating for two now. She still had some pregnancy books at home, she would have to reread those. And the nurse had given her some papers to read too. This was just bizarre. It was like once they stopped trying to get pregnant, it happened.

Her appointment was in the mid-afternoon, and she went home after getting the prescription filled. She put on something comfortable, some knit pants and a cropped top she'd had for years. She couldn't stop rubbing her abdomen as though she was somehow comforting the fetus. Then she rubbed lotion onto her belly as the skin was going to have to stretch in the next seven months.

Her husband found her out on the patio sitting on the porch swing, with her hand still resting on her midsection. Prosecutor was dutifully curled up next to her.

"What's the matter, does your stomach hurt?" he asked when he saw how she was sitting. "Didn't you go to the doctor today?"

She inhaled deeply and smiled slightly.

"So, what did he say?" He pushed the dog off the swing and sat down next to Yvonne. She didn't answer, she just put his hand over her navel. His hand warmed her cool skin. He laughed, "Prosecutor likes it when I give him a belly rub. Is that what you want?"

She shook her head but held his hand beneath hers. Yvonne heard Debbie's voice in her head from many years ago saying, "boys are idiots." She raised one eyebrow. He'd figure it out.

He slowly studied her face then his gaze drifted to her belly. "You're pregnant?" he whispered. She couldn't contain the grin that broke out all over her face before he brought her lips to his.

The next morning, he fixed her a hearty breakfast. She didn't have to go to work until nine o'clock, so she had time to eat. He slid eggs, bacon, and toast onto her plate, and poured her some milk instead of coffee.

"I'll never eat all of this. I was reading one of the books last night and I don't have to eat twice as much as normal," she said. "But thank you for making breakfast."

"I'm still in shock that we're having a baby. Maybe I shouldn't say it out loud, will that jinx it?" he said, pouring coffee for himself.

"I know. I can't believe how easy it was."

"What?" He nearly spat out his mouthful of food. He choked it down with some coffee and gave her a wide-eyed look. "What part of last summer and autumn from hell did you find easy?"

"Oh. Well, the side effects weren't easy. But I guess I had to take that drug to get to this part where I got pregnant within two months."

"At least you didn't have to take fertility drugs. Who knows what those side effects would have been," he said.

"Was it worth it?"

"We'll see in about, what did you say, seven months? That's about Christmas then?"

"Somewhere around then. Maybe a week after, not sure. But I don't want to tell anyone. Not until I am busting out of my clothes and everyone just thinks I am fat."

"You haven't been fat a day in your life. This will be fun to watch," he said, and she stuck out her tongue.

CHAPTER FIFTY-FIVE

Yvonne liked her job at Lincoln Telephone Company. Most of the time there was very little pressure. She enjoyed the other people she worked with, mostly women. The only thing she didn't like about being an operator was the variable shifts. Since she had little seniority, she was working a star shift, which meant working someone else's regular shift on their day off. Now that she was pregnant, she tried to avoid early shifts that started at six or seven in the morning. Most people liked those, so she was always able to find someone to trade her for those assignments.

Which is how she came to be working at eight that evening in late May. Most of her calls were routine, customers placing credit card calls where she had to key their telephone card number, or collect or person-to-person calls where she announced the call to the answering party. Or she just spent time explaining how the telephone industry was changing to customers who had questions. Sometimes people just called in to have someone to chat with.

Yvonne didn't know what the young girl needed, who just dialed "O" to reach the operator. She wasn't calling from Lincoln, but one of the towns around Beatrice. It could have been one of several different towns or a house in the country.

"Long-distance, this is Yvonne. May I have the number you are calling please?" Yvonne answered.

"I'm not calling lon' distance. I just dunno what ta do." The quaver in the girl's voice caught her attention right away.

"Do you need help? Do you need the police or an ambulance?" Yvonne had emergency services numbers ready for her area to connect her to.

"No! Don'cha call the police, please. I thought I done the right thing. But what if nobody finds her? I'se scared. Jus' tell the police to find her without reporting me."

"Um, sure," Yvonne told her. She stood to signal to the operator at the next position, mouthing "Call the service assistant for me." Service assistants helped with complicated situations.

"What is your name, Honey?" Yvonne tried to keep her voice calm. The caller's speech was becoming more rapid, and her breathing was audible.

"Nuh-uh. I don' think I should tell ya. Call me Missy."

"How old are you Missy?"

"I'se fifteen. Sixteen in July."

"What is your phone number? It isn't coming up on my display." By this time a service assistant named Mary was plugged in listening to the call with Yvonne.

"Dunno. Not at my house. It's a church phone."

"What church is it? I can look up the number."

"No, I don' want the police to find me. I want 'em to find her. I don' want 'em knowing who I am. Can you help me?" Missy sounded like she'd started crying.

"Who do you want the police to find, Missy?" Mary asked.

"Who zat?" Missy said.

"That's just my service assistant, Mary. She is here to help us," Yvonne said.

They heard Missy take a deep breath. Yvonne feared she would hang up. "I want them to find my baby."

Yvonne looked at Mary wide-eyed as a lump formed in her throat. No one at work knew Yvonne was pregnant yet.

"Your baby? I don't know what you mean. Is your baby missing?" Mary asked, taking notes.

"Not zactly. I didn' know I was preggers. I gained some weight, I guess. I had terrible stomach pains, so I went home from school today. My baby was born this afternoon. I was so scared. I didn' know what to do. I tied a string around the cord by her belly button. I saw that on TV." Missy sobbed and was hard to understand.

Yvonne blamed her hormones for the tears welling up in her own eyes. "Did you tell your mother or father you had a baby?"

"No, it's jus' Mom and she was at work. She works at the diner in Beatrice."

"Missy, where is the baby?" Yvonne asked.

"I took her to the hospital. I wrapped her up and took her to the hospital in Beatrice. I figgered someone would find her, I figgered she'd cry. But what if she don't cry loud enough?" Missy's words came out in ragged breaths. "I didn' want her to die. I just wanted to give her to someone else. Some people want babies, you know? But I can't take care o' no baby. I'se fifteen years old."

"Okay." Yvonne took a deep breath. "You took her to the hospital in Beatrice. Did you hand her to someone there?"

"Oh no. Nobody could see me. I was 'fraid to go inside. They might even have cameras or guards," Missy sniffed. "I took her 'round the backa the building by the dumpsters. I figgered someone would bring out trash pretty soon. But I dunno how soon they takes trash to the dumpster. Or when the garbage man takes trash from the dumpster. I was just terrified and I didn' know what to do."

Mary unplugged her headset from Yvonne's position and had the next operator calling the Beatrice hospital.

Yvonne felt warm tears streaming down her cheeks but willed her voice to be strong. "Okay, Missy, where exactly did you put the baby? In the dumpster, beside it? Was there more than one dumpster? If someone looks for her, what is she wrapped in?"

"There was three dumpsters. It was the middle one. I put her inside, stuck next to big trash bags, but so's her mouth wasn't covered. So she would cry to alert someone. But not until I left. She was wrapped in a big red quilt. It was on my bed, but I got blood on it. I didn' have any bottles or diapers or nothin' to take cara her. But what if they don't find her?"

"We are trying to get someone to go look for her right now, Missy," Yvonne said. Missy started crying harder again. "Don't hang up, Missy, okay? We're trying to help you."

Yvonne heard Mary nearby talking to someone at the hospital, and relayed the information Missy had given her about the baby's location. When she looked back at her screen, the caller had hung up on her. She made her position busy to stop the next call from coming in and checked to see if Mary needed anything else. Then she made a beeline for the bathroom.

As soon as she closed the door to the stall, the dinner she'd eaten half an hour ago started reversing course. She didn't even know she had to vomit. Afterward, she sat on the toilet and started crying. After a few minutes, Mary stood outside the stall. She knew it was Mary because of her godawful shoes. They were brown and white and looked like golf shoes. Or bowling shoes. Mary was a dear but no woman alive should have shoes that ugly.

"Yvonne, are you all right?" Mary said. "The hospital will call me back to tell me what they found."

Yvonne came out of the stall and washed her face and hands. Her gaze flitted around the room. "I have been trying to have a baby for over two years. You can't believe the hell I have been through, the hell I have put my husband through, just to have a baby. And this idiot girl," She pointed her finger as though the girl was in the room and jabbed the air, "this girl has one she doesn't even know what to do with it. She puts her in a goddamn dumpster!"

She shook her head and looked at the two of them in the

mirror over the sink, hissing out her words. "And then, she feels guilty? Or it occurs to her she might be committing a crime? She still doesn't want the baby. Now she wants it to go to a good home. If the baby survives, that is. What is wrong with these girls?" Her hands were balled in fists.

Mary studied Yvonne. "Do you need to go home, Yvonne? That was a lot and it is clearly bothering you."

Yvonne nodded. "I think I should. I'll call my husband to come to pick me up." She wiped her eyes. "I can't believe how calm you are Mary. You were a big help."

Mary patted her arm. "I have had years of practice."

Thirty minutes later when she got in the car beside Daniel, she crossed her arms over her chest.

"What happened at work tonight? I thought this was a low-stress job," he said when he saw her face.

She told him about the phone call. There were privacy rules in place to protect customers, and normally she wouldn't have discussed anything that would reveal a customer's identity. However, she didn't know this girl's identity. Then she told him about how she got sick and ranted to her supervisor.

"But maybe you helped save a baby," he said softly.

"Maybe it was too late. If she'd been in Lincoln, I would have wanted to drive there myself and look for the abandoned baby. That's crazy though, right? I should be more like Mary and not let this get to me," Yvonne said looking out the window.

He took her hand. "No, I think it is perfectly natural it got to you. You're pregnant after all. And you have a finely honed sense of indignation. It's one of the things I find endearing about you. But you can't change all the injustice in the world."

"Why not?"

His mouth curved. "That's my job."

CHAPTER FIFTY-SIX

Leading up to the Fourth of July, Yvonne had nothing to wear that would fit her. She'd been holding her pants together with safety pins and wearing baggy sweatshirts over her tops to try to disguise her expanding midsection. Everyone kept asking her why she wasn't hot wearing all those layers.

She called her mother the weekend before Independence Day. "Mom, do you have time to go to Omaha to go shopping with me? I need something cute to wear for the July Fourth party. There is a new store at Westroads I heard about and I want to check it out."

"Oh, you mean the one for tall sizes? Sure, that sounds like fun," Connie said.

When they got to the shopping mall, Connie searched the store directory to find the store she'd mentioned. Meanwhile, Yvonne took off in the opposite direction, as if she knew where she was going.

"Yvonne, I think it's down here," Connie called.

Yvonne just motioned for Connie to follow. When she disappeared into the maternity store, Connie was surprised. She walked into the store herself and Yvonne jumped out from behind her. "Surprise, Grandma!"

Connie instinctively put her hands on Yvonne's middle. "Really? How far along?"

"Four months, more or less."

"Oh my goodness. You kept this a secret for four months?"

Then they were hugging and dancing in the maternity store.

The clerk started laughing.

"Sorry. I just told my mom I'm expecting." Yvonne flushed, not able to control her beaming smile.

"No problem. We see this all the time. What can I help you find?"

Yvonne found some cute clothes including some festive T-shirts and dresses that were on sale. As Yvonne had anticipated, Connie was so excited, she wanted to pay for it all.

Daniel and Yvonne planned to tell the rest of the family at the barbecue on the fourth. Since Debbie and Robert were home visiting with André, Jamal, and Chantelle, it seemed like an ideal opportunity. For many family events, the lines had blurred between the Adams and Edison families, so Connie, Harold, Clark, Annette, and Matthew were also invited.

Yvonne checked herself in the mirror before leaving for the party. "They'll be able to tell I'm pregnant in this dress, won't they?" She tilted her head side to side as she smoothed her hand over the small mound on her belly. The bright blue print sundress was gathered full under her bust line.

"I don't know if anyone is going to look at your stomach. They will wonder how your breasts got so big though," Daniel said, admiring them in the mirror as he stroked the back of his fingers down her arm. "But there are some things you should just appreciate without question."

"It is very odd. My boobs practically disappeared last year and now they have grown more than my belly has. My mother told me the same thing happened to her when she was pregnant with Clark," she said. "But here's the deal. If they don't figure it out, you have to make the announcement."

Once they got to the Adams' house, it was controlled chaos

with everyone milling in different places, catching up individually. Debbie hugged Yvonne and started talking about her children. Clark had been promoted to head barbecue chef and was wearing Bernard's apron. Finally, Daniel had to call for everyone's attention.

"I'm glad we could all get together today. First, I want to salute my father, Bernard. He has had a rough year with his heart surgery, but he looks great today and has even been out to the nine-hole golf course a few times. *Salud*, Dad!" he hoisted his beer can, and the others echoed his toast. "And then there is Yvonne," he reached for her hand. "She has had a very difficult year too, ever since the miscarriage last year, then the demon drug that just about did us both in." There was a chorus of agreement. "But now I am very pleased she is back in good health and is carrying our child."

For a moment, it was so quiet, the noise from the neighbor's cap guns could be heard. Then pandemonium set in with everyone descending on Yvonne and Daniel, asking questions and congratulating them.

Debbie and Yvonne finally had a moment to talk about twenty minutes later.

"How have you been feeling? How long have you known you were pregnant?"

"You know I haven't felt very sick. Part of it may be I feel so much better now than I did when I was on the Danocrine, that my tolerance is much higher. In fact, it makes me nervous I feel this good like maybe I'm not really pregnant. But every time I see the doctor, there's a heartbeat that isn't mine. I was two months pregnant before I even went to the doctor. I thought I was still having infertility problems."

"You don't look like you are showing yet, since you are so tall and thin, but you certainly look healthier than you did in January. I can see that pregnant glow they talk about," Debbie said.

"Well, Daniel keeps telling me that, but I don't see it,"

Yvonne said. "I do seem to get tired more often."

"Then you should be sitting down, taking care of yourself." Daniel came up behind her and put her in a nearby chair.

"He keeps fussing over me. I love it."

"Daniel, I think you should come over and babysit our three wild ones tomorrow just to get a taste of fatherhood," Debbie said.

"Gosh, that sounds tempting but I'm afraid I have a court appearance tomorrow. Raincheck."

CHAPTER FIFTY-SEVEN

Yvonne continued to be surprised at how easy her pregnancy was going. She was more comfortable now she was in maternity wear with expansive panels in the front of her pants, and loose dresses and shirts. She had a doctor's appointment every month and Dr. Mayer always seemed optimistic she could carry the baby to term.

In late September, she had an appointment for an ultrasound which Daniel wanted to attend. She was told to drink a lot of water before the ultrasound so she would have a full bladder. The nurse told her that this helps move the uterus up for a better view.

Yvonne was scanning the waiting room repeatedly and tapping her knee before the exam when they didn't call her to come in right at the appointed time. She grabbed Daniel's hand.

"They shouldn't make anyone wait too long when they've asked you to drink this much water. It's an accident waiting to happen."

A few minutes later they were shown to the exam room and Yvonne climbed onto the table. The technician put cold gel on her abdomen and ran the wand over it. Her nametag said "Cindy."

"We have only had this machine a year or so," Cindy told them. "It takes a little bit to warm up to get a good picture."

Daniel moved over to be closer to the screen. "Oh my gosh, is that the baby?"

"Yes, you can see the head there and the torso. There are the arms and legs." They saw the image appear and disappear as Cindy moved the wand around. It was grainy and odd-looking, but it resembled a baby.

"Okay, the other one is over here. You can't see as much of this one, more the backside . . ."

"What?" Yvonne's eyebrows shot up, eyes wide.

"What do you mean, the other one?" Daniel peered at the screen. "Are there two?"

Just then Dr. Mayer walked into the exam room, eyeing the ultrasound image. "Good morning. How do you like the show? Are the babies cooperating or are they shy?"

"She just said there are two. Two babies," Yvonne pushed her hair from her forehead as she grew pale.

"Yes, let's see if we can get a look at both of them." He took the wand from the ultrasound technician and had Yvonne lean more on one side. "Okay, here is the second baby, a little behind the first one." The baby that was in the back was slightly more visible, and the doctor attempted to rearrange them by pressing on Yvonne's abdomen.

"Ahhh, that hurts. A full bladder, remember? But you never mentioned there were two." Yvonne knitted her brows. Daniel stared at the screen slack-jawed.

"I heard two heartbeats, but it is better to wait for the ultrasound to be positive. Don't you want more than one child?"

"Yes, but twins. That's two at a time." Yvonne said.

"It's amazing. What are the odds?" Daniel scratched his jaw.

Dr. Mayer looked at Yvonne's medical chart. "How long were you on fertility drugs?"

"I didn't take any fertility drugs. Just the Danocrine." Yvonne frowned.

"Well, then you were lucky to get pregnant at all. This is a bonus. We'll want to see you every two weeks now that the twins are confirmed. We'll talk more about your due date in future visits, but it will probably be a little earlier." Dr. Mayer left the room.

Daniel took Yvonne's hand, as she started to tremble. "Can we see both of them again?" he asked Cindy, and she complied, and gave them some crude photographs of the images.

After the appointment, they both sat in the car and stared at each other.

"You know you're probably going to get enormous." Daniel stared at her belly.

"That's all you're concerned about? I just can't believe the doctor didn't tell me."

"I suppose he was waiting for me to come to an appointment, you know, because the husband is the important part of this equation. You're just the womb." If she hadn't detected the sarcasm in his voice, she would have hit him.

"But what are we going to do? Two babies. We don't even know if it is two boys or two girls or one of each."

"Well, the first thing we should do is talk to my parents. We're lucky we know someone who has gone through this."

Yvonne blew out her breath. "Yes, that should help. Isn't it unusual to have a twin father twins though? And what about the house? We only have three bedrooms, and we were lucky we didn't just get two. But now, we'll lose the office."

"We can always buy a bigger house. This is going to be a good thing. If things had gone the way we planned, we probably would be having our second child by now anyway. This is like a two-for-one deal."

"I just can't believe it yet," Yvonne sighed and leaned back putting her hands on her belly. He put one hand over hers.

"I think you'll believe it when they start kicking up a storm."

CHAPTER FIFTY-EIGHT

After her next doctor's appointment, Yvonne picked up some pizza for dinner. She didn't feel like cooking.

"Daniel, we have to talk," she said as soon as he came home. He sat at the table and helped himself to some pizza before it got cold. She twisted a lock of her hair, waiting for him to be settled.

"This smells good. Valentino's always gets it right. Did you get some garlic rolls?"

"I went to the doctor today. This feels like déjà vu. He gave me a list of problems you can have when you are carrying 'multiples.' As if having twins was just like having sextuplets. He made me feel like I'm having a litter. Sometimes I don't like him much, which makes it hard to trust him to deliver the babies."

"I think you are just getting cranky because you are uncomfortable. I mean it makes sense that it's harder the closer you get to the end. I can see how the skin on your ankles is getting tight at night. That's gotta hurt." He patted her hand while he stuffed hamburger and sausage pizza into his mouth.

"Well, you're right. Edema is one of the common problems

of any pregnancy." She pulled a list out of her purse. "But here are the ones that are higher risks for me because of the twins: leg cramps, shortness of breath, varicose veins, vivid dreams, insomnia, urinary tract infections, heartburn, stretch marks, snoring, or numbness in your fingers and toes."

She went on, "But those aren't the dangerous ones. What you mostly have to worry about is high blood pressure which can lead to preeclampsia. That can cause severe headaches, rapid weight gain, or seizures. Then there is gestational diabetes, which can throw your blood sugar out of whack. You're more likely to have excessive bleeding and intestinal problems, and premature labor, which may confine you to bed rest. And the chance of having a Cesarean section is much higher. If the babies do come early, and most twins do, they could have immature lungs, low birth weight, digestive problems, nervous system problems, or difficulty with feeding. Hearing all that scared me." Yvonne ran her sweaty hands down her pant leg.

"I don't know, Yvonne. If I learned anything about you in the past year, it is you are a trooper. Stubborn as all get out, but a trooper, nonetheless. I don't think I could have endured half of what you did taking that drug. It's going to be fine." He put a hand on her wrist.

"I'm at about thirty-one weeks. Every day I don't have a complication is good. Once we get to December, the doctor said I could go into labor at any time, but we should hope for December 17."

Yvonne woke up on December 1 with tightening pain in her abdomen. She didn't recognize her abdomen anymore, it was a mountain of moving flesh now, obscuring her view of the lower half of her body.

"Daniel, wake up. I think I'm in labor." She started doing the panting breaths they learned in Lamaze classes.

"How do you know it isn't one of those practice labor pains, what are they called? Braxton-Hicks. That sounds like a case citing to me."

She breathed easier. "I don't know. When is Debbie coming?"

"Not for another two weeks. If you want her here, you'd better cross your legs." He closed his eyes again and snuggled closer to her.

"Just to warn you. No jokes. Don't try to make me laugh in labor. It will be hard enough just to breathe."

"Got it. No fun today." He sat up, yawned, and stretched. "Just screaming, panting, and waiting."

"Maybe cussing."

"You're planning on cussing?"

"Well, the Lamaze instructor said not to rule it out. Aaaaaahhhh!" Yvonne screamed, grabbed his arm, and then remembered to do her panting.

"I might start laughing if you start cussing."

"Screw you," she said, and he chuckled obligingly.

They'd already packed her bag to take to the hospital with a few clothes, a bed jacket, and things to focus on during labor. Daniel called the doctor's office and the nurse told them to go to the hospital to be checked out. But her labor pains were about ten minutes apart, so it didn't seem urgent.

Once Yvonne settled in a hospital room, the labor seemed to calm down. About every twenty minutes, a nurse came in to check on her.

"I'm not sure we should be here yet. It doesn't feel as strong now. Maybe it is just a strong version of Braxton-Hicks contractions," she said.

"We're here now. Let's just see what the doctors tell us." Daniel held her hand and put his other hand on her bulging belly.

"Did you bring your guitar?" Yvonne asked, leaning back on the pillows, and closing her eyes.

"No. But I did bring my Walkman and headphones. I thought it might help you to listen to music."

She beamed. "Play something for the babies."

He reached for the blue and silver cassette player and looked through his cassette case for some Mozart.

He put the headphones on her belly and tried to turn the earpieces down so that the vibrations or beat might be felt at least.

"This is a piano version, not an orchestra," she said. "Who is playing the piano?"

"It's me. I recorded it a couple of weeks ago. I had to practice a little. I have gotten rusty."

"You recorded music for our babies? That's so sweet."

"Well, I thought you could play it on the boombox when I wasn't there. It's never too early to develop some taste in music. Unlike the Police or Journey you like to dance around the kitchen to."

"You said you liked watching me dance around in my leotard."

"Well, there was that one night when you started taking off the leotard and —Oh, Dr. Mayer. Good morning." Daniel stood abruptly and shook Dr. Mayer's hand as he came into the room.

"How are you doing this morning?" Dr. Mayer said and put his hand on Yvonne's arm. "According to the chart, your contractions are getting farther apart. Let's just have a look and see if this is a false alarm."

After he examined Yvonne, Dr. Mayer sent her home with

orders to be on bed rest for the next ten days to try to stop contractions. She was only allowed to leave the bed to use the bathroom and take quick showers.

CHAPTER FIFTY-NINE

Daniel had Cablevision install an outlet in the bedroom, and he moved the television to the bedroom dresser. Yvonne made a list of library books he could pick up for her as she tried to stave off boredom. Connie and Bonnie stopped by several times.

Bonnie's eyes gleamed when she sat in Yvonne's bedroom. "I remember how excited I was right before the babies came. Back then they didn't know I was having two babies. Little Daniel came out and I thought I was done, but the labor didn't stop. Debbie was only a few minutes behind him, and I couldn't believe it. To have both a boy and a girl was like a miracle. They didn't let Bernard in the room, so he didn't get to see them until after they were cleaned up. You know how on television they always show the nurses giving the father the first glimpse of the swaddled baby, but I wanted to see his reaction. He came into the room, and I was holding Debbie in a pink blanket, and he thought we had a girl. Then after he sat on the edge of the bed, another nurse brought Daniel wrapped in a blue blanket. I will never forget the look on his face when he saw the second one. He nearly fell off the bed." Yvonne couldn't help laughing as Bonnie mimicked Bernard's shocked expression.

Connie was laughing too. "I remember that Clark was hard. I was in labor for about eighteen hours and they finally used the forceps to turn him. That was terrible. I don't think they do that anymore. Yvonne was a little angel compared to that. Only had about five hours of labor and I didn't even push very many times. Clark was nearly nine pounds and Vonnie was only seven, so that

266

made a difference too. But I don't know if having two at once would be any worse than having a two-year-old running around when you have a newborn. Both are still in diapers and crying a lot."

Why do women tell you their labor stories? Yvonne fingered the gold cross she'd resumed wearing around her neck when she discovered she was pregnant. Dr. Mayer had assured her he wouldn't let her labor for days on end. That would be too risky, and he'd perform a cesarean before that happened. But then her recovery would be long, and she'd still have to take care of two babies. She shifted the pillows around in the bed, trying to get comfortable.

She made it through all ten days of bed rest without anything more than the minor contractions. She was glad to be able to move around again but her muscles were stiff when she tried to walk around the house. The baby load weighed her down. Doing anything made her tired.

On December 14, a pounding headache reminded her of the ones she'd had a year before. Her ankles were still pretty swollen from the night before. They often were better in the morning. She rolled onto the bed, hoisting her feet up with some trouble, and pulled the phone into her lap.

What's wrong with my fingers? She tried to call Daniel, but the buttons on the phone seemed to fade in and out. The headache tightened its grip, and now her belly was riddled with pain. Was this labor? The telephone clattered to the floor when she moved onto her side and started gasping.

She didn't know how long she laid there, unable to budge. Her head was pounding, and her vision blurred. She had to reach the phone to call for help. She should have let one of the mothers stay with her, but yesterday she'd felt good.

The dog jumped on the bed and tried to nuzzle her. When

she tried to push him away, he began barking. Prosecutor must know something is wrong too. The barking faded away as she lost consciousness.

She was marching in line with the other twirlers. It must have been in high school. Yeah, it was that Veteran's Day parade in downtown Lincoln. There was Debbie next to her, and Joann and Barbra. A frigid wind made her bare legs blue. Hard to twirl a baton when your fingers are turning to ice. The band started playing "Yankee Doodle Dandy" or "Seventy-six Trombones" or both, combined. The twirlers were doing windmills. Easy.

But wait! They started tossing batons in the air. First Barbra tossed her baton, then Joann, then it was Yvonne's turn. *We can't do that! We're marching down a street with forty band members behind us. Spectators are lining the streets with young children. There is no way I can gauge where to throw the baton so that I can catch it.*

But she spun her baton aloft anyway. Then magically she had another baton. She tossed the second one up in the air too. There were traffic lights and power lines overhead. How was she ever going to catch two batons? Barbra caught hers. Debbie caught hers. But they each had only one baton. Yvonne had to catch two.

Her husband was talking. Was she dreaming?

"Baby, what's wrong?" Daniel rolled her onto her back as she cried out in pain. "Jesus, are you in labor? What is it?" He picked the phone off the floor and called an ambulance. "I've been trying to reach you for hours and just got a busy signal. The operator said the phone was off the hook. She heard the dog barking."

Her lips were trembling but she couldn't speak. She wanted to tell him how much her head hurt, how she couldn't see him clearly. Someone was screaming. Was it her?

Am I dying? I should tell him how much I love him. Then commotion. Adrenaline coursing through her. Someone slapped a mask on her face and told her to breathe in. Strong arms picked her up and strapped her to a gurney. There was a blood pressure cuff on her arm. Too tight. Where was Daniel? Where was she going? She wanted Daniel. A blanket was thrown over her and then they were outside. Shouting, cold air on her face, snow blowing, lights, sirens. What was happening? Daniel. She heard him then, shouting and grabbing her hand. She couldn't see him but she knew his hand. He was with her. She could relax a little.

Maybe she fell asleep. When she opened her eyes, a nurse was putting an intravenous needle in her arm.

"This will help with the edema," the nurse said.

Yvonne just groaned.

Daniel stepped up to the bed. "Yvonne?" She looked up at him with a tight smile. "God, you scared the hell out of me. What happened?"

"Head hurt. It still hurts. I couldn't see clearly. I tried to call you."

"They think you have preeclampsia. Dr. Mayer is on his way. They may have to take the babies by C-section."

She just groaned again and put her hand on her belly arching her back. "Oooohhhh!" She started panting and he matched his breathing to hers. A monitor beeped over and over. *What's that wire attached to my belly?*

She relaxed and dozed for a minute. When the pain advanced again, she clenched Daniel's hand and started whimpering. He started panting in her face, nodding until she did likewise.

"I need some water. My mouth is like a desert."

"I don't think you can drink anything in case you have to have surgery. Here, try this." He wet the corner of a washcloth and put it to her mouth.

Dr. Mayer came in. "Well, this looks like labor. I thought we were going to the operating room. It's time to get those little rascals out. Do you want to wait and see if the labor progresses? If it doesn't move along in the next hour, we'll have to go ahead with the cesarean. After the next contraction, I can do a quick exam to check your cervix."

The obstetrician was willing to gamble on the labor delivering the babies after finding she was mostly dilated. "It is getting close. I won't lie to you; it is going to be a rough ride. Is that what you want to do?"

"But can't you give me something for the pain?" Yvonne asked.

"No, it is too late. We couldn't do that earlier because your vital signs were shaky. Now your blood pressure has come down some. But we still need to get this done pretty quickly. You say the word, and I will bring the anesthesiologist in here. Or you can tough it out. What's it going to be?"

She took in her husband and doctor with frightened eyes. "What is safer for the babies?"

"Doing a vaginal birth is safer, but twins present their own risks. That's why I like to let Mom choose, if at all possible," Dr. Mayer said.

"What's safer for Yvonne?" Daniel asked. "We can't let anything happen to her." He twisted his wedding ring on his finger.

"There is always a risk when you put someone out. If it was my wife . . . well, I'd try the natural way first. Based on the ultrasound, I don't think either baby is over six and a half pounds."

"Then no C-section. As long as I get to wear a bikini in St. Tropez next year." She managed a wan smile.

"We'll go to St. Tropez, I promise. Don't know exactly where that is, but just think about a warm beach every time you get a—." Daniel broke off when another contraction hit her and he started panting again.

Her labor went on for another forty minutes. Her blood pressure and pulse had risen again and the doctor looked less encouraging. Yvonne was sweating, crying, and wearing out.

"I need to take a short break, Mama. When you have a contraction, just keep doing what you have been, no pushing while I am gone. I hope we can have you push when I get back," the doctor told them.

CHAPTER SIXTY

As soon as he left the room, Yvonne grabbed Daniel's arm. "I'm going home. This hurts too much. Help me get dressed."

His eyebrows shot up, but before he could respond, Debbie waltzed in carrying coffees. She already had a hospital gown covering her clothing.

He turned to her instead, "They just let anyone in here?"

"Nice to see you too, Brother. What's happening?" She kissed him on the cheek and handed him a cup of coffee.

"Yvonne wants to quit. It is too hard," he said.

"Of course, it is hard. How could it not be hard? Daniel, you have no idea what she's going through."

"I took the Lamaze classes. I know exactly what she is going through."

"Just leave us for a minute." He scowled at her, but Debbie pointed to the door.

Debbie sat on the bed, eyes glistening, and panted with Yvonne through the next contraction. She grasped Yvonne's hand

and held it tightly next to her face. "Listen, Sweetie. I've done this. It isn't fun, but you can handle it. You were the girl who always knew what she wanted. You weren't about to let any boy's carnal desire get in your way. Remember that? You told Nancy, Linda, and I that we should have had more will power. Maybe you were right. But you had it in spades. You and Daniel went through hell taking that drug, but you didn't give up." Debbie's voice cracked as her tears fell onto their hands. "But it was leading up to today. Today you are going to hold those babies in your arms. It is just going to take a little more."

Yvonne leaned her head on Debbie's. She was in the middle of the next powerful contraction when Dr. Mayer came back in with Daniel on his heels. The doctor sat at the end of the bed and announced it was time to push. It took another ten minutes before he could hold the first baby's head in his hands, and he rotated the shoulders out. Debbie and Daniel stood wide-eyed, mouths agape.

"Well, Mama. It looks like you have a beautiful daughter," the doctor said to Yvonne. "Here now, Dad, just hold this baby right like so until I see what else we have hidden in here." He put the newborn on her side on Yvonne's chest and laid Daniel's hand on top of her. Tears were running down Daniel's cheeks now too.

After a few more pushes, the second twin emerged. "Okay Sister, you are in charge of this one right now. Just hold him steady like the other one. How'd ya like that? One daughter, one son. Sound familiar?" He put the second baby right next to the first on top of Yvonne and had Debbie hold him in place.

"Oh my God," Daniel's shoulders relaxed and he stared in disbelief at his children.

The doctor and two nurses clamped and cut the cords and finished with the post-delivery procedures. In a few minutes, a nurse came and took each newborn, weighed it, and cleaned it off, before putting it back on Yvonne's chest so she could hold onto them.

Yvonne's voice came in ragged breaths. "They are perfect, aren't they? All their fingers and toes and everything?"

Daniel gave her a quick kiss. "Good job. Perfect. Both perfect."

"Daniel, do you think it was like this when we were born?" Debbie asked stroking the baby girl's blondish hair.

"No, I think I was the perfect one and you started screaming at me as soon as I beat you out the door." Yvonne and Debbie both laughed. Dr. Mayer said, "Hold still if you want these stitches nice and tidy."

Later, when the babies were checked thoroughly and had diapers, long-sleeve shirts, and pink or blue knit hats on, they were swaddled and returned to the exhausted parents. By this time, the grandparents had been allowed in the room, and Debbie had gone back to her parents' home to be with Chantelle. Robert and the boys would be arriving in a few days by plane so they wouldn't miss school.

"Did you decide on names yet?" Connie asked, holding the baby boy, while Bernard had the girl.

"I think we settled on Thing One and Thing Two, didn't we?" Daniel winked at Yvonne.

"You keep forgetting. No laughing today. It hurts to laugh." Yvonne grimaced.

Daniel nuzzled her neck. "How about kissing? Is there a ban on kissing today too?" She shook her head and he pulled her into a long kiss, just as Clark and Annette walked in.

"Egads, you two. Get a room," Clark said shuddering.

"We did," Daniel said, "This is our room. Deal with it." He stifled a smirk and added, "Oh, and no laughing, Clark. This is a strictly no laughing room by maternal decree."

"They haven't named them yet, Clark, before you ask," Connie said.

The next morning, Daniel opened up the baby names book on Yvonne's lap. "I still like Genevieve for a girl, pronounced the French way, Zhahn-vee-EV."

"Genevieve Constance Adams. Do you like that?" Yvonne leaned her arm on his shoulder.

He nodded. "I always thought your name sounded French and so will Genevieve, even if someone pronounces it the English way."

"Do you still like Jesse for a boy? Jesse Bernard Adams?" she asked.

"Yes. I am surprised Debbie didn't use Bernard for a middle name. Anyway, Genevieve means 'God's Blessing' and Jesse means 'The Lord exists'. Both of those hit close to home. For a while there, I thought I was going to lose all three of you." He closed the book and took her hand.

"But you didn't. You found us, you saved us all. Last night when I was half-delirious, I dreamt about that Veteran's Day parade we did when we were juniors. It was too cold and dangerous to toss our batons. But in the dream, I did it anyway. I tossed two batons up. My fingers were frozen but I caught them spinning, both of them like I had done it a hundred times. I think it was like an omen. You take a risk and prepare to catch the spinning baton no matter where it lands."

"Even when it slams into you?" Daniel said.

"You recover." She smiled at him as the nurses brought in their babies.

Just as a nurse gave baby Jesse to Yvonne, two of Daniel's co-workers arrived. Yvonne knew Daniel's secretary, Judy Thomas. She was ten years older and had two sons. The nurse handed Baby Genevieve to Judy as she settled into the chair next to Yvonne's bed. Daniel was chatting with the man who had accompanied her.

"Oh my goodness, they are just adorable, Yvonne. You must be over the moon," Judy leaned in for a better look at Jesse. "And Daniel said his sister came for the birth too. Be sure to take gobs of pictures. Two generations of twins are something rare."

"Oh yes, everyone has taken pictures of Daniel and Debbie with our twins. Like I'm not important here. I'm just the one who gave birth. Twice." Yvonne shook her head, laughing. "I don't necessarily want my picture taken until I can fix my hair and put on something nicer than a hospital gown."

"Yvonne!" Daniel raised his voice.

"What? What's wrong?" She pressed Jesse's face to her neck and gave Daniel a sidelong look.

Daniel grinned. "I have just been trying to get your attention. I want you to meet Mike. We lured him away from the Attorney General's office last month. I told you we played racquetball. Michael Conyers, this is my wife Yvonne. She's been preoccupied of late, as you can imagine."

As he moved toward her, Yvonne stared once again into Michael's luminous hazel eyes and the bouquet of daisies he held. Her mouth flew open.

Twirling Fire is Debbie's story, coming soon. You can read an excerpt from it on the next page.

SNEAK PEEK AT *TWIRLING FIRE*

April 1961

Debbie glanced at the clock and groaned. She was already tired of the exercise belt jiggling her waist and threatening to curdle her breakfast. Her mother had a friend whose daughter lost four inches off her waist and hips, and Bonnie had become a faithful user of the Walton Master Craft Belt Vibrator. Debbie had used it three times in the past week and couldn't tell it made any difference.

Her latest humiliation about the shape of her nine-year-old-body began when the students in her classroom sat cross-legged on the lunchroom floor waiting for the annual height and weight check done by the school nurse. She was thankful that her best friends, Yvonne and Janine were in her class this year, and her brother
was not.

"Tommy Sanders, fifty-seven inches, eighty-one pounds!" Their teacher, Mrs. Hunt, called out loudly enough for the nurse, Miss Benson, to hear where she sat at a desk across the room.

"Janine Meeks, fifty-two inches, seventy-three pounds." Janine scrambled back to sit with Debbie and Yvonne. Janine cringed although she was clearly within the average range of the girls in their grade.

"Martha Glencocks, fifty-four inches, 109 pounds." Debbie saw poor Martha turn bright red as she plopped back down at the edge of the group separating the boys and girls in their class. Debbie had been getting to know Martha better this year and offered her a small smile. She was the heaviest girl in their class.

"Eddie Perkins, fifty-nine inches, ninety-two pounds." Eddie grinned taking his seat.

"Yvonne Edison, sixty-two inches, ninety-three pounds." Yvonne's downcast face told Debbie that being the tallest kid in their class bothered her.

Then it was Debbie's turn to smash her backside up against the height chart on the wall and step on the big scale like the one at the doctor's office. She bit her lip as the teacher fiddled with the counterweights, willing herself to weigh less.

"Debbie Adams, fifty-three inches, ninety-two-and-one-half pounds!" Mrs. Hunt seemed to say this as though it was unlikely anyone her height and age could be so chubby. Debbie had glanced at the door briefly, wondering if she could escape. But at the moment, she felt she was so huge, there would be nowhere she could hide where they wouldn't find her. Instead, she slinked back to try to gracefully sit down next to her friends, who patted her knee in sympathy.

When she refused to eat dinner that evening, Bonnie had drawn the story out of her.

"It wouldn't hurt you to eat a little less," Bonnie suggested. You could eat just one cookie after school. And if you'd get a little more exercise, that will make you feel lighter. But you can't skip meals altogether. That isn't good for you. I haven't seen you out on the trampoline lately. And Yvonne is outside playing ball with her brother and Daniel. Maybe you should join them."

"But Mom, Vonnie's a tomboy. She said so herself. I am not. I'd rather read or play make-believe in my room," Debbie said.

But she had agreed to try the weight loss vibrating belt. It was boring. If only she could be more like Yvonne or Daniel and enjoy running around the yard. But playing ball meant she'd fall, and that hurt. Or she'd have dirt and grass stains on her clothes. At least she took their boxer, Grover, for walks. He loved her no matter how chubby she was. And Yvonne was usually eager to come along.

December 1967

Barry Whitaker was coming over to Debbie's house to watch television. Barry could best be described as average. He was average height, a little taller than her five foot six. He was about average build. He wore nondescript glasses and had unruly blondish-brown wiry hair. He was the guy you'd cast in a teen movie to play the awkward best friend. But he'd noticed her, and that set him apart.

She talked to him by their lockers almost every day. His locker was two away from hers. She had replayed the previous day's conversation in her head at least fifty times.

"What's happening, Blondie?" Barry had asked.

"Debbie. My name's Debbie," she laughed.

"Oh, I know. But you remind me of that comic strip, *Blondie*. You know the one with Dagwood and his huge sandwiches. You have the blondest hair I think I've ever seen. Except for maybe Marilyn Monroe."

Debbie didn't mind being compared to Blondie, the sensible wife of the bumbling Dagwood. She read about them in the newspaper regularly. And who wouldn't want to remind a boy of the late M.M. She smiled at Barry. Maybe that's what emboldened him to keep talking.

"If you aren't doing anything on Saturday afternoon, I thought I might come over. You know, to see what you were up to," Barry said. He seemed to freeze for a moment, and swallowed hard, perhaps realizing how clumsy it had sounded.

"You could come by. I'm probably not doing anything important," Debbie crossed and uncrossed her arms. "And I'll probably be done around two o'clock. Do you remember where I live?"

"Sure. I've been to your house. When I was in Boy Scouts, your brother was in my troop."

And now it was Saturday, almost two. She didn't know if she was ready. Her father had taken Daniel ice-skating. At least he wouldn't be around to heckle them. Her mom had baked cookies, so the house smelled wonderful. She had fixed her hair and put on mascara and lipstick. She rarely wore much makeup, but she had to admit, she liked the effect. Maybe if she batted her eyelashes and pouted her lips, he wouldn't care she had an extra fifteen pounds on her. After all, M.M. had been curvy and she seemed to have many admirers.

Barry was late. Debbie began pacing the floor by 2:05 p.m. A few minutes later the doorbell rang, and Debbie opened it with a big smile.

"Hey, Debs. What are you doing today? Gee, you smell nice," Yvonne said, standing on their front porch.

Debbie spotted Barry walking up the driveway before she could answer. A blush rose to her cheeks. Barry stopped in his tracks when he saw Yvonne. "Yvonne, you have to leave. Now."

Yvonne whirled around and saw Barry, who was still hesitating. "Oh. OH. Listen, I wanted to check if your folks were giving me a ride to the basketball game tonight. Six-thirty?"

"Yeah, sure. Whatever," Debbie motioned with her head for Yvonne to retreat to her own house. Debbie never wanted a boy to compare her to Yvonne. She loved Yvonne, but she had morphed into someone closely resembling a fashion model, once she had started wearing contacts and grew her luxurious reddish-brown hair past her shoulders.

Yvonne backed away, turning in time to see Barry's cautious approach. She waved at him and left without another word.

"Did your plans change?" he asked. "Were you and Yvonne supposed to—?"

"No, it's nothing. It was about tonight. Come in, Barry."

They settled on the sofa in the basement with a plate of cookies. *King Kong* was showing on the afternoon movie. Debbie had seen this 1933 black-and-white film a few times, but it always made her jumpy when the monster gorilla roared or thundered his way through the jungle.

"You aren't scared, are you?" Barry asked.

She gave him her best wide-eyed look, like the movie's lead actress, Fay Wray. "It doesn't scare you, Barry?" she asked.

He put his arm around her shoulders.

Debbie was encouraged. This was going well so far.

"You're as bad as my little sister. She always wants to cuddle up on the couch when we watch scary movies," Barry said, grabbing another cookie with his free hand.

Debbie was about to put her head on his shoulder when she got an image of him sitting with his sister. Had he been thinking about kissing her or had she imagined that? She took a deep breath.

When she did, she caught him suddenly looking at her chest. She was wearing a mohair sweater but she didn't think it was unladylike. She supposed it did show off her generous breasts. It wasn't like she could hide them completely, although she'd been looking for a way to do that since she was thirteen and she caught a boy in class snickering at her.

Barry suddenly leaned away from her, moving his arms around to hug his sides.

Just when Debbie thought things couldn't get worse, Daniel came bounding down the stairs. Debbie heard her mother calling after him, to try to stop the interruption of her date, but it was too late.

"Are there any more cookies down here, Deb? You didn't eat them all, did you? I am starving!" he said bouncing off the last steps and launching himself toward the plate with two cookies left. "Oh, hey, Barry. What are you doing here?" Daniel sat down next to Barry on the couch and glanced at the console T.V. "*King Kong*. I love this part where he climbs up the Empire State building."

"Daniel Morris Adams, didn't you hear me calling you? Come back up here right now!" Bonnie hollered down the stairway.

Daniel stood up. "What's her prob—oh. I see. Sorry," Daniel said, grinning knowingly. He started laughing as he climbed the stairs, polishing off the last cookie.

"I suppose I should go," Barry said, getting to his feet.

"But the movie isn't over," Debbie protested.

"Would you like to go to a movie at the theater next weekend? I think the basketball game is out of town."

Debbie's face brightened. "Sure. That'd be swell." She stood close to him, not wanting their time alone to end.

He stared into her eyes then kissed her on the cheek. Not what she had been expecting, but maybe a step forward. She could still hear her brother making noises in the kitchen, so she didn't follow Barry upstairs to say good-bye. She stayed on the couch and watched Kong battle the dive bomber biplanes. Just once she wished the big ape would win.

ABOUT THE AUTHOR

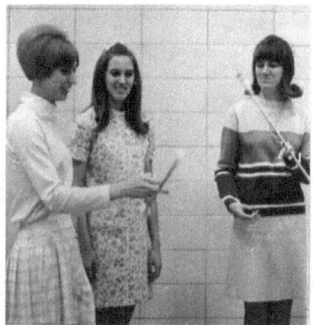

Claudia Johnson Severin lives on a farm in southeast Nebraska. She grew up in Lincoln, Nebraska, in the Eastridge neighborhood. She went back to her high school twirler days for this series. Like her main characters, she found hours of practice together developed friendships which led to many adventures outside of school.

Like Yvonne, she graduated from the University of Nebraska with a journalism degree. She also worked at Lincoln Telephone Company. The infertility storyline is based loosely on the experience of college friends.

This is the first of the Twirler Quartet series. She previously wrote *Her Side of History—Finding My Foremothers' Footprints*, an anthology of historical fiction about four of her family's female ancestors.

Writing about past decades gives her a chance to rewrite history and gives the characters a chance to benefit from lessons learned in the time since. She loved the 1960s, but wouldn't trade her smartphone for a teen line or her SUV for her old Volkswagen Beetle.

Thank you for reading my book. You can contact me through my website at https://claudiaseverin.net. Feel free to add a review for my book on Amazon or Goodreads. In the meantime, life's a whirlwind: catch it spinning!